1

It was a yoga day when I first met Brenda, and based on my experience, I expected her to die by month's end. I am retired, and after thirty-one years of working in academia, I have allowed myself the disciplined luxury on Monday and Thursday afternoons of heading to the local community centre for an easy Hatha class. In some sessions there are other men in the group, but mostly I'm the only guy, so the energy in the room is very yin, unlike in the weight room down the hall, which is full of grunts, slamming barbells, and yang. Thursday is also my day to visit the hospice; that is where I met Brenda.

Somehow my dog, Lacey, knows that Thursdays are special, and she comes to sit at my feet when I enter the house after yoga. Maybe it's because I'm wearing my exercise togs that she knows what should come next, but she never does the sitting thing on Mondays. Not a particularly smart dog is my Lacey, so how she knows it's a hospice day is a mystery to me. She's a fifteen-year-old cocker spaniel–poodle cross, and at twenty-two pounds she could lose a few. My two daughters would kill to have hair the colour of Lacey's: strawberry blonde with caramel highlights.

Insistent, she always sticks her head out, eager to don the "Animals Care" bandana and get started, so I slip it over her ears, and then she does a full body shake to settle everything in place. She waits by the door while I tend to a quick shower and sandwich, after which we hop in the car and head to the hospice. It's a payback thing, this hospice visiting. I had a brain tumour more than three decades ago and am so thankful for every day that I have a chance to give back. Also, the visits help me from falling into the abyss when I try and deal with the issue of my wife.

A hospice is not as dreary a place as you might think. The residents may be dying, but they are also trying to live their final days to the fullest, so we often have some good moments. The low-rise, ten-room hospice is sheltered in a grove of Douglas fir trees with a nice big garden for those residents still able to push or be pushed along the concrete path. The back garden is currently in a state of flux. The pond installed when the building was first erected has since filled in and become overgrown. A very eager volunteer gardener is in the process of bringing the garden back to life; at this point, though, it looks like a bomb crater.

Normally when Lacey is on leash, she walks beside or slightly behind me, but on hospice visiting days, as we leave the car, she is always out front leading the way along the sidewalk. After we enter the building, she wriggles a greeting to the receptionist, who voices an enthusiastic hello and rubs Lacey's ears. We chat briefly and then stop in to see the volunteer coordinator, who also gives her a welcoming pat.

Today as we head out into the hall, the chaplain meets up with us. Two residents have died in the night and he has been dealing with the families, one of which has taken the death particularly hard. The chaplain looks a little drawn as he kneels to engage the dog. I tell her to stay and then I duck into the lunchroom to grab my name tag from a drawer. When I return, Lacey's tail is sweeping broadly, and she's got a happy pant going. The chaplain now wears a smile. When he comes back up to a stand, his aspect is brighter as he enters his office.

Lacey and I continue down the hall and stop in to touch bases with Elizabeth, the Director of Care, who is just hanging up the phone. It is a busy day, what with the two deaths and consequently the two open beds to fill. She leaves her chair to greet Lacey and sinks to her knees, enjoying a very brief hiatus. Elizabeth tells me which of the residents have died, one of whom, Candace, had always been eager to receive a Lacey visit. She raised purebred Irish setters on her farm a few miles from here but had to give it up a year ago. Our visits were filled with talk about dog training, feeding, grooming and pretty much everything canine related. I learned a lot from her and will miss our time together.

"And yesterday we had a new admission, Brenda Leamington," she says. "A very nice lady. No family here. Still very bright, but quite frail. I'm sure she would love to see you two."

We move to the nursing station and say a brief hello. Lacey takes the opportunity to hoover the floor for the odd crumb that may have fallen. I pull out the notebook in which we volunteers record the details of our visits. The notes give the volunteers a running non-medical history of each of the residents: preferred topics of conversation, who is eager for visits, who is not, and who is fading. I chat with the nurses to make up a visit plan, then Lacey and I move down the hall together.

I give a little rap on the door and stick my head in. Beatrice is a long-term resident. Well, it's relative I guess; she's been here for just over a month. Today she's sitting quietly atop the bedclothes, watching a talk show on TV. She is wearing sweatpants, a tee shirt, and a lovely hand-knit sweater. Though only fifty-two, she has fought a long, losing battle with cancer. The skin on her face makes me think of tea-stained crepe paper. When Bea sees the dog, her face lights up. I see profound gratitude in her eyes as I lift Lacey up onto the bed. They give each other their full attention, and then after a couple of minutes, Lacey lies down with her head on Bea's lap. As we talk, Bea's right hand fondles the dog's ears continually. I have the feeling she's working up the gumption to say something difficult. "It's just that Lacey seems a little, I don't know, low energy today. Is she okay?"

I speak before I can think to hold it back, "Probably missing my wife. Makes two of us."

"I'm sorry Colin, I didn't mean…"

A knock on the door interrupts her and two of her friends step into the room. After brief introductions we all chat about dogs for a while. Then Lacey and I say our farewells and duck into the next room.

Dennis is almost gone. We have been visiting him for over a month, and at the beginning he delighted in having visitors. Now, though, he is pretty much just a shell. His wife and son have gone to catch a quick late lunch and will be returning shortly. He smiles weakly as we enter, and Lacey quickly settles onto the bed. Heavily medicated for pain, he strokes Lacey's back while I talk about a fishing trip I recently took with my cousin. Dennis was a fisherman here on the West Coast, and after hearing my story, he tells one of his own.

"...so he gets out the twenty-two. Fish is on the surface. You gotta kill 'em before you haul 'em aboard. You don't want a two-hundred-pound halibut bouncing around on the deck. Break your legs with one flop of the tail. Billy aims the rifle but the boat is bouncing around in the swell, really rockin' cause I got her in neutral so we can haul this thing in...." and abruptly Dennis is asleep.

Lacey joins him in dreamland and begins to snore. We went for a long walk this morning and she has some catching up to do. I close my eyes and try to slip into Zen. It's an effort to stop my mind from spinning. Night-time is the worst—it takes me forever to fall asleep, and when I do, my wife is always dying.

A few minutes pass and Dennis wakens. "But he pulls the trigger anyway. Shoots the line clean through." His chuckle is part gasp for breath. "Now the fish is just lying there on the surface of the water, doesn't know he's free. Exhausted, you know, from the fight and from coming up from so deep. So I grab the gaff and while...."

This cycle of wakefulness and sleep continues for some time, and it amazes me that each time, he picks up mid-sentence exactly where he left off. Somehow his brain simply goes into pause mode; then a few minutes later, something in there pushes play.

"So, Billy figures he should try again to shoot it in the head before I gaff it. He's holding the rifle real tight while he takes aim, just as a big wave hits and then over he goes. In them days we didn't bother with life jackets and Billy was a lousy swimmer."

I said in jest, "So did you save Billy or the halibut?"

Dennis gasps for breath, willing himself to get to the end of the tale. He coughs and then manages in a growl. "Oh, they both flopped around in the water for a while, but I have to say I never had so much fish and chips."

I should have laughed. In better days, I would have roared. But I still couldn't. I managed to force a toothy grin. Dennis lay there wearing the self-satisfied look of a man who has brought the house down.

His wife and son eventually return to his room and are relieved to discover Lacey and me at his bedside. They express their thanks that he has not been alone. We chat for a few minutes, then I rouse the dog. As we walk down the hall, a young Asian woman steps out from her mother's room.

"The nurses told me that you were here. My name is Vera and I was hoping you two could stop in and see my mum. You see, we have a dog at home, but Barney is too big and unruly to bring in here." Vera hesitated as her gaze shifted to the floor. "She misses him so much. The thing is, my mother doesn't speak English."

"Not a problem," I say, "Lacey understands pretty much every language. We'd be happy to visit."

We enter the woman's room. When she first glimpses a six-foot-tall male stranger, her face shows a flash of concern. Vera explains our presence as her mother catches sight of the furry, panting face at my feet and breaks into a lovely smile. I sweep Lacey up onto the bed, and she soaks up the attention both women lavish on her. They are chatting now in Cantonese, spattering the conversation with laughter.

I pull a dog treat from my pocket and give it to Vera, who offers it to an eager gaping mouth. After much nodding of heads and smiles, I accept a translated request for us to visit her next week. We head for the room of the new lady.

Sometimes when you meet a person, something clicks. It was like that with Brenda.

"Hello," I said. "My name is Colin, and this is Lacey. We volunteer here." I swing the leash around and bring my partner into view. "Are you a dog person? Would you like a visit?"

Unlike the tiny, delicate frame and thinning white hair that conveyed her illness and her age, her eyes met mine with strength and vibrant focus. I've noticed that for many people over the age of eighty, their eye colour has faded to a ghostly pale. Brenda's eyes, though, were still a deep, almost emerald green with a dark band around the iris. Her smile wrinkles were fully engaged as she replied, "Oh please do come in."

I lifted Lacey up onto the bed and she immediately set to licking the elderly lady's right hand.

"Bits of jam from the toast, I expect." She freed her hand and extended it to me. "Brenda. Not much oomph left in my grip, I'm afraid."

The dog nestled into the quilt that lay across Brenda's legs. Despite her quiet time with Dennis, Lacey hadn't had a chance to really settle into her afternoon nap, so she licked a front paw and then her lips a couple of times, let out a big sigh, and closed her cataract-filled eyes. She would be snoring again soon.

"It's my pleasure to meet you. Do I detect a hint of Britannia?"

"London, born and bred."

"It has changed a lot since you were born, I'm sure."

"Yes, well, the Germans remodeled it significantly when I was a child."

"So were you there during the war? The Blitz?"

"Indeed, I was fifteen when the bombing started. September 7, 1940 at five o'clock. Still light out. Imagine the effrontery. Later on they mostly bombed at night. You know, for the terror." She idly toyed with a furry ear, then looked up and met my gaze. "Are you a religious person?"

"Sorry, no."

"Good, I don't do religion either. Come here often do you?"

"Weekly, on Thursdays. For several years now."

She eyed me carefully. "As a volunteer you must hear a lot about peoples' lives. On your visits here they must tell you a lot about significant things that happened to them, yes?"

"A few of them do. Most just like to have light everyday conversation, though a couple of people have told me some pretty amazing stories. One fellow laid out in great detail how he had escaped from behind the Iron Curtain. He swam miles to freedom."

"Nothing too intimate then? No confessions or clearing of consciences?"

"No, I think most people leave that for the chaplain or family."

"Well, as I said, I'm not a believer."

"And no family nearby?"

She shook her head, then asked, "You have children?"

"I do, yes. Two girls. Both out in the world. Thankfully, doing well."

"You must have been good parents. Doing well doesn't just happen."

"No, I suppose not. I credit my wife for that."

She glanced at my left hand "Still married I see. The ring."

I looked at the gold band on my finger. "Widowed actually."

Our eyes met. "Oh, I'm sorry. Me too. Love of my life." She sighed, and then added, "Gone."

I nodded and heard her pain echo through the silence that followed.

A loud snort from Lacey broke our separate reveries. "My girls have been a big help. They really are chatter boxes. I think it helps them to get things off their chests."

Brenda focused those intense green eyes on mine and said, "I think there may be truth in that."

"I have to tell you that I'm a good listener —pretty much a vault. And I'm really bad with names, so I never remember who said what about whom."

There was a brief silence. I could tell Brenda was weighing the thing in her mind. Then she met my gaze and asked, "Would you like to hear my story?"

I moved from standing at the bedside to sitting in the recliner chair and eased back. "I would love to hear your story."

She reached over to her bedside table and picked up a small glass of water. Putting the straw to her mouth, she took a long draw and then set the glass down.

"For some of the crucial beginning parts you must give me some poetic license. There are bits I have had to fill in with what I thought must have transpired. Also, there are some terrible things that happened that I still don't understand."

She inhaled deeply, letting it out as a cleansing breath that would purify the slate upon which she was about to indelibly write her life.

"One tends to paint oneself with a rosy glow, but the reality I must stress at the outset is that my palette is a combination of disgrace, dishonour and embarrassment. Many of the folks that know the truth of the matter were killed at the time, so please bear with me."

2

1940

The big break for Albert Biggins came during the bombing raid the night of October 1, a full two weeks into the seemingly endless nightly Luftwaffe bombing runs. This night found him deep under the earth. He sat propped against the smooth tile wall of the London Underground platform, feeling as much as hearing the shudder and thump of bombs pummeling his city. As far as he could see along the curving tunnel, people were lying down or sitting, some on the tracks. Everyone was waiting. Waiting, wishing, and hoping.

To fill the time, Albert slowly dragged on his penultimate cigarette. He breathed the smoke in deeply, triggering a chest-racking cough. Christ. Another bloody war. Hadn't the last one been the war to end all wars? Hadn't he given up his lungs and a leg then for Britain? And what had he got for his trouble? Poverty. That's what. Always struggling for the next shilling.

On his right, two little girls sitting beside him with their mother continued to whimper and whine. On his left, four school-aged boys listened intently to a white-bearded gentleman grinding away on an out-of-tune fiddle. Exasperated, Albert pulled himself to a standing position and allowed the knots in his bad hip to loosen, then he picked his way through the crowd. As he reached the top of the stairs, the all-clear sounded and Albert was one of the first to exit the Aldwych Tube Station. The orange glow of fire was reflected in the smoke-filled night sky to the north and he set off in that direction, dodging fallen walls and smashed vehicles. His looting success to that point had been somewhat limited by Air Raid Precaution wardens, whose role was not only to ensure blackout but to limit pillaging from bombed-out buildings. Albert was keen enough, but his bad leg limited his ability to sprint away from pursuers. Physical limitations forced him to be very selective in his choice of targets.

Turning a corner, he saw a dark human shape sprawled in the middle of the street. The area was lit by a firebomb that continued to burn, its thermite and magnesium core hissing in the gutter. Albert approached the inert mass and knelt beside what he could now see was an ARP warden lying on his side. The head was bent back at a hideous angle and the sight triggered the gorge to rise in his throat. He had seen too many bloody deaths in the trenches.

Albert scanned the street and, seeing he was alone, quickly stripped the corpse of a canvas kit bag and dark blue overalls.

"Sorry about this mate. I need this more than you do now."

He picked up the dented helmet sitting several feet away, its chin strap torn and useless, popped it on his own head, and then slid into a nearby alley.

§

"Oy! You! Yes you, laddy!"

The teenage boy stood caught in the headlight intensity of the ARP warden's voice.

"You. Here you dirty little bastard!"

The warden pointed his truncheon at the hunched figure scrambling out of the wreckage of a row house, one of many now converted into irregular masses of brick and timbers smoldering in the dark. The boy looked around, hoping some other wretched creature might be the target of the vitriol, then took a few steps forward. All the while his eyes cast about, seeking possible escape routes.

Albert shifted a few paces to his left, effectively cutting off the most likely path. He took great care not to limp.

"Now!"

The boy scrambled over the last pile of rubble and stood uneasily in front of Albert but well away from the swing of the truncheon.

"What's in the sack then?" Albert said, pointing with his stick at the satchel hanging over the boy's shoulder.

"It's mine. It's from my house!"

"What's in the sack then? Tell me or I'll ram this rod so far up your arse it'll knock out your teeth!"

The boy shifted the satchel, and Albert could see that his small, white-knuckled hands had begun to shake.

"It's me mum's. Some jewelry and stuff."

"Yours you say. That house. Right there." The boy turned to look at the hulking carcass of the building, then swung back with a defiant stare. "Yes!"

"Right then. What's the address?"

The boy's mouth fell agape, and no sound came out. The pause stretched too long. Albert moved forward and swung the stick. The boy ducked, dropped the bag, and scrambled wildly into the smoky blackness. Albert pulled a torch from his kit bag and quickly examined the satchel contents. A matching set of sterling silver candle sticks and a tangled mass of gold chains and sparkles glinted in the beam.

"Well done me," he said and then shoveled the plunder into his own kit bag, slung it onto his shoulder, and limped off into the night.

The next morning found Albert emerging from the Liverpool Street Underground station and heading east. He was dressed in his weary wool suit and worn-at-heel, spit-polished brogues. A flat tweed cap topped his head. He scuffed his way eastward till he found his way to Cutler Street, known in the trade as Loot Lane.

Propped up by a soot-blackened stone wall was a thin mustachioed figure in a shiny black suit whose glance fell far too heavily on each young woman that passed by. He flicked the ashes from a nearly spent cigarette and caught Albert's glance with a bounce of his wiry eyebrows.

"Bertie my lad. Good to see you still with us. Still shifting coal?"

A spasm of distaste curled his tongue, but Albert eased up beside the man and spoke quietly but clearly. "No, Ray, I have here items whose provenance has been assured, but the owners' wish to discretely transfer them to more liquid assets."

Ray barked a laugh. "Just because you nick stuff from the toffs don't mean you need to talk like 'em, Bert." He spat on the pavement, then ground the butt of the cigarette under his heel and met Albert's gaze. "So, no more scrumping rotten apples and rusty screwdrivers then?"

"Afraid not Ray. I do have some items with me today of some significant value. Rather easily transformed into the King's capital, I should think."

Ray shook his head and said, "You may be a wordy bastard, but you have my interest, Bertie. What say you come into my office and we have a look see, yeah?"

Albert nodded and followed the man into the shelter of an alleyway.

8

Robbie Leamington felt the searing heat on his face from the rampant fire. He was one in a crew of nine from Auxiliary Fire Services laying sections of six-inch steel line from a standpipe a thousand feet from the conflagration. It would take them less than twenty minutes. This piped section could supply up to five separate streams of rubberized hose for fire pumps and the two-wheeled portable ladders. The Thames provided an endless supply of water; the AFS just had to get it to the fires. Bombs regularly severed the in-ground water lines, so the forty stationary pumps scattered along the river kept the more easily repaired above-ground lines well supplied. It was back-breaking work, but if he really focused on joining the pipes together, he just might be able to ignore the sounds of gas lines exploding nearby. The fires were creating tremendous whirlwinds of searing smoke and ash, and he coughed up black spit into the gutter.

"Robbie! ROBBIE!" His mate behind him bellowed but his voice was lost in the din. The man stepped up to Robbie, patted him on the shoulder to get his attention, then leaned in and placed his lips to his comrade's ear. "That wall up ahead is gonna go! We should cross over to the north side!"

Now no longer supported by cross beams or roof, the wood and brick wall hung at an inevitable angle. The shuddering impact of collapsing buildings anywhere in the vicinity would ripple through the earth and soon bring the flaming mass to the ground.

Robbie nodded and ordered the crew to route the course of pipe on a different path.

"We need an elbow!" he shouted to a burly man on his left and pointed. "There's one on that truck!" Then, on top of the din, came the sound of a woman shrieking. Robbie's head spun to source the sound just as the wall gave way. He stood eighty feet from the crumpling mass, and when it came down, a devil's breath of fire and cinders roared across the gap and engulfed the crew. A superheated ember smashed into Robbie's left eye socket and he went down. From across the street, two men on a hose saw the plasma of fire and burning air swallow up the piping crew and immediately turned the nozzle on the men.

§

Nurse Dorothy Leamington sank into a hard oak chair and sighed at the comfort. The windows had all been blacked out, but she could tell it was morning by the spring in the steps of the nurses just coming on shift. She had been on her feet for sixteen hours straight, as she had every day since the bombing had begun. Patients were jammed along hospital corridors so full it was difficult to pass. She shuddered to think what would happen if the hospital suffered a direct hit. The ward matron sat slouched beside her, looking as wan and drained as Dorothy felt.

"Bedpans and dressings then bedpans and dressings then more bedpans and yet more dressings. This isn't nursing, it's...I don't know. I'm so tired I can't even think."

"Go home, Dotty. Tonight will come too quickly." The heavy-set woman reached out and patted Dorothy on the shoulder. "Off you go, pet."

Dorothy needed no more prodding, and as she stepped out of the hospital, she drew in a deep, cleansing breath. The outside air was redolent with the smell of coal fires, bombs, and wood smoke from burning buildings but mercifully free of the leaden admixture of feces, urine, suppurating sores, and bleach. She took a Greenline bus homeward, stopping to queue outside a bakery, where she proffered her coins for a sad-looking loaf of bread, then farther down the block picked up a bunch of carrots, some blighted spuds, a spongy onion, a small brick of cheese, and much to her delight, the forequarter of a rabbit.

Recently, game meats were more easily found for sale than beef or lamb, most of which went to the armed forces. But even venison and rabbit were not available every day, and Dorothy eagerly searched her purse for the requisite coins. Her salary of four pounds a month didn't stretch as far as it had before the war. Fortunately, her husband's salary was quadruple that and they were able to manage.

With dinner secured in her net bag, she finished the rest of her journey on foot to Gretton House on Globe Road. She climbed the stairwell to the second floor and crossed the threshold, calling out to her children: "Lawrence! Brenda! Up now! School!"

Dorothy entered the kitchen and would have smiled if she had had the energy. The stove was lit and hot, the room warm and cozy. Robbie had been home at some point in the early hours before going back to the fire hall. She turned up the gas on the Silverette, set up the toast rack, sliced the bread, and searched out a precious block of butter and the marmalade. She turned on the water tap but as had been the case yesterday and the day before, no water flowed.

Dorothy reached for a milk bottle that had been refilled with water and poured the contents into a kettle.

Her young son shuffled into the kitchen. He was fully dressed but looked as though he had slept in his clothes. Dorothy straightened his cardigan, spun his ten-year-old frame around, and tucked in the back of his shirt.

"You need a haircut," she snapped, her tone suggesting hair growth was a moral failing.

"No, Mum. It's fine."

"On Saturday. I'll cut it then."

He turned around to face her, his eyes narrow, and through tight lips repeated, "No, Mum. It's fine!"

"Alright, Sunday then," she said and attempted to tamp down a wayward cowlick. "That curl is a tyrant. It's why you need it cut." Dorothy slid the kettle onto the stovetop. "Rabbit stew tonight. And the toilet pails and water bottles need filling when you get home from school."

"Some big bombs last night," he said, deflecting the possibility of yet more chores. "People in the shelter said Gerry blew up the chemist shop. If I help with the cleanup, I bet they'll give me a bob or two."

"Just don't be taking anything without permission. Even bits of wood. You'll be in jail for looting faster than you can blink but not any faster than I can smack you. And make sure you get to the shelter at dusk. No waiting for the sirens. You know the agreement.

Early to shelter or we ship you out to your aunt's at Windermere for the duration."

"I know, Mum."

A dark cloud in the shape of a teenage girl drifted into the room. Her head hung laxly, causing her disheveled brunette hair to obscure her face and green eyes, which squinted out the light. She was fully dressed, in a white blouse with school plaid tie, jacket, and skirt. Her slippers scuffed along the floor with a staccato hiss. Lawrence met his mother's glance and smirked.

"Did you see your father this morning, Brenda?"

She shook her head. "I got three hours' sleep," she replied, as if that would clarify her response. "Lawrey and I got back from the shelter at six o'clock." She slumped into a chair at the table. "I want to go back to bed. How can I learn anything at school if I feel this tired?"

"Sleep in the Tube station like I do," said Lawrence.

"I can't, can I? I'm sitting there keeping my eye on you. Making sure you don't get in trouble or do something stupid. And this has gone on every night since the beginning of September! I just want to sleep."

Dorothy let the complaint hang in the air before replying, "Tea will be ready in a tick. I just put the water on. Here, have a piece of toast."

Brenda's day in class was long and boring, but lunchtime was full of chatter about the bombings and the air war. Several times during geography she had nodded off with her hands propping up her chin, only to snap awake and find drool slipping from the corner of her mouth.

After school, Brenda made her way home and unlocked the front door, dropped her satchel by the stairway, and was struck by the luscious aroma of stew. She quietly made her way to the kitchen and lifted the lid of the pot on the stove. It was bubbling quietly and she deeply breathed in the smells. Replacing the lid, she scanned the countertops for anything to roll back the overwhelming pulse of hunger that gnawed at her stomach. A bowl of apples held promise, and Brenda carefully selected the least scabby. She gave it a vigorous rub on her blouse, bringing the skin up to a satisfying shine. There was no sign of her brother. No doubt he was fetching water. Her mother would be asleep for a few more hours, so Brenda bit deeply into the fruit as she quietly stepped outside. The door latch closed with a satisfying click.

"Afternoon, Brenda. Off to the library, dear?"

A heavy-set woman in her forties was coming up the stairs as Brenda was heading down.

"Yes, Mrs. Teal. How was your night? I didn't see you at the Tube station."

"No. I was across town helping my sister. She's expecting a babe soon, and what with four already, well, she needed a bit of a hand. Then the bombs started falling so we spent the duration in an Anderson shelter in their back yard."

"Bit cramped was it?"

"Oh dear it was. A bit like sardines we were. Lots of blankets, though, so we were cozy."

Brenda nodded and asked, "Have you seen Lawrey?"

"He and my Jimmy went out to search some water. I told them to be back by five."

Brenda thanked her neighbour and headed down Globe Road, then turned onto Roman Road and walked the short distance to the red brick mass of Bethnal Green Library. The bulk of the place, full of knowledge, reinforced for her the weighty certainty that Britain would endure. Since its reinvention in 1922 as a library from its original incarnation as the Bethnal House Asylum, it had been a repository of the documented prowess of the Empire. Surely no bomb would dare mar the façade, never mind obliterate the contents. Brenda had held onto her finished apple, the fruit nibbled down to a slim, browning core and now she threw it as far she could onto the treed green sward that fronted the building. A rook swooped down and pounced on it while voicing its desperation. Brenda climbed the three low-rise steps and entered between the paired columns that the architect had crowned with elegant terracotta pilasters.

She made her way to the sorting area of returned books and met with one of the librarians, Evangelina Babcock, a brittle and sour spinster who used words instead of little steel daggers.

"Ah, at last. There may be a war on, Brenda, but there is no excuse for tardiness. Look at this pile. If we all whimsically rattled around without notice of others' greater needs, we would be French."

She pointed with a hooked finger at a large wooden box on wheels, brimming with returned items. "Onto the carts and out to the stacks. Your visage is somewhat drawn, so let's make alacrity the watchword for today shall we?"

"Yes, Miss Babcock."

Always keen to avoid the woman's acidic censure, Brenda worked quickly, all the while ensuring the librarian's fastidious standards were maintained. She found that the repetitive lifting and stooping required to replenish the cart had dissipated the leaden mental torpor she had been battling all afternoon. Now she felt buoyant and engaged in her work.

Up in the stacks, a thin, middle-aged gentleman with a slight overbite and wearing wire-rimmed glasses approached her.

"I don't suppose you could help me? *Civil Engineer's Reference Book*. Trautwine the author. Published in thirty-seven. Here is the call number." He handed her a slip of paper. "The librarian says it is not out on loan, but I'm afraid I can't find it in the stacks." And then as if to imply the urgency of this request, he added, "I need to calculate some truss stresses and beam rupture moments."

The man's Oxbridge accent revealed his educational roots, while his suit and posture informed her of his class. His greying hair was combed straight back. He wore a bow tie.

"Normally I'd be at my college, but I was at a meeting when inspiration hit and, well, one must respond to the muse when she calls, mustn't one? Any thoughts where it might be?"

Brenda smiled broadly and bravely met his gaze. "I do. In fact," she said, pausing to bend down and reach to the bottom shelf of her returns cart, "I was in the process of reshelving it." She handed him a leather-bound volume. "I think this is what you're looking for. A whole chapter on force in rigid bodies, I believe."

The man started; incredulity emblazoned across his face. "Oh yes, splendid."

"Good luck, sir. Glad to be of help."

He nodded, spun on his heels, and began eagerly flipping through the pages of the tome. Brenda was pleased with the man's reaction and with herself for remembering the book's table of contents glimpsed when the book had fallen open as she was loading it onto her cart.

Some time later, she was down to the last book on her last cart: Havelock Ellis, *The Psychology of Sex*. Brenda thumbed through to the table of contents, and finding a chapter titled "The Sexual Impulse in Youth," she quickly scanned the stacks for possible interlopers who might correctly interpret her reddening cheeks. Seeing no one near, she indulged in several daring minutes of reading and rereading the more titillating and informative passages. Details on erotic dreams and self-stimulation were particularly revealing and to some extent, reassuring. Her impulses of late as she lay in her bed at night had been so uncharacteristic and intense, that Brenda had feared that maybe something was wrong with her. Even if she didn't understand the subtleties, here was medical proof. She wasn't a deviant after all.

Then, sensing the distant and impatient presence of the librarian, Brenda reluctantly closed and shelved the book before making her way back to the reference section, where the mass of an *Oxford English Dictionary* rested heavily on an oaken pedestal. Based on her quick read of Ellis, she flipped through to specific enlightening entries but terminated her research when, looking up, she saw her supervisor glance over to her while holding a pencil vibrating between her long, narrow fingers. Brenda turned the current page into the anonymous depths of the textbook and then approached the librarian's desk.

"Four carts re-shelved, Miss Babcock."

"Two bob for a job well done, Brenda. Shall we see you on time tomorrow?"

As though the exchange of money from hand to hand was somehow unseemly, the woman had left Brenda's wages lying on the counter.

"Yes, Miss Babcock," she replied, picking up the coins just as the bow-tied gentleman from the stacks approached.

"I'll sign this out, if I may," he said and proffered the engineering manual to the librarian.

Evangelina nodded, "Yes, of course."

With brisk efficiency, she processed the loan and was rewarded with a warm, "Thank you again, ladies," as he slipped a black homburg hat on his head and headed for the exit.

"Do you know who that is, Brenda?"

"No, Miss Babcock, I do not," she replied before slipping into her coat.

"Good. He was not here."

Hunger had knotted her stomach and Brenda hurried home. The thoughts of a hot meal made her dizzy with longing. As Brenda stepped through the door, she was met by her mother and brother. Dorothy was dressed in her nurse's uniform, her face drawn and tense. Her brother was attached to his mother's waist, tears on his cheeks.

"I've just got word that your father's been injured," Dorothy said. "Last night. Bit of a burn on his face, apparently. Not to worry. I'm off to the hospital now, so look after your brother. There's lots of stew for both of you." She grabbed her handbag and made for the door.

"No. We'll come with you. I want to see him."

"Not yet. Just do what I say, will you? The hospital is too hectic right now. Let me tend him tonight and then we'll see what's what."

"But we want to come too!"

"Shut it. You'll only be in the way. We'll see where we stand tomorrow. Have I been heard? Are we clear?" Her mother shot her daughter a no-nonsense nurse's glare, then marched down the hall, leaving her daughter and son to make their way together through the perils of the night.

8

Albert stood upright and still in what might have appeared to his fellow churchgoers like pious contemplation. The holy voices of the choir and congregation in evensong reverberated throughout the vaulted dome of Saint Paul's Cathedral, the gilt surfaces reflected the easing of the evening light. The final hymn ended, dissipating into the minds of the devout. He watched his fellow Londoners file out into the darkening sky, then made his way along the north aisle and into Saint Dunstan's chapel and sat on a bench. A candle beside him flickered and glowed. Albert shifted his sagging satchel to the floor by his feet and made to read the *Book of Common Prayer* that had been sitting on the bench. Scanning the Psalter, he thumbed his way through to the ninth psalm and read, *"For the poor shall not always be forgotten : the patient abiding of the meek shall not perish for ever."*

"Well, I've been poor and abiding for too long," he said, his voice merely a breath. He snapped the book shut and checked his newly acquired wristwatch. "Far too long."

In the solitary emptiness of the chapel, Albert slipped out of his shoes, scrambled into his ARP coveralls, and strapped his helmet on tightly before stepping into a pair of well-abused leather boots. Then he slung his satchel over his shoulder and headed for the exit. An elderly priest in full choir regalia of cassock, surplice, and tippet stood at the door, blessing the remaining supplicants as they departed.

"Bless you for the work you do, my son." He reached out to shake Albert's hand. "May God bless you and keep you safe."

"Thank you, Reverend. If the Germans come tonight, I'll be ready and waiting."

A slip of glow hung in the western sky as he began his journey to Belgravia, the upscale borough to the south-west of Buckingham Palace and north of the Thames. It would take Albert an hour on foot to reach his target, but any other mode of transport put him at risk of being identified or, worse, seconded into real ARP duties.

Darkness settled on the Strand and the sidewalks emptied; those pedestrians still out and about hurried to their destinations. The weather boded well for yet another night of bombing.

Albert turned right off Grosvenor Place onto Chapel Street, passed by Belgravia Square garden, and with the Spanish Embassy on his left, continued on to the corner of Belgravia Mews, where he paused. Down that street was the Star Tavern. His stump was throbbing, and couldn't he just go for a pint after all this walking? He closed his eyes to fight off the wanting of it. No, he could never be seen in this neighbourhood.

Albert squeezed his fists tightly and crossed over to Lowndes Place and the elegant, white-faced row houses brimming with wealth. He scanned down the block; many of the residences were fronted with wrought iron railings, Doric columns framing the doorways. Albert crossed over to a home that sat midblock. A sliver of light was sneaking out from the sill of a front window. He climbed the six stairs of the stoop and gave the lion's head knocker what he hoped would be interpreted as an officious rap. Moments passed till finally the door cracked open.

"Good evening," said an elderly gentleman in servant's livery, who eyed Albert carefully by the muted light spilling over his shoulder.

"ARP. I'm checking up on blackout violations. You've got a wee beam slipping out your front window. Don't want to give Gerry a target."

"Yes. Yes of course, Warden. I'll tend to it immediately."

"Thank you, sir. The neighbours, are they at home and secure?"

"Most have gone elsewhere actually. I'm here by myself with Cook."

"So not much problem with blackout for your neighbours then?"

"Well, to my right, that's been locked up tight since four o'clock. A single gentleman who makes it a habit to leave town for the night and return in the morning; however, he takes his valet and cook with him it seems," he said with a resentful tone. "So no lights on there. On my left, Lord Meldon has taken his whole household to his estate in Berkshire for the duration."

"And beside them?"

"I am told that the Earl has returned to his estate. Somewhere in the Cotswolds, I believe. Next to them is Colonel Rease-Jones. He has decamped back to India."

"You've been very helpful. There is every likelihood that the Germans will bomb tonight. Do you have adequate shelter?"

"Indeed. Cook and I will head for the wine cellar rather than the public shelter."

"You'll both be in good company then."

"Sir?"

"The Rothschilds."

"Sir?"

"The bottles of Bordeaux."

"Ah, yes. Sadly not for me to drink, sir."

"Wouldn't hurt for a rattle to shake one loose, I should think."

The man at the door pursed his lips but did not reply.

"Alright," said Albert. "Well, good night then, and please tend to that window."

The door shut with a quiet click, and Albert stepped away and walked down the block.

"The earl it is then," he thought. Buffered by two empty homes, whatever noise he might make would not be heard. Of course, if and when the bombing began, he could play a drum kit and nobody would hear a thing.

The moon was a waxing crescent and low in the sky as it settled toward the horizon. The day had been gloriously sunny, and the night sky was still free of clouds. It did not bode well for the city. Albert found his way to the portico of the earl's residence, his presence obscured by a column and the darkness. Then, with a weak and low whine that pitched up to a loud and frantic wail came the sound of air raid sirens in nearby Hyde Park. The searchlights blinked on, the beams streaking in wild arcs in pursuit of the coming German bombers. Minutes passed as a frisson of excitement increased his pulse. At last, the rumble of the planes in the distance rolled across the city. Albert reached down into his satchel and extracted a pair of leather gloves and a small pry bar. The bombs started exploding miles away.

"Goin' for the docks again," he thought and was about to give the door a try when he heard the pounding of feet on the sidewalk. Fear grabbed his breath. There was the sound of crying, accompanied by a woman's voice and the staccato sound of high heels and little feet striking the pavement. The steps faded as the pair fled down the street and around the corner.

Suddenly there came deafening blasts from the anti-aircraft gun emplacement in the park. He smiled, rammed the pry into the door jamb at the latch, and heaved with his shoulder. With a loud crack it gave way and he entered the house.

Albert closed the door behind him and was immediately enveloped in a deep and consuming blackness. Unmoving, he stood and waited for his eyes to adjust, but the absolute dark remained.

The subtle tingle of disorienting vertigo coupled with the mad thumping of the antiaircraft fire hurried his reach for the torch in his satchel. He snapped it on and felt a wave of relief as the narrow beam bled light into his surroundings.

To his right was the living room, elegant and serene. A large, ornately framed landscape hung on the wall.

"Is that a Turner?" he whispered.

Albert knew he lacked expertise in works of art, but this piece bore the requisite sunset, ships, and Thames, and he had seen something just like it in the National Gallery. He moved further into the home and noted a gilt and crystal teardrop chandelier hovering in place over a rosewood dining table replete with chairs for twelve. The tall walnut and mahogany eight-day longcase clock kept silent watch over the room, its mechanism absent the weekly twist of the key. Albert turned right, stepped beyond the small but ornately faced elevator, and climbed a flight of steps. Haughty-faced ancestors hung on the stairwell walls, mute and unperturbed by the air campaign being waged outside.

On the second floor, he chose to turn left and was rewarded with what appeared to be the master bedroom. A tall, Georgian walnut-and-tulip chest of drawers caught his attention. Sitting squarely on top was a wooden box crafted from bird's-eye maple. Albert flipped back the lid and examined the contents. Tie tacks and jewel-studded pins were neatly aligned alongside two gold fob watches and some pinkie rings made of what appeared under his torch to be platinum. The box was a keeper, he decided. Well, maybe not. Too traceable. He emptied the contents into his satchel, then replaced the box and moved on to the chest. Underwear pressed and folded. Next drawer, garters and socks paired and arranged by colour. Next drawer, collars and dress shirts pressed and folded. Next drawer, casual shirts pressed and folded.

"I'll have to get me a valet one day," he muttered.

Beside the walnut four-poster bed was a rosewood table banded in rich mahogany. Sitting in its center was an ornate silver dish brimming with half crowns, florins, shillings, pence, and the detritus of the earl's emptied pockets. The coins went into Albert's pocket and the dish into his satchel.

He crossed the room to a wide armoire and rifled through the inner and outer pockets of bespoke jackets and pants, finding nothing. Outside, the bombing suddenly sounded closer and urged Albert onward.

"This must be where the missus spends her lonely nights," Albert whispered as he repeated the rummaging process through the room across the hall. From the top drawer of a walnut chest he withdrew a dainty, lace-trimmed silk undergarment and felt his groin pulse. Albert brought it to his face and breathed in the delicate floral scent. Lilac filled his lungs and repulsed, he flung the garment to the floor. This was his mother's scent. He made his way to a dressing table and to his delight was rewarded with rings, earrings, broaches—and the crowning glory, a necklace heavy with diamonds and sapphires. It was so breathtakingly beyond his experience that he felt a powerful impulse to simply put it back in its case and leave it be. By merely touching it with his glove he was contaminating it. Mind you, he wouldn't have to hock it though, would he, just keep it as a secret treasure. Maybe one day he would even have someone worthy of it. Albert poured all the jewels into his satchel.

Up the next flight of stairs and oh, this looks like an office and this looks like a safe. What could be in the safe that was more precious than the necklace? He tried the handle. It was locked, so he attempted to shift the black mass. Two hundredweight if it's an ounce, he thought. Self-aware enough to know that he would never play in the premier league, Albert reluctantly dismissed the possibility of opening the safe, spun on his heels and headed down the stairs.

8

Brenda eyed her brother sitting at the kitchen table with his nose deep in the newspaper. "Lawrey, come and dry the dishes."

"It says here that boys are putting out the incendiaries with garbage bin lids and sand!"

"Yes, well it also says that there is terrible risk with such things and that under no circumstances would such activities be permitted for unauthorized persons, certainly not the likes of you."

"It says that simply cutting off the oxygen supply puts them out, and that the AFS is putting sand bins and pails on the streets to make it available."

"To make it available for firefighters like Daddy, not little boys."

"I'm not little and you know it. I just want to do my bit."

"Well, right now your bit is to come here and dry these dishes."

"Don't be so bossy. Let God dry them. He doesn't do much else around here."

She let out a loud deep sigh. He stared at her and flung the paper to the floor. "And," he continued, "why does God allow bad people to drop bombs on good people?"

"Free will. God gave us all free will. They'll get punished in hell."

"Great, but how does that help us now? And why does God let bad things happen to good people like Dad? If God is so all-powerful, why did he let Dad get hurt? Where was his guardian angel? It's not fair!"

Brenda looked again at her little brother. He wasn't so little anymore. Lawrence was now almost as tall as she, and he was three years younger.

"No, it's not fair," she said and wondered whether she should tell him her thoughts—that she'd come to feel that while a spiritual mind might believe in God, her rational mind could not, certainly not the wantonly fickle one worshiped in the Bible. Would voicing these doubts make Lawrence feel even more at a loss or would it have some other consequence? Brenda hugged him and said, "It's time to go to the Underground. Put a scarf on; it'll get cold tonight. I'll get the blankets and pillows while you get your coat on. Bring your history textbook."

A knock at her door revealed their neighbour Mrs. Teal and Jimmy, her son.

"Good evening, Brenda. I was wondering if you might take Jimmy with you to the Tube. You're just heading out, yes? You see, it's my sister, the one I told you about. She gave birth today and there were complications, dear. I'm going to have to head over there and set things right." She sighed heavily and continued, "Best if my lad is elsewhere, if you know what I mean. I'm going to have to bring the clutch of them back here in the morning," she said with little enthusiasm.

"Of course," said Brenda. "We'd be happy to have Jimmy accompany us."

"Ooh, you're a love. He's been fed, watered, washed, and here are his bedclothes, so he'll be no trouble," she said, pushing forward her son, who was clutching a pillow and two blankets.

Schoolmates and back-alley chums, Jimmy and Lawrence bore wide, satisfied grins as the woman turned to take the flight of stairs.

At the Bethnal Green Tube Station, the three children found a well-lit spot inside on the floor, directly under a light hanging from the ceiling. Brenda spread out their bedding and the trio settled in to read. The Underground line was still under construction, but the station had been requisitioned as a bomb shelter. It was sparsely occupied when they arrived but would fill rapidly when the sirens sounded.

With her brother snuggled in beside her, the quietude of reading melded with the soporific effect of a full stomach and she slipped into a deep sleep. A dream formed, clear and disturbing. Brenda was being pursued naked through the stacks of the library, a leather-bound book gripped tightly in her hand. She felt a panicky need to find its spot in the shelves but it lacked a reference number on its spine, and each attempt to file the book resulted in her knocking other books to the floor. Her pursuer, an unseen and relentless menace, was getting closer at each failed attempt. Brenda fled and suddenly there was her father, standing at the library door. His face was both hideously scarred and simultaneously completely wrapped in white bandages that oozed bloody fluids. Abruptly, the scenario changed and she found herself in church, standing in the nave with goose bumps covering her naked skin. The choir in full regalia turned and in unison raised their arms, fingers pointing in admonishment, their collective voice a single note growing louder and higher into a shrill scream.

Brenda snapped awake at the sound of the air raid siren filling the night. People were scrambling into the space, some voices pitchy with excitement, some frantic, most in stoic silence. Little children were crying while mothers and their elderly parents scrambled for a place to claim. Lawrey and Jimmy were gone.

"Went to find a loo; they said to tell you."

Still dragging herself to full wakefulness, Brenda looked quizzically at the young woman beside her.

"The two lads. Gone for a pee. Must have been half an hour ago now."

As Brenda pushed herself to her feet, the shudder of bombs rippled through the earth.

§

For the boys, the night sky was transcendent—alive with flashing arc lights, exploding anti-aircraft shells, the bass line of bombers, and mid-range wavering drone of fighter planes; the symphony only lacked a melody line to perfect the spectacle.

"Look at that!"

"Heinkel!" yelled Lawrey in a vain attempt to be heard above the din. They were both pointing into the sky at a flaming bomber tracking across the blackness, its rear fuselage and port-side wing ablaze in yellow and orange plumes. It sank from their line of sight as a load of incendiary bombs impacted blocks away, filling the rooflines with glowing smoke.

"C'mon!" Lawrey shouted, and the two boys sprinted toward the newest source of fiery enchantment.

Guided by their radio operators, the Heinkel pilots rode a radio beacon, its strong, clear tone transmitted from the coast of France. Where and when that signal transected a second beam from a different position, the bombardiers had but a few set minutes before releasing their load. Regardless of clouds or black night, the invisible pied piper led squadron upon squadron to London town.

The Luftwaffe pilot listened to the radio chatter from the incendiary bombers already returning from their runs. Flying above the ack-ack, the planes had encountered little initial resistance, and the thousands of two-pound, fourteen-inch, roof-piercing incendiary armaments had released a firestorm. The pilot checked in again with his radio operator, bombardier, and gunners, giving them a heads up on the level of resistance to expect as they flew up the Thames. His aeroplane hauled a payload of eight two-hundred-and-fifty-kilogram high-explosive bombs across the night. Not only had the planes radio beacons to follow; London was now lit up by so many fires that targeting would be grossly simplified. Smoke from the burning buildings might obscure some specific targets, but they would be in the ballpark.

"Acht minuten!" shouted the radio operator through his head set as time seemed to slow. The bombardier took over the controls and began sighting the ground below.

Brenda ran down the street screaming at the top of her voice for her brother. It was difficult to see; the air was full of choking smoke; the only light was that reflected from the fires on the ground. She turned off Cambridge Heath Road onto Three Colts Lane. Here incendiaries littered the tarmac, the sidewalks and the buildings but Brenda had no idea where the boys might be fighting the bombs, hiding in shelter or collapsed in fear. Now onto Dunbridge Street, she could see the glowing orange ribbons of the Great Eastern Railway tracks.

"Zehn secunden!"

She pleaded for her brother to appear as she ran, her voice now just a raspy wail. A big black dog ran toward her, frenzied-looking and panting, its tongue lolling, his eyes frantic. Brenda called to it, but he ran from her.

"Bomben weg!"

Released of the tonnage, the plane leapt upward as the bombs fell free. The pilot banked the Heinkel back towards the Fatherland, his objective met. He blanked from his mind any thoughts of the vapourized, charred and shattered bodies far below him. Instead, he imagined his wife Greta and little Stefan, deep asleep in Dresden, as the compass guided him home.

Brenda heard the bombs coming, the speed of sound outstripping their free fall velocity. With terror as a specific intent, the German armament manufacturers had riveted a set of inexpensive but effective cardboard whistles to the explosives' fins. As the bombs fell, the shrieking harbingers foretold all Londoners of the impending devastation they would soon wreak. She leapt into the shelter of a doorway just as the world around her erupted and disappeared.

3

Deep in sleep, Lacey was dreaming; her paws trembled, and her upper lip twitched. Brenda stroked the animal's ears softly to settle her. "My scalp was scorched; all the hair on the left side of my head was burned off. And three ribs as well as my right lower leg were broken."

"I can't imagine how scared you must have been. A situation like that is so far out of my realm of experience," I said quietly and then espied a thin, angry ripple of scar running from somewhere behind her left ear down her throat to her clavicle.

"I was lying in my hospital bed, feeling very sorry for myself with my head all bandaged. My leg was in a cast from my toes to my groin and it was difficult to breathe because they had taped my chest. At this point, no one had told me that my brother had died. My father marched into my room, wearing a bandage over his left eye. The very first thing he said when he saw me was, 'Why weren't you with your brother?' I was stunned at first. I didn't know how to respond, so I said nothing."

Feeling the weight of loss, Brenda bowed her head, I think from shame.

"He died, my little brother did; doing his bit."

Brenda's eyes brimmed with tears, but she continued, "After my father left the room, I thought more about what he had said. Did he mean that he thought I should have been with Lawrey and that I should have died too? Or did he mean that I was at fault for not being with him and protecting him? Did my father really have the gall to believe that I would abandon my little Lawrey as if I had been outside in the middle of an air raid just having a bit of a lark? Or was it that I would be so irresponsible as to give the lad permission to go outside when bombs were raining down?"

"He didn't ask how you two had become separated?"

"Never did. I told my mother, of course, but by then the seeds of guilt had flowered—a bouquet I carry to this day. Stuck in the hospital, I didn't even get to go to Lawrey's funeral. Of course, in the end, what my parents thought didn't really matter."

Brenda looked up and met my gaze. "But I get ahead of myself."

She roused the dog on her bed and asked, "Do you mind if we call it a day? I'm fading a bit and could use a nap."

"Pain okay? Shall I call a nurse?"

"No, dear, I'm fine." She reached out to grasp my hand. "I'll see you next week, shall I?"

"We'll be here with bells on, Brenda. You take care and we'll see you soon."

When we got home, I announced to the house, "We're back!" Ever the hopeful one, Lacey trotted into the family room, the kitchen, and then upstairs to the bedroom. My wife wasn't there, of course, hadn't been for more than two years. Still, it was our ritual and felt like the completion of our outing.

It was a beautiful May day, so I took a cup of tea into the garden and soaked up a bit of sun. The chickadees were making fuel runs back and forth to the birdhouse that hung from our much cherished styrax japonicus, their babies frantic for grubs. In a couple of weeks, the little dangling bobbles would burst into bloom, flooding the whole garden with a scent unique unto itself—but if I had to put a label on it, I would say the hills of Grenada. We stopped off there while on a cruise several years ago. On an outing we visited a fruit plantation. The air was tropical and heady, yet somehow delicate. The birdhouse was a bit of a fun. My wife painted it from a Caribbean palette, lime green being the primary wall colour with trim in bright orange, teal, and sky blue. I sat and watched her paint it. She was so immersed in her task that she forgot I was there loving her. Finally, she looked up and laughed when she saw the expression on my face.

When our teenage girls were getting too big for the small bungalow we lived in, financial circumstances allowed us to purchase a post-war stucco box on a well-situated lot. We knocked down the old, rotting cadaver and built something more suitable. Pretty much every living plant in the garden had been planned, selected, planted, and coveted by my wife. She loved the act of gardening, sometimes staying out till long after dark, literally rooting around out there. When the girls had fledged with careers and homes of their own, she spent endless hours cajoling the perennials.

One day she was weeding in the dahlia bed on her knees, right hand supporting her weight, left hand pulling up the damned weeds and horsetail. Suddenly her forearm gave way and she screamed in pain. She walked into the kitchen carrying her arm like a dead cat. I took her to the hospital, where they took X-rays, then a CT scan, then an MRI, then a nuclear medicine scan. Cancer of the fallopian tubes that had metastasized to pretty much everywhere was the diagnosis. When you absorb such a verdict, the world suddenly shifts, and every truth you held up to that point is violated. You float in a miasma of isolation, fear, and fury. For thirty-five years, she was my main support and everything that I counted on to battle the nasty weather life threw at us as a couple. You know what happens to a tent when the centre pole comes down.

Tuesdays are Bereavement Walk days. We are a small group who have lost loved ones, spouses mostly, but some have lost a child. We get together and go for a walk that ends up at a coffee shop by the water. The Community Place coordinated it; they are an organization sponsored by the city and the hospital. They provide the trained volunteers who come along to guide us through the grieving process.

"You can't go around grief, you have to go through it," is their mantra. I agree, but it is a messy process. As I say, it's been over two years now—well, twenty-five months, four days, and six hours, and if I look at my watch, I can tell you to the minute. You'd think that all the grieving we did together before she died would count for something after she died, like some kind of down payment. Not so, at least not for me. If I had thought it was bad before, I had no idea what was coming down the pipe after her death. That is part

of the problem with grieving. It's like, what the hell, where did that come from? No sleep at night. Zombie all day. Lose weight, then gain weight, then lose weight. Lacey would look at me with her big, dark eyes, and I would hear a little whimper, and then I'd lose it for three hours, just weeping out of control. That is part of it, the trauma of grief; it is overwhelming. It comes from the slightest of triggers or sometimes no trigger at all. Just a tsunami rolling over the horizon and suddenly you are awash. The dog and I helped each other, though, mostly just by being there for each other. Of course, the girls were affected too, and I had still had to be their father.

Not long after being widowed, I went through one of my weight-loss phases—no interest in food whatsoever. One day, as I was sitting in the family room, staring at the wall, Lacey came up to me and started whining for her dinner. When I ignored her petition, she more insistently and repeatedly pawed at my foot. I lost it and screamed, "Leave me alone, dammit! You stupid idiot." She cowered and fled with her tail between her legs and then hid behind the sofa. I burst into tears, ran upstairs, and slammed the bedroom door. That first year was a shambles.

"My sister died when we were kids," said Amanda, one of the ladies in the walking group. We hospice volunteers are not allowed to talk about specifics of what we hear when visiting, but I had just mentioned to our intrepid troupe of grievers that someone I knew had lost a little brother during the war.

"She was nine and I was seven," Amanda continued. "I recall being truly sad when she died; but if I'm honest, I also remember feeling relief. She had been sick for so long, and my parents spent what was to me an inordinate amount of time tending her. Children are so egocentric. I just wanted to have a normal family."

"Truth be told, when Alistair died of prostate cancer, I felt relief." Lisa was a heavy-set, elderly lady who always wore a long dress and running shoes on the walk. "The cancer had gone to his brain by that time and he wasn't my Alistair anymore. I had to say goodbye to the love of my life, but he was just a shell of his former self when he died," she said. Her hands were clasped tightly in front of her. I could see that she still wore her wedding ring.

"The long decline was torture. The fatigue of tending to him wore me down. If I had to lose him..." she said as tears came to her eyes, "if I had to lose him, I wish he had had a heart attack and not had to suffer all those months."

The ladies in the group are great at hugs; they hug everybody, and they swarmed Lisa. Being hugged by a clutch of emotive women is very reassuring, but originally, I found hugging random guys a little off-putting—part of the problem for men, I think. It is tough to share physical intimacy with an unfamiliar man after a lifetime of masculine internalizing. The guys in the group are getting better at it, but it does not come naturally to us as it seems to for the women.

It took me more than a year to figure out that it is not the hug itself that helps. It is the emotional connection that comes with the contact that brings some sort of relief. I told this guy Ben who was having a really rough time, "Without a mate, your daily touch count drops to pretty much zero. You feel empty. A hand on your shoulder and a good solid handshake is a good place to start. But there is nothing like a bear hug to let you know that somebody really cares about you."

4

Yoga Thursday again and we've got a new yogi. Brent, our long-time teacher, has left for greener organic pastures, and for the last several weeks we have suffered at the hands of a series of wannabe Deepak Chopras. I like the meditative centering that comes with yoga, and I enjoy doing an *om* at the start and end of the class, but the militant vegan thing some of them are into is a bit too much. Today's teacher, on the other hand, is almost anti-yoga, with her brush-cut hair and bodybuilder's profile. She's all business, and we start the class with no *om*, diving right into some heavy-duty stretching exercises. Already I'm not liking her. I'm deaf in my left ear from the radiation treatment on my head those three decades ago, and she speaks far too fast with a heavy accent that I cannot parse. I turn my head and see lots of confused faces. This will not do.

When I come in the door after the class, Lacey is asleep and doesn't hear me. She is old in dog years—eighty-something, I think—and not only have cataracts diminished her sight but her hearing is also pretty much gone. I had taken Lacey for a brisk morning walk, so she was sleeping off the exercise. Brisk was a relative term, mind you, what with her nose being engaged at every post and her desire to shuffle rather than stride along our route. When I woke her, she saw that I had my yoga togs on and immediately jumped off the sofa. We did the drill of bandana, shower, and lunch, then headed for the hospice.

The sky had filled in and now the first drops of rain were falling. By the time we got to parking the car, it was really coming down and puddles had formed all along the sidewalk. We shook ourselves off at the front door, and after we had said our hellos to the administrative staff and nurses, we sought out Vinda, the laundress. She keeps the linen clean for ten beds and ten bathrooms; no small feat when one is dealing with the dying, who endlessly ooze, seep, and excrete. Vinda is always ready with a smile and a towel to dry Lacey. Nobody wants a wet mutt on their bed.

I left Lacey at the nursing station for a minute, as I had forgotten to pick up my name tag. Back at the entrance, I also stopped to take a quick look at the memorial table. There were three paper place cards atop it, folded and standing like little headstones. In a vase behind each one was a long-stem red rose. I read the labels and found that Vera's mum, the Asian lady, had died since our last visit, and so had Dennis. No more fishing tales. The third name was of a chap I had never met. He came into the hospice with a specific request for no volunteer visitors, family only. As I read the names, it struck me how little impact their deaths had on me. I don't mourn not having a second chance to talk to people I meet at the grocery store or on the subway. We just yack on for a bit then go our separate ways. Maybe it is the same thing here, I don't know. Maybe I just add the hospice deaths to my existing chasm of grief that is already so deep that I don't even notice.

When I returned to the nursing station, Lacey's nose was to the carpet. No slouch when there are crumbs to be found on the floor; she had scanned the area with fastidious efficiency. Off to the rooms we went, making Bea our first port of call. The door was ajar and the room dark, with no artificial light. She was deeply asleep when I peeked in and looked so much frailer than the previous week. We backed out and headed to the next room, where a new resident had moved in the day before. I knocked and, hearing no reply, stepped into the room. I saw the back of a young man standing by the bed, looking down at the occupant. When he turned, I opened my mouth to introduce myself, but he had seen Lacey at my side.

"No dogs! Out!" He pointed to the door as his face turned into a snarl.

I was quite taken aback and simply gaped for a moment, then nodded, turned, and left. Grief is a funny thing; social niceties go out the door sometimes. I stood outside the room for a few moments, framing how I wanted to express to this man that although his mother was dying, this was no reason to be rude and that he should control himself. Then I realized that he was being rude because he had no control, not of himself nor of his situation, and telling him as much was not going to give him any. Of course, Lacey took no umbrage at his outburst, despite being the target of the man's ill temper. She looked up at me as if to say, "What's the holdup?" and so we went down the hall to see Brenda.

She was looking much better. Brenda had been fighting her cancer battle by herself at home, and now that she was getting three square meals a day and nursing care 24/7, she had put on a pound or two, though she still had the diminutive body of a starving adolescent. I suspected I might have to adjust my first estimate of her longevity.

You just never know. Some people come into the hospice and you think they will be good for weeks, then they end up dying four hours after admission. Others have such a rabid desperation to cling to a life of pain and anguish that their tenacity can be shocking. My wife was a fighter until she decided she'd had enough.

Lacey and Brenda fussed over each other for several minutes. Then apparently, a dog nap was in order and as Lacey settled into the folds of the quilt, Brenda looked up at me expectantly and said, "Are you at all interested in another instalment of my saga?"

"Absolutely, but it's kind of dark in here today," I said. "What say we open these drapes?"

Brenda nodded assent, so I inched them open and saw the gardener, also a volunteer, out in her patch, moving a barrow full of crushed gravel down a pathway. It looked miserable out there; the rain was still pelting down. "You have to give her credit for her resolve."

"I have been told that she's from Ireland, originally; they're good at being wet, the Irish," she said and laughed brightly.

I sat down in the recliner chair, tipping it back till the foot riser came up, and she began.

"I was laid up in the hospital. After three weeks or so they cut off the first leg cast and replaced it with a shorter one. The burn did not amount to much really. Eventually I began hobbling around on crutches. My mother would pop in from the wards several times a day, but my father came just once more during my stay. He could have come more often if he wished, as he couldn't work as a firefighter with only one good eye. His eyelid had suffered terribly, and his cornea had been scarred beyond full healing. I think there was damage to the lens of his eye as well. The ember had cooked it like a three-minute egg—instant cataracts. They needed the beds in the hospital for the more immobile patients, so he'd come in to get the bandages changed and so on; it wasn't like he couldn't stop in to check on me. I don't know what he did during the day. It wasn't work, though I suspect drink or the bookmakers. In any case, as I say, I only saw him the once after his initial visit."

Brenda began to fidget with Lacey's collar, rotating it slowly around the dog's neck, and in response, the dog grunted softly.

"My aunt came to the hospital one day to take me to Windermere. My mother told me that the arrangement had been made because I couldn't make my way on crutches to bomb shelters in a timely way, so I was at risk. That may well have been true, but I suspect it was also that I would have to spend a lot of time at home recuperating with my father, who was not terribly keen to even look at me with his one good eye."

"Your aunt, was she your mother's sister?"

"No. She was my father's younger brother's wife. Fiona was only ten years older than I, to the day. Other than sharing the same birthday, though, we were pretty much opposites in every way. Maybe that's why we got on. Where I was short, Fiona was tall, almost six feet. Where I was what my mother called 'bird boned,' Fiona was solid and broad of shoulder. She wore her long, blonde hair in a ponytail. I always imagined she was blessed with royal Norse blood, a Valkyrie."

"So she came to fetch you and take you away to Valhalla?"

Brenda laughed. "Hardly. No, we lived in a little cottage in a lakeside Cumbrian village. And whereas I was a taciturn teenager, she was open, warm, and mothering. She was the first person in my life I felt actually cared about who I was, rather than what I could do to ease my parents' burdens."

She took a sip of apple juice and again her fingers quickly found Lacey's collar.

"According to my mother, her marriage to my Uncle Michael was a bit of surprise to them all. That is all she would tell me, though later I found out the reason. Anyway, while Uncle Michael was at war, Fiona was there on her own and was happy for my company. We got on famously, partly I think because the maternal side of her was budding with her first pregnancy. My mother said that Fiona had been aching to get pregnant and my experience was that she simply vibrated with the joy of it."

5

1940

It had taken the travelers two days to make the train trip from London to Windermere, what with the bomb damage to tracks, the unscheduled stops, and the sheer distance. They arrived at the end of the line and then transferred to a bus that took them the remainder of their journey to Sterness, a small village on the largest natural lake in England. Much deference and assistance had been shown to the women, what with one on crutches and the other obviously with child. The last leg of the journey from Sterness was made slowly on the back of an empty hay rig being pulled by a brace of massive horses that were guided by the deeply veined hands of Mister Dreagle, an ancient troll of a man. Dark rain clouds thickened above them while he delighted in the opportunity to ramble on, seemingly aimlessly, about the vicissitudes of the war effort. Much of the chatter was lost to Brenda, her ears not being tuned to the heavy Cumbrian brogue.

"Here you are, ladies," he said finally with beaming satisfaction. "Elterwater Cottage."

Fiona eased Brenda down to the ground and handed her the oak crutches that would be her companions for several weeks yet.

"Here, let me do that, lasso! I'll carry those inside."

"No, Mister Dreagle, these bags are quite light, and you've done so much already. Really."

"Tell you what; you take in't house tha' box of scran and I'll bring along them suitcases."

Fiona picked up the crate bursting with food items she had purchased in town and in reply presented the man with the shimmering radiance of her smile. In blushing response, he firmly gripped the handles on the suitcases and tucked a small leather portmanteau under his right arm, saying, "I forgot to ask how the Doctor is doing out there on't sea. Splendid I'll bet. Mad for the water that one."

"Out storming around the Atlantic somewhere, I suspect. He can't say where or on what, but the last letter was just a month ago and all was well."

"Well that's just grand. I'll say a special prayer at kirk for him."

A wooded area surrounded the proud little building made of squared grey stone that supported a slate roof. An arbor with stone columns and wooden cross-tresses led from the front door to the hard-packed crushed gravel drive that looped past the front of the building. Brenda commented on the thick shafts of wisteria that had wound their way up the supports and onto the upper trellis. There was little foliage left now that autumn had fully set in, but the twisted vines held their own beauty.

Fiona smiled and said, "That's my father's handiwork. He loved putting structure into the garden. You'll see more in the back."

They entered the home through a heavy wooden door hinged and bolted with black wrought iron. Fiona and Brenda expressed their thanks to their driver, and as the sound of clopping hooves diminished in the fading light, they closed the door.

6

1938

Launched in 1925 in memory of the greatest naval commander in British history, the battleship HMS Nelson was arguably one of the most formidable warships afloat. She had been designed by the Admiralty in 1922 and laid down at the Armstrong-Whitworth Navy Yard, South Tyneside. After her commissioning, the following months included outfitting and shakedown cruises till she joined the main fleet in the area called Scapa Flow in the Orkney Islands. As political tensions grew in the late 1930's, she joined the fleet in the North Sea patrolling for German ships running the naval blockade.

As a junior medical officer, Michael Leamington's rank was surgeon lieutenant, and his role and that of his colleagues, was to tend to the more than 1,300 crew on board. He was on middle watch, midnight till four, when a knock on the infirmary office door lifted his attention from a copy of *The Lancet* he had been reading.

"Come!"

A heavy-set clerk in a too-tight uniform stuck his head through the doorway. "Sir, we've got a lad here that's pulled something in his leg. Limped up here from the engine room."

"Very well, put him in a consulting room and have him drop trou." Michael closed the journal and stood. "Oh, and Ranford, when you are done there, would you be so kind as to tramp down to the officers' mess and ask Budgie for those horrid biscuits he promised me? And then what say you make us up a pot of tea?"

"Aye sir. On my way sir," said his clerk with vigour, always keen to tap into additional rations.

Michael made his way to the consulting room and found a lean young man wearing only underwear and sitting in a metal chair. He had short, blonde hair, fine features, bright blue eyes, and full lips that smiled broadly when Michael greeted him.

"Done something to your leg, sailor? What's your name and what's happened?"

"Aye, sir. Keating, sir. I was carrying a bucket of sand down in the engine room and didn't see that there was a patch of oil on the gangway. I slipped and my legs sort of went wide apart in a funny sort of way. I went down and felt a sharp pain in my left leg. Up here," he said, pointing to his upper thigh.

"Right. Well, Keating, pop up here on the table and let's have a look."

The young man obliged, wincing as he sat up on the cushioned surface, his legs dangling.

"Shift back a bit and just lie down." Michael guided him to a prone position and gently laid his hands on the man's ankles. "So, no discomfort anywhere in your right leg or left ankle or knee?"

"No, sir, just here in my thigh," he said, his voice almost a whisper.

"Did you hear anything like a cracking sound or feel anything snap when you went down?"

"No, sir. It just hurt like hell when I stood up again."

"Well, that's probably good news. Spread your legs a little bit and then I'll stop you from closing them, but I want you to try."

The sailor obliged and then gasped with discomfort.

"Okay, now the reverse. Stop me from opening them."

The sailor strained against the resistance. "Not as bad sir."

"Okay, let's have a feel," said Michael and laid his right hand on the man's thigh, sliding it up under the boxer shorts. He probed the deep muscle, feeling for swelling, and evoked a grimace in the process. Then Michael slipped his hand to the other thigh for comparison and watched as the man's penis began to slowly grow turgid. It was large and bulging under the material. Their eyes met. Seconds ticked by until a hint of a smile began to grow across the sailor's lips as the physician wrapped his fingers around the now rigid cock.

Michael had hidden his sexual orientation from his family, his university, and the navy. He had witnessed the abuse, subjugation, and mistreatment of his gay classmates, friends, and lovers and had learned to find his outlets with singular caution. A more permanent subterfuge had presented itself to him one night two years previously while he was still attending London University medical school. He and a paramour had slipped into the Gateways Club, a safe, discreet meeting place for lesbians and gays, on Kings Road in Chelsea. With its limited ventilation, there was a heavy fug of cigarette smoke in the place, and on that night, someone was plunking on a piano in a jazzy sort of way. It was crowded and there was little space to sit, but one table had two empty chairs. Michael approached and asked to join the two women already seated there; Fiona was very tall with long, blonde curls and Colleen, her partner, was shorter and more masculine looking, with short, brown hair creamed back.

The two women introduced themselves as university students, and Michael's companion Barry, always a great wit, had the four of them laughing riotously within minutes.

"So what they say about the navy is true then?" asked Fiona with a grin.

"Absolutely, no question," said Barry and raised his glass in a toast "We love our country and all the men it!"

"Can we refill your glasses ladies?" asked Michael as he stood to go to the bar.

"No, I think we were about to head off," said Colleen, her voice tainted with a possessive cadence.

From Fiona came a sharp, "What? Why? No!"

More drinks were ordered.

"How long have you been in the service Michael?" asked Fiona.

"Pretty much all my life. I joined as a lad in the Navy League Sea Cadet Corps and just kept with it. Now that I'm nearly finished my medical studies, my intention is to become a ship's medical officer. I love being on the water, any kind of boat, sail or power. My passion, though, is racing. In fact, when this term ends, I'm going up to the Lake District." Excitement quickened his voice. "Barry here is from Kendall and has a dandy motorboat we're going to race. Well, truth be told, he's going to drive and I'm to be the ballast."

Fiona sipped from her drink and was forced to raise her voice above the increasing volume of alcohol fueled chatter that filled the room. "Where is the race?"

"Lake Windermere. They have a club there on the lake for motorboat racing."

"I know! My mother lives there, at Sterness," said Fiona while ignoring Colleen's rampant scowl.

"Well then you both should join us. It'll be a loud and wondrous spectacle."

8

Fiona watched the race from the lake edge under the protection of a marquee; it had turned out to be a miserable day, with rain and wind buffeting the huddled spectators. Colleen had declined to suffer the long train ride and the separate bedrooms on offer in Fiona's mother's house, so Fiona stood with the other onlookers, stolid against the elements. Tea and biscuits were her armor against the chilling winds.

The course was set in the bay as a grand ellipse, with bright red buoys marking the route. There were six entries in this race, handicapped based on boat length, horsepower, and some other factors Fiona could not remember. Barry had explained it all in a flurry as she was introduced to the boat at the dock. It was a beautifully hand-crafted mahogany and teak affair with a large inboard motor. With the rain pelting down, she had given Michael and Barry a hug for good luck, then had retreated to cover to watch the race.

For the boaters, especially Michael and Barry, things did not go well. From the start, the water was choppy and the driving rain made visibility a challenge. At high speed, the boat often left contact with the water, leaping into the air with teeth-grinding discomfort as it bounced from wave to wave. On the third lap of the course, the engine coughed, then ran, then sputtered, and then the launch stalled altogether. They bobbed idly in the waves for twenty minutes till the race ended and the boat could be towed back to shore. Soaked by rain and spray, the two men hurried to the clubhouse to change and then joined Fiona in Barry's car for the drive to Elterwater Cottage for dinner. Much to her surprise, the two were laughing and chatting about the event.

"Dirty petrol, I'll wager," said Michael.

"That or the bloody distributor," said Barry. "It's happened before."

With a grin on her lips, Fiona eyed the two and then asked, "Where exactly comes the thrill from driving a boat in circles?"

The two men glanced at each other and burst into laughter.

After the short drive along the lakefront, Fiona led her two guests through the front door of her family home and introduced the pair to her mother. She too was tall, but unlike her daughter was waif thin. By way of introduction, Barry offered a magnum of champagne to his hostess. "This was to be opened upon our victorious domination of the entire flotilla, Mrs. Corium, but instead may I present to you a token of our appreciation for taking in two drowned rats?"

Smiling in thanks, she replied, "Call me Ellen, please. I am afraid that with Fi here as well, you two will have to share the back bedroom for the weekend."

"Not a problem, Ellen, not a problem," said Barry and returned her open gaze with a broad smile.

Back in London weeks later, Fiona had joined Michael in a Kardomah Café at his request. They chatted about friends and her university classes for a few minutes, then Michael said, "I have something to ask you, Fi, and before you say anything, please hear me out completely. Please?"

Curious, Fiona agreed.

"There is another war coming, and I'll soon be posted to a naval vessel. Sailors are away from home and family for long stretches of time, and especially with a war on we'll only see each other every now and then—and for only a short time on those few occasions. We've become good chums, you and I, and well, here's the thing. A bit selfish really, but I was wondering if you'd consider marrying me."

Fiona did her best not to react. Michael rushed on. "Being married will give the two of us insulation against questions of morality, if you know what I mean. Being a married couple would put full stop to any rumours," he said, meeting her eyes. "Life could go on pretty much as it does now for us, you with your partners and me with mine; but Fi, we would be safe. Also, having a ring on your finger would stop you being hounded by friends and relatives about who you were socializing with: 'When are you going to get married?' or 'What about kids?' That sort of thing. And this would mean that you won't ever have to be with a man, you know, in the biblical sense." He smiled and laid his palms flat on the table. "So there it is. What do you think?"

Fiona was gripping her cup of tea, enjoying the warmth radiating through the porcelain. She sat with her head bowed for some time. He could tell she was giving his offer her full attention and carefully leafing through the implications. Finally, she looked up and said, "But I do want a child. I don't want to go through life without living that part of being a woman."

Michael paused in thought for a few moments, then said, "I'll give you whatever you want, Fiona, though I hadn't honestly considered fathering a child. Is it a good idea? I have to say that I'm unsure." He paused to take a sip of tea. "It's not that I can't be with a woman though, is it?"

And then he looked out the café window and fixed his gaze as though measuring the distance to a faraway object. "But I will give you a child. I promise," he said, meeting her eyes. "Also, you could live in your rented flat here in London if that would be your choice, or you could move into mine. It's bigger and I own it. I'm never there. Of course, I'd support you and a child if you truly want one. And who knows, maybe when our passions became dissipated in our dotage, we could end up living out our lives together. You'd have complete freedom to live as you like and where you like, no ties at all. I think it could work."

"We shouldn't have to do this."

"I know, but what and who we are is illegal."

"It will still be that way if we get married."

"True, but we will be sleeping under the artifice of respectability, and that is a very thick blanket."

"I'm sorry, Michael, but I cannot give you an answer now." Fiona sighed heavily and set her teacup in its saucer. "This has really come out of the blue, and I'll have to take some time to think it all through." To take the sting out of her evasive response, she added, "You are so very kind to suggest it."

"Any answer but a straight out 'no' right now is a tremendously positive response in my mind. I had feared you might throw that tea in my face. That's why I waited for a few minutes before I popped the question, to let the tea cool."

Fiona laughed and said, "If only you were a woman."

She decided to take the weekend to visit her mother at Elterwater. Fiona would be riding the train most of her time away, as she just had the two days before classes on the Monday, but she felt a need to see her mother. When Fiona finally arrived late on Saturday, Ellen was sitting in the garden on a wicker chair, looking out at the lake. To Fiona, she looked drawn and tired as she rose to greet her.

"Mum, you look unwell. Is everything alright?"

Ellen eyed Fiona carefully for a few moments, judging the depth of her question.

"Just a touch of something," she said.

"Maybe you should eat more and exercise, get out for walks or something. It would make you feel better."

"I'm a little too tired for that," she said, and sensing the oncoming storm, folded her hands in her lap on a quilt they had made together. The air was cool, her fingers white with the chill.

"Well, that's just it. If you got out more and exercised, you wouldn't always be so tired," Fiona said, her voice holding a note of irritation.

Ellen could sense that her evasiveness would not placate her daughter's growing ire and knew that leaving her in the dark about the true condition of her health was unfair to them both. Continuing down that path would only lead to resentment. It had been a nice, safe bubble while it had lasted, a pretense of normalcy.

"Sit down with me for a minute, Fiona. I have something to tell you."

Fiona sensed the change in her mother's tone and noticed the sudden look of resignation on her face. Her mind began to race. Had she found out about her girlfriend, or perhaps Michael and Barry? Fiona felt her stomach forming a tight knot as she eased down beside her mother. Ellen took Fiona's right hand in hers.

"I've always felt a little guilty about having you live with me. How is it that I was blessed with such a wonderful child? You've brought so much joy into my life, every single day. Privileged is how I would describe it. I have been privileged to raise you, and somehow it seems unfair that I alone should be the focus of your love. Few people experience such wonder and satisfaction in their child."

Fiona smiled in recognition of her mother's love but wondered where Ellen was going with this conversation. Would she still feel this way if she knew who or what her daughter really was? It seemed to Fiona that her mother's eloquent words were leading up to a big "but." Relationships always seemed to be full of these little twisty grey zones wherein nobody was completely sure what another was thinking. Life was complicated, and it took time and experience to learn the subtleties. But her mother had raised her well, and Fiona always had a sense of complete and unconditional love from Ellen; this was especially so at this moment. Yet there was something dark and full of portent looming behind her mother's heartfelt words. Fiona suddenly felt a second wave of tension as she perched on the edge of her chair. Her mother's grip tightened as she began again.

"When your father died after the Great War, you helped me get through the loss. Your presence kept me connected to him, his memory. I see his face in yours and his bright, eager mind in everything you do."

Her mother followed Fiona's gaze to the framed picture of the couple that Ellen held in her lap. The ache Ellen felt suddenly pulsing through her was unrelated to the malignancy. It was the sorrow of acknowledging she would not remain to finish the job she had set out to do: to see her daughter well and truly launched on her adult path.

"I am very proud of you; I want you to know that. As you go through life, I want you to remember that you are special. The gift you have for caring so deeply about people draws them to you. It is also a burden—one that you must learn to bear with compassion for yourself. Hurt hurts. It is supposed to, and we all must learn to accept it in the end."

Fiona looked into her mother's eyes as the truth of her words assailed her. She had already known it at some deep level, of course, but had never allowed herself to completely understand the basis of her mother's fragility and failing health.

"You're sick, Mum," she said. A simple statement.

"I'm dying. It is not likely that I'll make it to Christmas," she said. "I just can't fight it anymore. I'm sorry, sweetheart."

Fiona fell to her knees and wrapped her arms around her mother, and together they wept.

§

That evening, the two women sat at a card table, playing a game of cribbage in front of the fireplace. Flames licked up and around the hardwood, and occasionally the logs would shift and settle. Each summer, Ellen engaged a local man to cut up windfalls on their acreage into appropriate lengths, and then later, Fiona would split and stack the pieces. When Fiona was a child, the man also did the splitting, but when she grew taller and filled out as a teenager, Fiona took great pleasure from the physicality of the process, despite her mother's protestations that it wasn't a feminine endeavour. It was enjoyable and hard work.

"Fifteen-two, fifteen-four, fifteen-six and eight are fourteen, and I'm out," said Ellen with a grin as she laid down her cards and counted her score. "That's three games in a row, sweetheart."

Fiona conceded the loss and then added, "I came here this weekend to ask you a question, Mum, but it turns out I've found the answer myself. I've been asked by Michael Leamington to marry, and I've decided to accept."

"Oh, how wonderful!" said Ellen. She clasped her hands together in delight, then said, "But my goodness, Fi, are you sure?"

"I am now, yes."

"I thought perhaps neither of you were the marrying kind."

"How so? What do you mean?"

"Well, you know. That is, I thought that you…or rather that he…well, both of you, really... Oh I don't know, how shall I say it? That you were less inclined to settle for the domestic life, so to speak."

Fiona's hands moved to reassemble the deck of cards. She did it slowly; her fingers were trembling. It took all her will to meet her mother's gaze. "So what you are saying is that you know about our...our lifestyles?"

"Fiona, I am your mother. Do you really think that I'm ignorant of your point of reference regarding the opposite sex? I've watched you grow up, and though I've tried everything in my power to subtly redirect your intense interest in female company, it's clear to me that you are immune to such influence."

"So all my skulking about and subterfuge has been for naught?"

"Well, let's just say that long ago I came to terms with this and have appreciated the discretion with which you have lived your adult life."

"I tried so hard not to be….It took me a long time to accept who I am. It turns out you beat me to it, but you didn't say anything."

"What could I say? I am not comfortable with it, but as I said earlier, you are my daughter and I feel blessed to have you in my life. There is nothing I could say that would change who you are, nor would I ever do anything that would put our bond at risk. I could not live with myself if you were forced to stifle what you truly feel," said Ellen. She stowed the counting pegs in the crib board and handed it to Fiona to put away with the cards.

"Mum, it would have been so helpful if you had said something positive when I was growing up. Something…anything to acknowledge what I was going through."

"Well, in some ways I was going through it too. As a parent you just bumble along sometimes. At first, I was hoping you would grow out of it when you found the right boy. When it became apparent this was who you are, I just accepted it." She raised her hands in acceptance of her culpability. "Besides, dying is not really the best pulpit to preach from. Oh, if I could wave a magic wand, things would be different, but from my current perspective, I'm just glad that you are forging a happy life for yourself. Nothing you are or do should jeopardize that. So, I ask again, are you sure you want to marry this man?"

"What I want most in my life is a child of my own. Michael is able to give me that and also give the child a legitimate upbringing. He is a good man, but I don't need him to be a good father. I've grown up without a father, and I know any child of mine will grow up with a strong moral compass, regardless of how much interaction he or she has with an absentee father. So yes, I want to marry Michael. I've decided."

7

1940

Robbie finished off another pint. He had been at the Sebright Arms since opening and if he'd been asked, he would have said that he was responsible for only a couple of empty glasses, whereas the real number was nine. From his perspective, the good news was that the other patrons had stood the rounds in recognition of the injury he had suffered. Before the bombing had started, the popular feeling in London towards the AFS was that they were slackers dodging the real war. However, once the bombing began and the firefighters were valiantly throwing themselves into the maelstrom, the perception changed, and they were looked upon as heroes.

"Bloody Germans killed my son," he slurred to the elderly gent who had just sat down across the table. "Bloody daughter left him to die in the street. Bloody wife couldn't keep control of them. What the hell? I'm out there losing an eye and all they had to do was sit tight in the bloody shelter."

"You've had a bad go of it all right; let me stand you a pint, lad," said the man, then pushed away from the table and carefully negotiated his way to the bar. Just as the barman caught his eye, the air raid sirens began to wail.

"Time, gentlemen!" shouted the barman and quickly set about turning off the keg taps and closing out the till. The patrons grumbled and with great bravado claimed to want to stay, but to a man they shuffled out into the evening and headed toward the Tube station shelter.

Robbie turned left as he exited, and like a number of other regulars suddenly struck with the urge to urinate, entered the passage that led to Hackney Road. With unbuttoned fly-fronts accompanied by loud sounds of relief, they emptied their bladders against the brick facades of the buildings along the walkway. While the others headed off in a group, Robbie's ale-numbed fingers fiddled unsuccessfully with the buttons in his fly as he fought for balance. By the time he was able to find relief, had shaken himself off, and was tucked away, his companions were long gone. He was alone with the sirens ripping the night apart. The sun had set, and the fading evening light settled on the city as he staggered down the passageway. On Hackney he made his way to Mansford until he washed up on the stoop of a row house, too intoxicated to continue. He closed his eyes and darkness fell.

"Oy! You! Get your arse to shelter!"

Robbie sat inert with his head leaning against a door post. Seeing no response, two ARP wardens approached; the larger of the pair grabbed him by the collar and gave him a shake. The smaller man shone a torch in Robbie's face, the beam cutting through the now fully dark night. "Clear off before I use my boot."

Dragged to consciousness, Robbie snarled at the pair and moved to lash out but was overwhelmed by the fierce grip of the giant hauling him to his feet. "Get moving. Gerry will be here soon, and we've got better things to do than shepherd around the likes of you." He gave the drunk a shove in the general direction of the Tube station.

"Pizz off, the pair of you!" was Robbie's garbled parting shot.

The blackout ensured that there was precious little light to guide even an attentive and sober man to a shelter, and after making many wrong turns and finding himself completely lost, he stumbled to a doorway and sat on the top step. His head was buzzing, and Robbie felt a wave of nausea while his world spun around him at high speed. To the sound of approaching airplanes, he lay back and for the second time that night succumbed to the black wave that swept him away.

ᔕ

In his stolen ARP regalia, Albert Biggins was again out and about in search of spoils. The haul from Belgravia had proven so much more lucrative than he had expected that he had decided not to cash in the necklace, instead sequestering the bejeweled treasure on his brother's property in Uxbridge. As his finances grew, so did his hope for the future. When the war was over, he would have the resources to elevate his station and no longer be forced to scrape and bow; others would scrape and bow to him.

On this night, the first squadrons of German bombers had roared through the darkness and released their incendiaries on a cringing city. As Albert pondered the wondrous riches within his grasp, a second wave of bombers carrying the heavy ordnance let loose. Three blocks south and one block east of him, a parachute bomb driven by the wind exploded over the commercial district. He felt the shock wave rumble through the ground, the detonation thunderous despite the cotton wadding packed in his ears.

Albert made his way to the crater site and was met with a scene of devastation 100 metres across. A water main was spurting its contents into the air and buildings were afire. Pieces of rubble were falling from the crumbling brick-and-stone walls of the surrounding buildings. It was the sign lying on its back in the middle of the street that caught his eye. A bank. Albert couldn't tell which institution it was from, as most of the bold brass lettering was missing, but it definitely was a bank. He scanned the area around him and realized the sign had come from the structure on his left. The front of the building had been sundered as though cleaved through by a giant's axe. Clambering across the wreckage, he made his way to the vault, whose door had been ripped off. It lay on the crushed teller's cage, its inner face toward the night sky. Inside the vault, a huge inner safe lay on its side, the thick steel doors open, scorched, and deformed. Dozens of safety deposit boxes had been smashed apart, and bonds, cash, and documents were strewn wildly across the floor. Turning his torch on the inside of the safe, Albert was greeted by the sight of heaps of bundled banknotes.

"Holy shite! This'll do, Albert, this'll do." He reached in and began madly stuffing his canvas kit bag with as many stacks as would fit. Then as he began cramming more money into the pockets of his overalls, he heard the growl of a fire engine approaching.

Reluctantly turning off his torch and keeping in a crouch, Albert made his way across the debris and away from the advancing truck and crew. The firefighters' attention was focused on the building aflame across the street, and Biggins was able to slip away unnoticed into the smoke-choked chaos.

Robbie roused to the thud of a single shock wave slamming into his chest. He sat up and fought to orient himself in the gloom and the fog of ale. After several minutes he pulled himself to a stand. Hearing the drone of an approaching flight of Heinkels, followed by the sudden burst of anti-aircraft fire, Robbie set off once more in his now urgent search for a Tube station or even an Anderson shelter. He came to an intersection and with his one good eye was finally able to make out a street sign. "Christ! Bloody Sclater Street." He had meandered too far south and west, so Robbie spun on his heels and now, knowing where he was, crafted a mental map back to safety.

For the first time since the war had started, Albert felt an inflating sense of hope and with that feeling came raw, unbridled fear. Now at last he had something to lose other than a life of poverty and squalor. He squeezed his bulging satchel, feeling the surety of it, the promise. The planes were now roaring directly overhead. The possibility he could lose it all had him shaking uncontrollably. His mouth felt dry as he hurriedly limped up Brick Lane.

From their separate locations, the two men simultaneously heard the shrieking whistle of the bombs shredding the air, the pitch of the sound getting higher and closer. Then the night exploded. The blasts seemed to crush the breath from Albert's lungs as it rammed a wall of air into his mouth and nose. He was struck by flying stone, mortar, and metal that severed his one good leg at the knee. His right hand was gone.

As he had at the Somme almost two decades earlier, Robbie waited for the barrage to end with hands pressed tightly against his ears and with his face to the ground. He had hidden behind a wrought-iron-crowned low brick wall only a block away from the blasts till finally, as a thunderstorm slides away, the bombs fell more distantly, laying waste to parts of the city south of the Thames. Emboldened by the receding violence, Robbie pulled himself to a stand, headed slowly up the street, and turned the corner. Buildings were on fire and reflexively he headed toward the conflagration. Rubble was heaped along the building fronts, and as the fires burned at supports and crossbeams, unstable walls gave way and thundered to the ground. The air was thick with smoke and dust, and with no tools or comrades to tackle the fires, he turned to find another route to safety. It was then he noticed the body of an ARP warden lying face up against a wall. The rim of the man's helmet was bent at an angle that in any normal circumstance would induce laughter, and his legs were obviously truncated and askew. Robbie called out as he approached. The man did not respond, but Robbie could see signs of life; his left arm was jerking and twitching, an unlit torch in his hand. Robbie knelt by the man and could see by the light of the fires that his face was horribly mutilated. His lower lip was dangling by a thin flap, and Robbie could see teeth and bare jawbone beneath;

bloody foam pulsed down his chin. The man slowly bubbled the words, "Take it...take it off me... Take it...take it off me... Take it..."

Seeing that a bulky satchel of some sort was lying partially beneath the man's right hip and was the probable source of the distress, Robbie pulled the strap from the injured man's right shoulder and carefully drew the bulging canvas bag free. As his hip settled to the pavement, the man wheezed, "You take it. You take it... You... T..." and then the eruption of bloodied bubbles ceased to form.

Robbie sat in stunned silence for several moments. Kneeling beside the body, he fought through the fog of alcohol and trauma to utter a few holy words. "God be with you," he said finally. Then he came to a stand, tossed back the flap on the satchel, and peeked inside. It was difficult to see, so he reached down to the corpse and picked up the torch. He flicked the switch on and off to no avail, gave it a few shakes, and was then rewarded with a faint yellow beam that he shone on the mass inside the bag. He was greeted by the sight of Britannia sitting proudly on the face of stacks of bank notes, spear and sprig of laurel in her hands.

"Crikey Moses," Robbie muttered as he felt his knees go weak. A hoppy burp rose from his gorge and he sank down onto his heels.

8

1940

"Well, what do you think about sleeping arrangements, Brenda?" asked Fiona. "We could put you on a sofa in the library, or you and your cast can brave the stairs and have your own room."

"Oh, I think my own room would be grand. The luxury of it!" she replied. "Lawrey and I," she began and then paused as tears came to her eyes. Brenda took a deep breath and continued, "Lawrey and I shared a room and it was rather close, so a room of my own would be brilliant. The doctors said I'm supposed to weight bear a little now, so if you are there to make sure I don't fall backwards on my head as I climb the flight of steps, that'd be a great help."

With a broad grin, Fiona nodded in agreement. "Just down the hall on the right is the loo and on the left is the bath."

"Speaking of the loo, I wonder if maybe...?" asked Brenda.

"Of course, how silly of me. You'll need a hand again. Not to worry—being married to a doctor, things are pretty down to earth here. Perhaps for the duration you could just consider me a ward sister."

She led her niece down the hall, and together they managed to get her situated on the toilet with her casted right leg akimbo. Fiona stepped out of the room momentarily while Brenda relieved herself and then returned to assist her out of the room.

"I've got used to bedpans and train station facilities now, so in comparison that was a great step up," said Brenda.

"My mother had the plumbing upgraded when we moved here permanently from Lancaster after the Great War. It was our summer cottage before my father died," said Fiona as she guided Brenda back into the hall. "I don't know what your family has told you about him, but he died just at the end of the war. The Spanish flu took him. He made his way through so many military battles but like so many thousands of others, in the end he died of influenza."

"Actually, I don't know much about my father's side of the family," said Brenda, "even you and Uncle Michael. My dad is not really the chatty type, and it seems that whenever the subject of Uncle Michael comes up, it gets dropped fairly quickly."

"Well, first let's get the Aga fired up so we can get some warmth in here and some food cooked, and then I'll try to fill you in."

"Oh my goodness, Aunt Fiona, that was amazing. I am so full; my tummy is bursting. I honestly can't remember the last time I had a piece of pork tenderloin."

"Well, don't get too carried away. It may not be too long before I hear, 'Oh no! Not pork again?' Of course, they're threatening to put rationing in effect soon, so we'll enjoy it while we can."

Fiona collected the dishes and moved to the sink.

"Oh, let me help."

"I think you've gone through enough today, surely. Getting here has been a trial. Instead, tell me about school or something while I do these dishes."

Brenda rambled on with stories of teachers and classmates, all the while carefully avoiding mentioning her brother. "And then after school I made a few bob at the library, stocking shelves. The head librarian was a bit beastly, but I liked being among the books. I'd often stay late and just read. My favourite was the *Encyclopaedia Britannica*. I would randomly pick a volume and crack it open and learn amazing things. For instance, did you know that you could fit forty United Kingdoms into Canada? Forty! I enjoyed reading about Canada. They have a province called British Columbia; wouldn't you love to go there? Oh, and do you know Chanel uses an essence from a sac under a beaver's tail to make their perfumes?"

Fiona laughed, pleased to hear vibrancy come into Brenda's voice for the first time since they had met. "I am so very glad you are here with me, Brenda. Since I moved back here to get away from the Blitz, it's been terribly quiet. We're going to have such fun. But for now, I think we should head to bed."

A scream yanked Fiona from a deep sleep and left her disoriented in the darkness. Then she quickly rose and made her way to Brenda's room; she knocked and then entered, finding Brenda sitting up in bed, weeping, her body shuddering. A slip of moonlight slid through a gap in the curtains, and Fiona could see that the hair on Brenda's good side was knotted and the bandages on the burns had come loose and were dangling from her scalp.

Through spastic gasps, Brenda said, "I had a dream."

"Oh sweetheart, how awful for you," and she sat on the bed and wrapped the child in her arms. "Tell me."

"I was running through the streets and the bombs came and Lawrey was standing there pointing at me. He just stood there and everything was on fire and he wouldn't come to the shelter. I kept calling to him but he ignored me."

"You tried so hard, didn't you?"

Brenda nodded her head. "This isn't the first time. For this dream, I mean. I had the same dream most nights in the hospital." Her breathing came more evenly, more quietly, and then she said, "It hurts when I cry. I mustn't cry."

"You have to cry; it's a normal reaction to what you've been through."

"No, I mean it really hurts when I cry. My ribs."

Fiona kissed Brenda on her forehead and rocked her.

Late the next morning, Brenda carefully descended into the warmth of the kitchen. Fiona was standing at the table, kneading dough, flour scattered about her.

"There she is. Did you get more sleep?"

"I did, thanks. A deep sleep. No more dreams that I can remember."

"Good. Porridge, tea, and toast?"

"That would be lovely, thanks," said Brenda. She moved to a chair at the table and looked out at the rills of water running down the window. "It's really coming down out there now."

"Well, it's rained heavily almost every day this month here. November is often wet, but this has been exceptional even for Cumbria. We were lucky to be free of it yesterday afternoon."

Fiona dusted the flour from her hands and laid out the food on the table. "You'll have to put up with my cooking. I am not very good at it. We had a day cook here when I grew up. Cora lived just up the road with her husband. She would come to Elterwater every morning and would leave after dinner. When my mother died, I moved to a flat in London. By then Cora was getting long in the tooth so she went to live with her sister in Lancaster after her husband died."

"When the war started you moved back here?"

"Yes. Your Uncle Michael was adamant that the baby and I be as far away from the fighting as possible."

"You lived here when you were a child?"

"Yes, hence the accent. I worked to tone it down; at university, if Londoners caught the slightest Cumbrian lilt I was literally classified. Although I guess it cuts both ways, really."

"Oh my goodness, isn't it so. Miss Babcock, a librarian at Bethnal Green, issues decrees in her Oxbridge timbre. She uses her tone as a weapon," Brenda said as she stirred her porridge.

"I put some cream and honey in that. You're such a tiny thing; you're what, five feet tall and ninety pounds."

"Almost. Well a long way from almost, but with the cast I bet I weigh in at ten stone!" she replied sipping her tea. "You said yesterday that this was a summer cottage but you had lived in Lancaster. What did your father do there?"

"He was a partner in a leather goods concern. Suitcases, belts, and the like. They owned a factory and distributed all over the country. When the Great War started, business was booming. So much work to outfit the troops. But he caught the fervour to go and fight for mother country. When he died at the end of it all, my mother was never the same. The battle over the estate was acrimonious to say the least; through all manner of legal machinations, his partner was able to claim the company mostly for himself."

Her aunt was back to bread making, and Brenda watched as Fiona's white fists punched deep pits into the dough before each fold over.

"The law was not my mother's friend," she said. "Oh, we did well enough. I went to a girls' school and then university. We sold the big house in town and moved here to the quiet of Sterness. It suited my mother." Fiona paused in her kneading and met Brenda's eyes. "The lake is a cure-all; I know you'll like it here."

There was a knock at the front door. "That'll be Doctor Malcolm. He's here for my pregnancy check-up. I've asked him to check in on you as well."

Leaving Brenda to finish her breakfast, Fiona went to greet the man. With pleasantries exchanged, the pair spent several minutes in the library while he assessed the progress of her pregnancy. Satisfied, he followed Fiona into the kitchen saying, "And the midwife will be coming every week now. If you have any problems, you just give either one of us a dingle."

Fiona nodded and then gestured towards her niece, who sat awkwardly on a kitchen chair, her casted leg askew.

"Well aren't you a wee thing," Malcolm said as he caught sight of Brenda. "Your aunt has briefed me on your history," he remarked by way of greeting. He was a short, red-haired man with an effulgent red nose and a broken-gate smile. "Let's have a look at you. Bit of a rag doll at the moment I see. Let's start at the top and work our way down, shall we?"

In the night, Fiona had done her best to reapply the cotton bandages over Brenda's burns, but when the doctor removed them he said, "Not much point to these anymore. Just this little strip from behind your ear we'll keep after. You'll have a bit of a scar there, but the rest will be fine and the hair is growing in nicely. Well done."

Brenda blushed modestly at the compliment, though she wasn't sure she had any particular power over her hair follicles.

Doctor Malcolm tended to the raw-looking wound and applied a new dressing.

"Now, I understand you've got a few broken ribs."

Brenda nodded. "Three. They've been re-taped twice. Not new each time. They just put new tape over the old ones that were slipping."

"Good girl, reporting the news. You should be a reader on the BBC. Beginning of October was it? Not too bad? No ends sticking out, that sort of thing?"

"No, just cracked. They said the taping was sort of a precaution and to help me not breathe too deeply. It only really ever hurts now when I cough," she said and met Fiona's gaze.

"Right, well, I think we're done with that," he said, rubbing his hands together. Brenda was not sure whether the action was through eagerness or simply to warm his hands. "This bit is not going to be fun, pet. Mrs. Leamington, could you please whip us up some hot wet towels? Not scalding hot, mind. We'll lay them on over the taped bits for a few minutes to soften the adhesive. You'll have to strip off that nightdress, lass."

The tape ran from the middle of Brenda's back, around under her right arm, and past the midline of her chest. After several minutes of soaking the tape, Doctor Malcolm started from the back and the adhesive began to give way. As the congealed sheet of tape came off around the front section, the doctor paused. "The bloody prats! This is going to sting a little. They didn't put any gauze over your nipple. Here we go, just the last bit now really."

Brenda winced as the adhesive slowly peeled away from the skin of her elfin breast. Finally, it all came away in one wet, drooping sheet.

"Ah, just here on the side you got hit, yeah? Hands on top of your head pet, and take a breath as deep as you feel comfortable." Brenda's cheeks flushed as the doctor placed his fingers over the site of the breaks and fading bruises. "And out, and then in again."

Doctor Malcolm smiled and handed Brenda her nightdress "Well, lasso, you are a grand healer. I'll wager that leg will be good soon as well. What say I make arrangements up at Calgarth Park to have them take that cast off. I'll try for the first week in December." He received an eager nod and then rooted about in his black medical bag. "Aha! Here it is. Some rubbing alcohol to take off the rest of that glue." He handed her a little glass bottle. "I'll give your aunt a call when they've set a time."

After the doctor departed, Fiona set to work with the alcohol to remove the remains of tape adhesive from Brenda's back and sides. She passed the bottle to Brenda to tend to her front herself.

"It feels so much better," said Brenda after slipping back into her nightdress. "So much freer."

"Now that the bandages on your head are gone, should we do something about your hair?"

"It is a bit of a tangle," said Brenda.

"And a bit lopsided," said Fiona. "Hang on a tic," she said and made her way upstairs, returning a minute later carrying a hand mirror. She passed it to Brenda.

"Oh dear, with the bandages off I look a little bit like Victor and Victoria," she said while comparing her two exceptionally different profiles. "Would you mind trimming away this matted mess, Aunt Fiona? Then I can start afresh."

A few short minutes with scissors left a small pile of hair on the floor and a smile on Brenda's face. With her hair now trimmed evenly at a length that would, with encouragement lie flat, Brenda eyed herself again in the mirror. "I look like Lawrey," she said and then burst into tears.

The dream came again that night and Fiona found herself rocking Brenda in her arms once more. After the shuddering lessened, Fiona said in an encouraging tone, "Tell me the whole story, Bren."

Brenda began with her mother telling her she was not permitted to see her father and ended with her entering the casualty ward at the hospital.

"So it sounds to me that you did everything possible to find and rescue your brother. Why do you think you keep having the dreams? Is there something that you're afraid to say, something you're not telling me?"

The question triggered a series of sobs till finally through her gasps Brenda said, "It's my fault. It's my fault he died. I had been running around out in the night, screaming at the top of my lungs. It was so scary and then bombs began to fall. She paused and then said in a quiet voice, "I was really mad at him."

"It's understandable that you'd be upset. You were completely at your wits' end."

"I was awfully angry and so just before the bomb fell, I yelled, 'I hope you do die you stupid boy!' And he did. It's all my fault; even my parents think so." The sobs came again.

"Brenda, the definition of a hero is someone who puts their own life in peril while taking great risks to save someone else. Without regard to your own safety, you went out into the darkness in the middle of an air raid to save your brother. I don't think I could have done that. You are a hero and you have to believe that."

Fiona cupped Brenda's face in her hands, "Look at me, Bren." The teenager raised her eyes to meet her aunt's intense gaze. "Every time those memories come up, I want you to say out loud, 'I am a hero. I did everything I could to save him. He died because he made some bad choices, but I forgive him.'" She paused to let the thought settle. "Can you do that? It could be your own little hymn to Lawrey."

Brenda nodded, her nose dripping onto Fiona's nightgown.

"If simply thinking hurtful thoughts could affect outcomes, Hitler would be long dead. What you thought and what you said had no effect on your brother. What matters in life are actions, not words. You know that to be true; you are a smart girl." Fiona kissed the child on her cheek and finally, exhausted from crying, Brenda gave way to her bed.

As she stood outside the closed bedroom door, Fiona strained to hear whether Brenda had finally settled. She was rewarded to hear a gentle murmuring, a mantra repeated over and over. Fiona made her way to her own bed, and it took some time for her to find sleep; her baby was kicking and shifting inside her.

After breakfast the next morning, Fiona said, "Come into the library. I want to introduce you to our books."

Using her crutches, Brenda followed Fiona and watched as she carefully shifted her maternal bulk to a kneeling position on the floor. She opened the flue, kindled a fire, and held out her palms to the warmth. As the fire ripened, Fiona worked herself up to a stand and then pointed to the far corner of the room. "I've put Michael's old medical texts over in a group on that shelf," she said, moving to a parson's chair by the window. "You may want to browse through them and read about your leg."

Brenda tottered her way to the shelves and scanned the titles. "*Gray's Anatomy*," she said as her fingers brushed the red leather binding. "May I?"

"Any book in this library is there to be read. What with you out of school and bored to tears from hobbling around in the house all day, I should think some good classics or perhaps some Brontë might go over well," she said while gently stroking her swollen abdomen and feeling the movements within. "Oh! I know—we have a copy of *Frankenstein* in there somewhere."

"I've read it. It's wonderful though, isn't it? Poor thing, so horribly outcast and alone. People can be so mean," she said as she ran her fingers over the spines of books. "What's this one, *The Well of Loneliness*?"

Fiona's hand stopped circling her tummy. In the following pause, the fire suddenly snapped and popped. "It's a story about two women; doesn't end well. Bit dreary, actually. The *Sunday Express* was not a fan."

"And you?" asked Brenda. "Did you enjoy it?"

"Hmmmm. It is one of those books where the theme transcends the prose," she said, resuming her stroking. Then suddenly, "I know! I bought a couple of books while I was in London. They're out there on the hall table. The Irish one is supposed to be quite good. It has an odd title that I can't remember, but the clerk found it remarkably funny. Grab that."

Brenda moved to the hall and shouted back, "*At Swim-Two-Birds*?"

"Yes, that's it. Give it a read and report back."

With book in hand, Brenda hobbled her way back to a chair and collapsed into it, her casted leg clunking against an ottoman. "What I liked about working in the library was the sense that if I set my mind to it, I could learn anything about everything. Of course, a little learning is a dangerous thing they say."

"So says Alexander Pope. The trick I guess is deciding what to focus on."

"That will be hard to do because I don't know what I don't know. There is a whole world of things that I do not even know exist."

"You know Bren, London is not the only place with a library. The one here in Windermere is quite good; Britannica and everything."

9

1940

Doctor Malcolm arrived in his dark blue Morris Fourteen on the Wednesday morning of the first week in December. It was raining and cold, and a bitter wind blew down the lake, driving the rain into their faces. After helping to wedge Brenda into the passenger seat, Fiona waved them off from the relative dry of the porch. Their destination was the Ethel Hedley Orthopaedic Hospital for Crippled Children, in Calgarth Park. Opened in 1920, the hospital was dedicated to treatment of childhood polio, tubercular bone disease, and other crippling disorders and was only a five-mile drive from Elterwater Cottage.

As they motored along, Brenda adjusted then readjusted her head scarf.

"It'll grow back in no time at all, lass," and he broke into a wide grin. "At least now you won't fall over with all the weight on the one side."

Brenda rolled her eyes, but a smile came to her face all the same. "How long have you been practicing medicine here?"

"Since I became qualified. Let me see, that would be fifteen years now in general practice."

"Do you like it? Medicine I mean."

"It's never dull, I can tell you that. I am healer, confessor, counsellor, and sometimes emergency veterinarian."

"Could a woman do it? Be a doctor." Her fingers were knotted and white in her lap.

"Well now, women have had their own medical school in London for more than forty years, so yes, they can and do. Are you interested?"

Brenda considered the idea for a few moments as the windshield wipers thumped an encouraging baseline rhythm.

The noxious odors and the sounds that echoed down the hospital hallways came back to her in a wave. Her mother smelled of it every day when she came home. Brenda pictured her father's one-eyed face. "I don't think so," she said finally. "I love problem solving, maybe something along those lines."

"My life is problem solving. To tell the truth, there are too many medical problems that I cannot solve. Drives me batty."

Malcolm drove the car over the Troutbeck Bridge and soon turned left down a stone-walled lane that led them to a large, three-story, white-fronted building. It boasted extensive two-story wings of grey stone and a long, colonnaded portico that overlooked a large lawn rimmed by woodland; it had a welcoming feel despite the rain savagely pelting down. Brenda could see no one moving about the grounds.

The doctor parked the car and with hunched shoulders dove into the rain. He moved around to the passenger side and eased Brenda out and onto her feet and crutches. Then together they made their way to the front entrance and were greeted warmly by a bulky woman in a crisp blue uniform fronted by a dazzling white apron.

"Now Brenda, while this nice nurse takes you off to have that cast removed, I'm going to be checking in on a lad taken down by polio—been sick about a year. Whoever finishes first will meet the other here at the entrance; sound like a plan?"

Brenda voiced her agreement and headed off down the hall on her crutches, led by the nurse. A boy Lawrey's age wheeled passed; he had no legs. Brenda felt her stomach flip and she stopped in her tracks.

"Come on love. You will be fine. Really."

Panic drove Brenda to gasp for breath. A buzzing sound filled her ears.

"Look at me," said the nurse and held her face, forcing Brenda to meet her gaze. "Follow my breath. In-hold. Out-hold. In-hold. Out... That's it. Keep going." A minute passed till Brenda felt calm enough to continue down the hall.

They made their way to one of the rooms near the end of the low-rise wings, and she was introduced to a middle-aged doctor with the thickest, most unruly grey eyebrows Brenda had ever seen. He wore silver-rimmed glasses with thick round lenses.

With the nurse's assistance they placed Brenda on a metal table with a small pillow under her head. She closed her eyes as her body began to shake. The nurse reached out to take her hand. "It's alright, pet, none of this is going to hurt," she said. "Correct, Mister Ostrand?"

"Only me if I catch my fingers," came the surprisingly high-pitched reply. Brenda had expected a grumpy, bass voice, but this was friendly and almost feminine.

The man picked up a pair of stainless-steel Stille plaster scissors about fourteen inches long with smooth oblong handles. The lower blade was shaped like an alligator jaw—flat, pointed, and covered with teeth-like ridges—and together with the upper blade were designed to both crush the plaster and cut the underlying cotton fabric.

The nurse released Brenda's hand and then lifted the girl's dress up to her waist. Tears pooled in the corners of Brenda's eyes as the doctor began at the outer aspect of her upper thigh. Ostrand spent several minutes cutting his way down the length of the cast and then repeated the process up the inside face of the cast and lifted off the top half-shell. He let his eyes run the length of the limb with an assessing gaze. Then, undeterred by a smelly layer of dead skin, the physician slowly slid his fingers down the length of the previously broken limb, probing and searching out the state of the mend. He looked up with a bright smile and declared himself satisfied.

"There is a very nice callous formed in the bone there at the break. We don't need an X-ray to tell me that the bone is straight and sound," he said quietly and then lifted her leg out of the bottom shell. "Now because you've not been able to exercise this leg, the muscles, tendons, and ligaments have weakened, and if we simply let you run and dance about as young girls are wont to do, things will most likely get strained or worse. So we'll fit you up with a short brace on an ugly and inelegant shoe with a Thomas heel. You'll only need to wear it for a few weeks and then you'll be good as new."

Brenda looked down at her legs. In comparison, her right limb resembled a knobbly-kneed stick beside her fleshy left leg. It was like looking at separate halves of two different people. Reading her horrified expression, the nurse said, "Not to worry, Brenda; that leg will fill out in a jiffy. Just you wait and see if it doesn't."

"And now a treat!" said the physician as he tossed the two plaster pieces in a bin. "Nurse, if you will draw this child a nice hot bath. She's been through the wars and deserves a good soak and scrub."

Finally free of her crutches, Brenda limped her way back into the entrance of the hospital and saw that Doctor Malcolm had preceded her. He was sitting in a chair reading and did not see her approach, but as she neared, his head popped up to the clumping sound of the braced shoe. The inside and outside metal straps of the belted brace ran from just below the knee and attached to the sides of the black Oxford heel. It was as Cameron had said, ugly and inelegant.

"You're reading *The Beano*!"

"No, no. Well yes, I guess I was," said the Doctor and immediately dropped the comic book on the table beside him.

"I thought those were for the children," said Brenda, taking the advantage. A smile came to her lips as he blushed.

Nonplussed, he jumped to his feet and quickly changed the subject, "All's well with the leg? Looks poker straight—should be, tibia wasn't broken. Still, healed well did it?"

"Doctor Ostrand says it has healed splendidly. I'm to put my full weight on it but with no dancing around. Well, at least not for two weeks and then I'll no longer have a need for this blessed brace."

"Good girl. Lovely. Let's be off and get you back to your aunt."

Moving freely under her own steam, Brenda felt a wave of elation and relief sweep over her as she stepped outside and lifted her face skyward into the rainy afternoon.

8

The dreams continued to come, but at least now she wasn't waking Fiona with her screams in the middle of the night. The content had subtly changed; now, rather than always searching for Lawrey, she was simply running. In these dreams, she was always wearing her leg brace, and it kept catching on things and slowing her down. In her most recent dream, Brenda had been running through the library, aware that she should do so quietly. But her brace was making such a clatter that it triggered Miss Babcock to hiss and whisper. The sound of an exploding bomb in the dream jerked her awake, and she lay in the quiet of the night, hearing only the patter of rain on the roof, the gurgle of the gutters, and the thumping of her heart. Despite the cold of the December night, she felt warm and safe under the covers. Here in Cumbria, she was far from the London bombings and far from parents that blamed her for her brother's death. Brenda rolled onto her side while imagined visions of her dead brother seeped into her thoughts. Unsettled, she flipped onto her back again and began to murmur her now reflexive mantra until she drifted back to sleep.

When she next woke it was morning, so she dressed, put on her shoes and brace, and made her way downstairs to prepare breakfast for herself and Fiona.

"Leg," said Fiona as she sat at the kitchen table, sipping a cup of tea. Brenda was standing at the sink, doing the dishes, and had shifted her weight to her good leg, leaving her weakened right leg bent at the knee and taking none of the load.

"It's tired."

"Good. The doctor said to exercise that leg, and tired means it's healing."

Brenda shifted to evenly distribute her mass and continued scrubbing a pot. "I was reading *Gray's Anatomy* yesterday. Did you know that we have 206 bones in our bodies? You have even more when you're born, but some of them fuse together as you grow."

"No, I did not know that," Fiona replied. "It's amazing what we don't know about ourselves." Fiona took a sip and then said, "Here's something for you. I was reading the newspaper yesterday, and did you know that the government is promoting pregnancy as a woman's contribution to national service? It's now our assigned role, according to Lord Woolton."

"Well, that's a good thing isn't it?"

"If the reason was something more noble than promoting another generation of cannon fodder, I suppose it would be a good thing. We pregnant women and new mothers even get to go to the front of the food line when they introduce rationing," said Fiona. "I'll tell you this: no son of mine will be the victim of a bunch of old men deciding that their so-called honour is worth more than my child's life."

"But how do you stop them from signing up? You said Uncle Michael has been keen on the navy since he floated toys in the bathtub."

"I don't know, Brenda, but there must be way. There has to be."

Though the midmorning was cold and the clouds ominous, Brenda stepped out onto the stone porch that ran the length of the back of the house. She was wearing her heavy winter coat and a woolen cap over her closely shorn hair. For the first time, the leg brace had been left beside her bed, and her first steps on the unfamiliar rough surface were tentative and measured.

On both sides of the garden, beech trees posing in their elegant nakedness gave way to thickly wooded areas. Empty raised beds rimmed with stone lay bare, awaiting the regrowth of perennials and the flush of annuals Fiona would plant in the spring.

From where Brenda stood, a path led down an easy slope to a stone and wooden dock that poked out into the lake. A large, slate-roofed stone outbuilding sat hunched near the shore. Brenda made her way out onto the dock and looked down the shoreline. To her right, perhaps a quarter of a mile distant, a rocky point jutted out into the water and obscured what lay beyond. To her left, the curve of the shoreline allowed for a view of bays and a scattering of other docks. The wind was chilling, so she made her way to the boathouse and with some effort opened the wide and heavy iron-strapped door.

Inside, a giant tarp-covered turtle lay in the middle of the floor, which as she approached transformed into a small upturned wooden sailboat. She estimated that it was the length of two sailors, and as she ran her fingers along the transom, she made an approximation of its width. On one wall of the boathouse hung two old bathing towels, several bulky-looking kapok life jackets, and a canvas sail strung from its tack to its head, dangling freely in the silence. On the floor lay the wooden mast. Along the other wall, garden tools were propped randomly and a hefty wheelbarrow still half-filled with dirt sat sulking in a corner. The space had a light aroma of soil, stone, and wood, mixed with a hint of mould.

Brenda climbed the flight of open wooden stairs that led up to a loft, her left hand sliding carefully up the rail. The weighty insular stillness gave Brenda the sensation that here were fading secrets not told outside these walls. Cobwebs reached across the one window, its panes covered both inside and out with the obscuring grime of weather and time. The first thing to catch her eye was a doll house teetering precariously atop a stack of old suitcases in the corner. To her surprise, inside were delicate pieces of hand-carved wooden furniture. Drawn to the house, she reached in and delicately lifted out a diminutive dining chair, mahogany she guessed. Just a few years ago, she would have been lost for hours in this miniature world. She slid the chair back into place.

To her left was an old wooden bench comforted by a side table whose top was covered with the multicoloured drippings of wax candles. Beneath it lay a sad-looking cardboard Burberry box that may at one time have held a birthday dress or coat; its top was concave and worn. Brenda wiped the dust from a spot on the bench and then, sitting, she leaned over and picked up the box; it had weight. She settled the container in her lap and opened the lid. Here were sheets upon sheets of pencil and charcoal drawings. The first was of a female face, young and brunette. The artist had captured the vibrancy of youthful eyes, eager and brash. The model was perhaps ten years of age. There were more of the same face and some of whole body poses, sitting or lying on the bench. In one, the subject lay on her stomach on the bench, her feet in the air. In another, this one clearly done at least a handful of years later, the model wore a bathing costume and her head was turned away from the artist. Deeper in the stack of yellowing pages was a nude in the same pose on the same bench, though in this image the head was merely hinted at, with the detailed focus on the line and form of the torso, buttocks, and legs. In the lower right corner were the two small initials of the artist, "F. C.," and the date, "1930."

The next pose caused Brenda to catch her breath. The nude model was sitting on the bench with legs wide apart, her elbow on her right knee and chin on her fist, staring at the artist. The gaze was a challenge, intense and sexual. The pose transcended what Brenda had seen in medical texts, wherein the nude images of the male and female forms reflected only cadaverous flaccidity. Brenda stared into the model's eyes, seeking clarification on a question she had no idea how to formulate. She was not captivated by the image—rather, it struck her as incongruous and vaguely off-putting. After several moments of inquisitive study, she put the sketches back in order and closed the box, returned it to its exact position on the floor, and then left the loft and the building to its secrets.

10

1940

For Christmas, Fiona gave Brenda her copy of Huxley's *Brave New World*, and in return, Brenda gave her aunt a pair of poorly knitted baby booties. Also included in the wrapping was a partly finished bonnet. "I promise I'll have it finished by the New Year," said Brenda. "And by then I'll know exactly how big to make it."

As Fiona was making tea at the kitchen counter on Boxing Day morning, her waters broke; the midwife was called. Brenda guided Fiona upstairs to her bedroom and settled her on the bed. A spasm made Fiona gasp for breath. Brenda reached out to hold her aunt's hand, unsure what else she should or could do to help.

"Not to worry Bren. All is good. Keep squeezing my hand." The contractions that rolled through Fiona's body came in separate and uncontrollable waves. Brenda found herself squeezing her jaw so tightly that her teeth ached. At the sound of a knock and a voice at the front door, Fiona gasped "At last!"

Daisy Frinton, the midwife, stepped into the room with a full understanding of the sudden relief she brought to the mother-to-be and the girl with the desperate look on her face standing at her side. Daisy had assisted at more than a century of births and was eager to add to her total.

"Well now ladies, let's get this wee bairn out into the world now shall we?"

Three hours later, Doctor Malcolm made his belated appearance. Finally, as daylight was fading, so too did Noel Michael Leamington, weighing in at just over nine pounds. Throughout the ordeal, Brenda held Fiona's hand, wiped her brow, and voiced her enthusiastic support. It was almost overwhelming for the girl; she found that if she kept her focus on the timing of the contractions, while trying to ignore the intense sounds, smells, and physicality of the birthing process, that she could manage her emotions. It came as a great relief when Brenda held Noel for the first time, he gripped her thumb while protesting quietly—not quite ramping up to a real cry—and she was smitten.

"What is that? What are you going to do?" asked Fiona and gaped at the physician.

Doctor Malcolm had removed a small, stapler-shaped steel tool from his bag. "It's a Gomco clamp. I can circumcise him now if you like, or perhaps you'd prefer to do it when he is christened?"

"No!" Noel's mother snapped. "He is perfect as he is. I will not have him mutilated in that way."

Her words hung heavily in the air for a moment.

"Right then," replied the doctor, his jaw tightening as he dropped the tool back in his bag.

"I'm sorry, Doctor Malcolm. I didn't mean to bark at you. We'll let him decide when he's older, shall we?"

The doctor nodded, packed up his gear, and with a quick wave and terse goodbye was gone, leaving the three caregivers to tend to Noel.

8

"Hello, Robbie," said Michael, as his brother answered his door. "Ship is in, and I got a wink of leave to go and meet my son. Fiona's had a boy, you see."

He had been smiling so much these last few days that his cheeks ached. "We've missed both Christmas and New Year's, but they've given me a few days while they refit and restock."

As though concussed, Robbie stood mutely on the threshold, his unbandaged eye blinking into the brightness of the daylight.

"Thought I'd pop in and say hello before heading north."

Without acknowledging his brother's pasty complexion and sagging shoulders, Michael turned to the man standing beside him, "You remember Barry, my old chum from school?"

Robbie turned his head slowly, nodded and drew them into the flat. "Yes, we got a letter from Brenda. Congratulations," he said stiffly.

Sensing the tension, Michael said, "How is the eye? Would you like me to have a look see?"

"Nay, the doctors at the hospital are at it several times a week. Just sort of tidying things up. Not much chance of seeing your silly mug through it anymore. What about you. Having fun out there?"

"Well, you know. We're holding our own, but as they say, loose lips sink ships."

The two visitors perched on a sofa in front of the blacked-out apartment window. They sat in awkward silence for a moment until Michael said, "Barry here is on Thames River Patrol, catching Gerry doing the breaststroke up to Battersea Park." Michael's companion barked a laugh and gave him a thumb in the ribs.

For the next while, the conversation came in fits and starts till finally Robbie said, "I wonder if you could do something for me Michael? I was going to put this in the post," he said, returning from the bedroom carrying a large suitcase. "It's for Brenda. Dotty has packed some of her clothes and there is also a package of my old firefighting manuals, photo albums, and the like," he said, tapping it possessively. "Not for her to open, just for her to keep safe for the duration. Never know when this place will be powdered."

"Sure, I'd be happy to take it with us up to Elterwater," Michael said and rose to a stand, relieved to have been given an opportunity to exit gracefully. "We'd better head out now if we're to catch the Windermere train. I'm glad to see you're on the mend," he said. Then while painfully aware he had not yet mentioned the death of his nephew or how his brother's wife was coping with the death of her child, he said, "I am sorry for your loss, Robbie. He was a great little chappie was your Lawrey. I know there is probably not a lot that I can say or do to ease the pain, but please know I will do anything I can to help," and he extended his right hand for his brother to shake.

Robbie's face blushed a deep red as his good eye welled with tears. "You are doing it, mate. Just get that case to Brenda."

"Windermere! End of the line," came the shouted command to disembark. As Michael and Barry stepped off the train to make their way to the bus, they were interrupted by a tweed-suited, middle-aged woman standing in front of a portable metal pen. Inside were three dogs; two lay huddled in a corner while the third, a liver-spotted English spaniel, sat up, eagerly eyeing each person that passed by. A sign hanging from the wire said, "Free Dogs."

"Gentlemen," said the lady, in a pleading tone, "would you give a dog a home? The Londoners are killing their pets, so that they won't be blown up in the streets."

Barry caught Michael by the sleeve, urging him to stop beside the cage.

"There will be no food rationing for dogs and cats, so the government is telling owners that they should put them all down. The government even issued a special pistol for the purpose, and people in London have been lining up outside the Peoples' Dispensary for Sick Animals to have their pets killed."

"Surely that can't be true?" said Michael, canting his head in disbelief.

"Oh, you can be sure it is, sir. During the first week of the blitz, hundreds of thousands of animals were put down or killed in the raids. The RSPCA is trying to find homes for some of them in the country," she said and reached into the cage so the dog could lick her hand.

"What say I get this one for Noel?" said Barry. "Every boy needs a dog."

"I'm not sure Fiona needs another mouth to feed. The number of inhabitants at Elterwater has already increased by two in recent days, and I hesitate to make it three."

"Well, he's not a puppy, and a fully grown animal is an asset, not a liability. Guard animal, best friend, foot warmer," said Barry, counting off on his fingers.

After several more minutes of persuasion from both sides, Michael found himself holding a piece of string attached to the dog. "Does he have a name?"

"Ummm… Spot," said the woman, clearly temporizing.

"Nelson," said Michael. "Lord Nelson of Elterwater."

With hugs all round, the greeting at the house was boisterous. When presented with the dog, Fiona simply shook her head and laughed. "Isn't it just so like you to give me another boy."

Brenda was enthralled. She and Lawrey had always wanted a dog, but her parents would have none of it. Now she sat on the floor of the kitchen with an old scrub brush in her hand, quietly grooming the beast. She cut the worst of the tangles out with scissors while Nelson lay sprawled on the doormat, eyes closed and breathing deeply. Whenever she encountered a knot or tangle, his left front paw would twitch, more in reflex than in distress.

"His ears are a bit of a mess," said Michael. "Fi, do you have some rubbing alcohol and a cotton rag; a small piece of an old bed sheet maybe?"

"We do. I'll get them," said Brenda. The dog's head rose as she dashed down the hall. She was back in a flash holding a cloth and a nearly empty bottle in her hand. "Leftovers from Doctor Malcolm," she said before plopping down beside Nelson. His head fell in her lap.

"Trim the hairs in his ears as best you can, then use the soaked rag to get all that goop out," said Michael. "He will love you for it."

Nelson gamely withstood her ministrations, till finally he sprang to his feet and shook himself vigorously.

"Isn't he wonderful, Aunt Fiona? I think he is wonderful. I am so glad you brought him home, Uncle Michael. He's wonderful."

"I do believe Nelson has a conquest," said Barry, then poured himself another celebratory glass of single malt. The whiskey bottle had passed through many black-market hands, each time increasing in value till it finally landed in Barry's. He passed the bottle to Michael for a top-up, but his companion declined.

Michael was sitting in a kitchen chair, his son bundled in his arms. "Thank you, Fi. As you know, I did not think that having a child was such a good thing when we got married. I didn't think it wise in the circumstance. But you were right, and I am glad you got your wish," he said and then brushed Noel's forehead with his fingers. "And I like the name you chose."

"He is a Christmas baby, after all," said Fiona.

After a meal of roast mutton, potatoes, carrots, and squash, Barry raised the subject of sleeping arrangements. "Fiona, where do you think Nelson should spend his nights?"

Brenda's attention snapped to her aunt as she awaited the response. The dog lay on his mat, working at the shank of mutton bone.

"Well," she began slowly, "all things being equal, that is to say, when you gentlemen are not here, I think he'll be with Brenda in her room."

Brenda's eyes went wide and a grin sprang to her face.

"But for tonight?" asked Michael.

Fiona looked cautiously at Michael, then at Barry. "Noel will be with me in our room of course, and obviously Barry with Brenda in her room won't work. Why don't you two sleep in Brenda's room, and she can sleep with Noel and me?"

"And Nelson?" asked Brenda.

"Yes, and Nelson."

"Are you sure, Fiona?" asked Barry. "Perhaps I should sleep on the sofa in the library."

Oblivious to the undercurrents, Brenda piped up, "Auntie Fiona, I can sleep on the sofa. Then you and Uncle Michael can be together, and Barry can have my room."

Fiona was quick to respond. "That may not be best if you have any bad dreams, Bren. And these two travelers will want a good night's sleep without being constantly woken by a fussing baby and a snoring dog."

"If you think that best, Fi," said Michael.

"It's a pretty small bed," cautioned Brenda. "At least Lawrey and I had separate beds," she said, mentioning her brother in casual conversation for the first time since her arrival.

"Not to worry Brenda, we sailors are quite used to being jammed together into tight spots. At the best of times, our bunks are only twenty-six inches wide," said Michael. "The one in your room is broad acreage in comparison."

Ablutions done, the men settled down the hall, and with Noel in his bassinet, Fiona settled in behind Brenda, who lay on her side, watching Nelson's inert form in the deep darkness. Brenda huddled into a ball.

"The fire will warm up the room in a bit," said Fiona quietly and wrapped herself around her tiny, shivering companion.

"Uncle Michael said that he didn't think it wise to have a child in the circumstances. What did he mean?"

Fiona lay silently for several seconds, her mind cycling through potential responses.

"Did he mean that because of the war it wouldn't be a good idea? Too risky? But it wouldn't be too risky, would it? Out here, that is. But it's not risky here at Windermere, is it?"

"No sweetie, it's not risky here. The war is a long way away from here. I'll keep you safe," she said and brought her hand up to stroke Brenda's closely shorn head. "I'll take care of you. I promise."

Later in the night, Noel stirred and began to fuss. Before he roused to a full cry, Fiona rose and swept him up in her arms. In the dim light of the fire, she changed his diaper and then settled herself back in the bed with Noel on her lap. She arranged the pillows against the headboard and opened her nightdress. Then she leaned back and offered her breasts to her needy son. Brenda did not stir.

As the full moon began to sink in the night sky, Fiona awoke to find Brenda twitching and spastically moving her legs. Garbled but insistent words slipped from Brenda's lips as she wrestled with the hallucinations of bombs falling from the sky. Raising herself to her left elbow, Fiona leaned forward and whispered repeatedly in her bedmate's ear, "You're a hero, Bren. You did everything you could to save him. This is just a dream."

Fiona kept repeating the words as she gently massaged her niece's shoulder. Finally, Brenda climbed out of her nightmare until she became aware of the hand rubbing her.

"I was dreaming."

"You were. Quite a physical one, I think. Where were you?"

"In the street. Bombs were coming closer. Lawrey was there."

"Was he pointing at you?"

"No. This time I was pointing at him and beckoning. And yelling for him to come with me."

"And did he?"

"No. He wouldn't come, and I couldn't get closer to him and drag him away. It felt like I was submerged in thick jelly and that I could only take steps backwards. I couldn't go forward. I knew my bomb was coming and we were running out of time."

"Was it as scary as your last bad dream?"

Brenda thought for a moment, took a deep breath, and then exhaled slowly. "It was just as scary but different. I felt less useless. I didn't get to the end because I woke up, but it was different."

As they lay in darkness, they settled into a wordless calm, each with her own thoughts. The fire had burned down to ash when Noel once again began to stir. Fiona rose to tend to her baby.

A thin winter sun was shining through the kitchen window when Fiona entered with Noel in her arms. Brenda had made porridge, toast, and tea for the men, who sat in their uniforms at the table. Nelson sat eagerly nearby, hoping for anything that might come his way.

Once sated, they all moved to the living room where Michael set a roaring fire.

"I was just telling Brenda that in all the to-do of arrival, I had forgotten to give her a suitcase her dad had us bring along for her," said Michael. "Mostly clothes and such, and a package of boring papers to put aside until such time as he needs them."

"Oh, that'll be grand, won't it Bren. I bet it will be some of your favourites," replied Fiona as she handed the baby to his father. "Mind his head."

"I'm sure the clothes won't be much. When I last saw them, they were pretty much done in, so I shan't be too excited," said Brenda.

"Just a tic," said Michael, immediately handing off the baby to Barry. "Don't drop him," he said over his shoulder and then fled the room, returning moments later with the large suitcase and three presents neatly bound in bright Christmas wrapping. He handed two of the packages to Fiona and the last to Brenda. "Right, then. There you go, ladies; have at it."

Fiona broke into a wide grin and stared at the packages as Michael retrieved his son from Barry. He gave Noel a little jiggle and was rewarded with a hint of a smile.

"Go on then," urged Michael. "The little one is for His Majesty."

Fiona opened the little box and was delighted to find a sterling silver rattle for Noel.

"That is as far as my imagination goes for newborn babies, I'm afraid," said Michael as he toyed with his son's hands.

The next present was for Fiona; it was a red cashmere cardigan. "I know you like red, and the lady at Harrod's said this ought to fit you."

"It's stunning, Michael. I love it," she said as she held it up to her chest. Then her hands dropped in her lap. "I feel terrible. I didn't get you anything. I am so sorry."

"A son, Fi. You gave me the greatest gift you could ever give me," he said, then rose to his feet, crossed the room with Noel in his arms, and kissed her on her cheek. Father and son joined her on the sofa.

Brenda peeled the paper from her rectangular package and revealed two books, *Learning to Sail* and *Swallows and Amazons.*

"You can't live on this lake and not know how to sail," said Michael. "In the boat shed is a fine little craft that you can sail from here all the way up to Waterhead."

"I saw the boat and the sail and all the other bits. It looks quite complicated," said Brenda. "I'll need this book for sure."

"We'll get you out on the lake in the spring. You'll love it," said Fiona. "It's easy once you get the hang of it."

Michael nodded, and added, "The other book is a happy little tale of some children who sail a dinghy into a grand adventure."

"Spoken like a true navy man," said Barry. "Michael, you do know that she is fifteen going on twenty. You might have given the lass a nice frock."

"Nae. Wear a dress for a season and it goes out of style. Learn to sail and it's with you your whole life."

"As Barry says, spoken like a true navy man," said Fiona. Then added, "Actually, it will be fun. This summer we will get the Swan out on the lake and sail out to some of the holmes. Brenda, can you swim?"

"No, Auntie. We went to the sea a couple of times, but we just sort of played in the water. I didn't fancy getting my face wet."

"It looks nice and clean from here. You do wash your face, Brenda?" said Barry.

She blushed and replied, "Yes of course."

"Leave the girl be, Barry. No one likes a tease," said Fiona lightly and picked up the suitcase sitting beside Michael on the floor. She passed it to Brenda. "Let's see what's in this massive thing."

Brenda laid the suitcase on its back and undid the buckles on the two leather straps that wrapped its circumference. Inside she found that her mother had packed some of her old dresses, blouses, cardigans, and underwear, plus a pair of shoes. Also, in the case was a large package wrapped in brown paper and tied with string.

"That'll be Robbie's firefighting manuals. Why on earth he boxed them up and had me haul them all the way out here I cannot imagine," said Michael. Under the string was an envelope that held a letter in her father's small, neat cursive. It advised her to behave appropriately in her aunt's home and to leave the bound package for him alone to open at such a time when he would come to visit. There was no addendum or attached note from her mother.

"Well, that was a bit anticlimactic," said Barry. "At the very least a 'Merry Christmas' was in order."

"They're still grieving," said Brenda as she wrapped her fingers tightly around her thumbs, then shoved her fists into her lap. "I think they are struggling."

"No excuse for it. Would not have been any skin off their noses to celebrate the fact that they still have a daughter," said Fiona tersely. "One that has literally been through the wars." She walked over to her husband and picked up Noel. "I think maybe I shall write them a letter."

"No, Fi. He is my brother. I'll deal with it," said Michael. "He's more likely to respond positively if it comes from me."

Barry jumped to his feet and said, "Sad to say, but we should head out soon, mate. We can't miss that train. But before we go, I think we should take a picture of you and your family. I brought my Brownie."

The sky was a pallid winter blue and the sun strained through a wispy mist that hung above the lake as Barry posed his three subjects on the front steps of the cottage. Michael in his navy best looked dashing, and with pride filling his face, he stood beside his wife and son. With the sun in his eyes, Noel began to fuss, and Michael said, "Barry, you'd better snap it soon before he gets to full throttle."

"Brenda, maybe you should jump in there," said Barry and motioned with the camera for her to join the small group.

"Absolutely not," came her reply. She rubbed her hand over her short hair. "I would prefer not to be memorialized looking like this."

He turned back to his subjects. "Right then. Smile!" said Barry. "Let me take two. One for each of you."

§

It was the second Saturday in January, and Robbie was eager to treat his wife to a fine early evening meal now that she had the day off and he had a fistful of money. Through one of his mates, he had heard of a small, private restaurant that had all manner of illicit food items on hand for those with deep pockets. At Christmas, he had surprised Dorothy with a new dress, winter coat, silk stockings, and shoes from Selfridges, and he had treated himself to a bespoke suit, a heavy woolen overcoat, and a new fedora. New Year's Eve had been a bust, as his wife was on duty at the hospital, so his plan for this evening was to splurge and try to put behind them the trauma of the previous year.

On their way to the Bank District, they had passed a Community Feeding Centre for bomb survivors, with the line-up extending down the block. "There but for the grace of God go I," whispered Dorothy to her husband as she stared at her countrymen huddling in the cold. She squeezed her husband's elbow more tightly and the couple hurried past the crowds.

It had just turned five o'clock when they entered Saint Swithin's Lane. "I think this is it," he said as they stopped in front of a stone-arched doorway. In the dusk light he could see that the door was painted a deep plum and the bottom was faced with a shiny brass kick plate. The building facade was nondescript and wood hoarding replaced windows that had once looked out on a busy sidewalk. He tried the doorknob, but it was locked. He gave the door a sharp triple rap.

"Leamington for two. I believe you are expecting us," he said to a dark-suited man who had cracked the door open. He looked askance at Robbie's black leather eye-patch at first but swung the door wide when, with a calculating headwaiter's eye, he assessed the worth of his clients' apparel.

"Of course, sir. Welcome."

Small and intimately lit with sconce lighting on the walls and candles on the table, the space boasted only four tables, two of which were already occupied. Robbie's and Dorothy's hats and coats were taken, and they were soon seated.

"This evening, sir, we have a set menu. Our first offering is a squash and cream bisque with just a hint of cinnamon. Then some delicate Dover sole sautéed ever so briefly in butter with a dash of pepper. This will be followed by the main course of beef Wellington and assorted vegetables."

As the waiter spoke, Robbie could feel his salivary glands pulsing. He swallowed.

"For dessert, we recommend a chocolate ganache cake, and to finish, we have a cheese plate that includes offerings from the continent. And of course, coffee."

"Real coffee?" dared Dorothy.

The waiter blinked, waited a beat, and then said coolly, "Of course."

Dorothy felt a blush flood her cheeks.

"Also, I can recommend a particularly good Bordeaux from Gruaud Larose we have the pleasure of featuring tonight. A nineteen thirty-five vintage. Very nice."

"That sounds like just what the doctor ordered, so we'll order it too," said Robbie and then indulged in a smile at his own joke.

"Very good, sir," said the waiter dryly, unresponsive to his patron's bon mot. "Medium well on the beef Wellington, sir, madam?"

"No," said Robbie tersely, "we prefer medium rare, if you would be so kind." He actually did like his meat done medium well, but he rebelled against the sting of implicit censure oozing from their server.

"Very good, sir, madam," said the waiter and disappeared down a short hallway to the kitchen.

"Robbie," hissed Dorothy, "how much is this going to cost? He didn't even tell you the prices of anything!"

"It doesn't matter, Dot."

"How could it not matter? It's not like we're made of money is it? We do all right, but this is just so...so...extravagant."

"Just sit back and enjoy the evening. Please?"

"How can I? Where is the money coming from? Where is all this money coming from? My Christmas presents, your new clothes, and this meal. You know these private restaurants are only permitted to serve three courses and charge no more than five shillings. Call me stupid, but this meal isn't going to be had for five shillings a pop."

Dorothy glared at her husband as he sat across the table, pursing his lips and quietly drumming his fingers on the table as the waiter served the first course.

"This soup is amazing," said Robbie. He downed his serving in short order, the silver spoon flashing in the candlelight. Drawn by the heady aroma, Dorothy finally submitted to the contents of the Spode bowl.

The sole was delicate, delicious and gone in a flash from Robbie's plate. As Dorothy finished her serving, she met his gaze and said, "You've spent more in the last two weeks than in the last six months put together. And don't tell me it's a disability payout for your eye. I know exactly how much that was."

"All right, I'll tell you," he said, then followed his response with a heavy sigh of capitulation. "But at least let me have some wine first."

The entrée came, and throughout Robbie slowly revealed the source of the windfall till finally Dorothy asked, "So where is the money now? Did you put it in the bank?"

Robbie waved her to silence as the waiter served coffee.

"How could I?" he whispered when the waiter was out of earshot. "The manager would want to know where a one-eyed firefighter comes up with fifty-seven-hundred pounds."

Had her mouth not been filled with hot coffee, Dorothy's jaw would have dropped open. As it was, she forced a swallow and in doing so, scalded her throat. "Fifty-seven-hundred..."

"I couldn't risk leaving it in our flat. If we got bombed, we'd be back right where we started. I had Michael take it up to Elterwater."

"You must give it back, Robbie!"

"Give it back? Give it back to some random dead man who gave it to me?"

"No, I mean give it back to...I don't know. The government. It's not right. You know it's not right; we didn't earn that money. Where did the dead man get it?"

"I have no idea. And I don't care. Maybe he was just trying to protect what was rightfully his."

Dorothy gently and with slow deliberation placed her empty coffee cup back on its saucer. "No honest man runs around at night in the middle of a bombing raid with a bag full of money."

"He was wearing an ARP uniform," said Robbie dully as he began to feel his imagined grand future slowly slipping away.

"Well that's it then isn't it? He was probably protecting someone else's money. From a bomb site I'd guess. Maybe even a bank. If we asked about it, I'm sure we'd find the answer and then we could return it. Imagine how you'd feel if you'd lost fifty-seven-hundred pounds."

"I think I'm about to find out," he said as the waiter brought round the bill and deferentially laid it on the table.

"How much is it?" she asked and then gasped as Robbie laid five one-pound notes on the table.

It had just turned seven thirty when they left the restaurant. As they made their way home, the air raid sirens began to sound, so they detoured to the nearest Underground station to wait out the attack. It was crowded on the stairs, but they eventually made their way to the platform, deep under the earth.

11

1941

On the third Sunday of the New Year, snow fell in knee-deep drifts, turning the usually grey and dripping estate into a mystical wonderland for Brenda and Nelson. Together they stamped trails into the wooded areas of Elterwater and far into the fields beyond, with Brenda imagining herself crossing the vast Arctic wastelands, her trusty spaniel turned Siberian husky at her side. With every step, she could feel her leg strengthening and her soul lifting. At the top of a hill, she could see the lake below; the shoreline was iced with rime.

"Lawrey would just love this, Nelson. If he were here, we could make snow angels together. He liked angels." Brenda gazed up into the sky, "He is an angel." She took in a deep breath and slowly released it as a frosty cloud. "He died being silly…and brave. He was brave. Like you." The dog raised his head from a hare track he had been snuffling and gave her a measured look. A treat did not appear to be forthcoming; he stuck his nose back into the snow.

They returned home and were greeted by a stream of smoke curling from the chimney. Suddenly struck with an idea, she rolled three great balls of snow. She struggled to stack them, but with much grunting and effort, a snowman took shape on the back patio. "In fact, here's Lawrey now," she said, finishing the arms with sticks. Fiona knocked on the window, a big smile on her face. She held Noel up to the pane.

The snow had hampered the rail lines and blocked many of the roads, so it wasn't till the end of the following week that mail delivery resumed. At the end of a long walk with the dog, Brenda had met the mailman at the bottom of the drive and now sat in the library, warming herself by the fire. Her aunt was just out of the bath after sharing the water with her son and was now up in her room, nursing Noel. For some time, Brenda's letters home had gone unanswered, and so she was feeling disappointed that yet again her parents had rejected her. She cursed them under her breath.

Then to her delight, in the stack of correspondence was a letter addressed to her, but the writing on the envelope was unfamiliar, rudimentary, and tentative. Brenda felt very adult as she used the letter opener to neatly slice along the top fold and pull out the single sheet. She began to read. It was from Mrs. Teal.

"NO! No. No." Her eyes welled with tears.

Noel had fallen into a deep sleep after finishing the right breast, despite his mother's prompting to relieve the fullness and pressure in her left. With bedclothes to her waist and propped up to a sitting position with pillows, Fiona had finally relented and laid her insensible son on the bed beside her just as Brenda burst into the room. Fiona startled as her niece flung herself onto her aunt's lap, crying uncontrollably.

"Oh my God, Bren, what is it?"

Overwhelmed and desperate, Brenda curled into a ball and continued to wail, simply seeking the haven of solace in her aunt's arms.

Fiona waited a few more moments before prompting Brenda again as her concern grew that somehow her brother's death had reached some sort of critical point, a point where her niece would be irrevocably damaged.

"What has happened? Tell me. Tell me now."

Through stuttering breaths, Brenda was able to manage, "They're both dead."

"Who?"

"Mummy and Daddy," she said and then again began to cry, curling ever more tightly into herself. The letter fell from her hand.

"Oh no. Oh no," cried Fiona and pulled the diminutive body to her.

Mucous bubbles formed below Brenda's nose as she stuttered, "They were at the Bank Underground Station and there was a direct hit," and then she burst into renewed sobbing.

In response, Fiona herself began to cry, overwhelmed by the sheer folly of it all, her sobs came deep and filled with anguish and the familiar despair of loss. She had long felt this same feeling after her mother had died, and it returned to her once more, memorable and raw.

Between sobs, Brenda managed to say, "I never got to tell them that I still love them. I never got to them how angry I am at them and Lawrey. It wasn't my fault!" Another wave of sobs wracked her little chest.

It came naturally, the rocking. To dispel the feelings of numbness and hopelessness, she rocked and rocked her niece until finally, sheer exhaustion settled their conjoined weeping. In response, Brenda's fingers had wrapped tightly around her own thumbs, making small self-soothing fists until at last, her breathing became regular and quiet.

Fiona saw that her turgid breast had been seeping milk down the curve of her flesh and drips had fallen onto Brenda's cheek and mixed with her tears. Combined, the fluids had formed beads at the corner of her niece's mouth. She reached for Noel's burping cloth.

Brenda quickly sat up, suddenly aware that her face was awash in mucous and milk. A wan smile passed her lips as she wiped her face dry.

"We are very leaky you and I," said Fiona, and then leaned forward to gently kiss Brenda on the forehead.

12

1941

In the midmorning June light, Brenda looked up from the desk in the library and said, "Did you know that with a piston diameter of thirteen inches and a stroke length of twelve inches at 330 revolutions per minute, combined with an average pressure generated per stroke of sixty-seven pounds, an engine generates more than 161 horsepower?"

Fiona looked up from the newspaper. "Surely you jest. I would have thought that it couldn't be a jot more than 150," she said and then laughed.

"No, it's true. I just calculated it. With a bit of help from this little book of Uncle Michael's. She held up a black-covered copy of *Audels Marine Engineers Guide.* "I'm practicing my maths."

"Good for you," replied Fiona and returned her attention to her paper. "Aha. The Birthday Honours list is out. They've given an Officer of the Order of the British Empire to John Fleetwood Baker, creator of the Morrison indoor bomb shelter; no doubt his boss named the thing after himself after Baker did all the work. This is right up your alley, Bren, the maths. Did you know that he created the plastic theory of structural analysis? Whatever that is—says so here. Look, here's his picture."

"My goodness, I know him!" Brenda said and stared at the photo. "Well, not really. I met him in the library after school one day. He took out a book. Miss Babcock had me forget his existence. All very hush-hush, apparently."

"Fancy that," said Fiona and put the newspaper down. She met her niece's glance and asked, "Are you missing school?"

"Not school per se. I miss the learning. I feel like the world of knowledge is racing on without me."

"Well then, I think we should get you back in school. There is a grand school for girls in Lancaster. You could start there in the autumn term."

"I don't want to leave Elterwater," Brenda said firmly as her eyes narrowed.

"Well, the local grammar school in Sterness would be a dead end for you—there would be little chance of a girl from there getting a scholarship at a good university. Besides, it wouldn't be so bad; you could go just for the weekdays and come home on weekends. Being stuck here with me, Noel, and the potatoes will get a little tedious. And you do love your cosines and secants, which I can't help you with. My degree is in art history—Raphael, Michelangelo, and Da Vinci."

Mathematics suddenly flooded Brenda's thoughts, pushing away the anxiety of leaving Elterwater. "Did you know that

Leonardo thought that the grand proportions in his Vitruvian man had a mathematical basis?"

"Yes. And did you know that he felt that the dimensions of man were linked to the dimensions of the universe?"

"No." Her right eyebrow arched. "I wonder what made him think that," said Brenda. She turned to look at her aunt, "I like playing 'Did you know?', don't you?"

"I do, but you seem to be so much better at it than me. For such a small package, you are brimming with information. Noel is so lucky to have you as a big sister."

"Cousin."

"Technically, yes, but not many cousins spend as much time with their counterparts as you do with Noel. He's a lucky boy."

Brenda snapped the reference book shut as a serious expression settled on her features. "How would I pay for school? There wasn't a lot left after the funeral and gravestones. My parents spent pretty much what they earned."

"Not to worry, Bren. We'll work something out. I do have a trust fund. We could dip into that if necessary."

"That wouldn't be fair to Noel. That's his legacy, not mine. I couldn't accept it." Brenda stared at her aunt with a stolid and intractable look. "I won't."

The next morning, as Brenda came in from the garden with Nelson on her heels, she was met by Fiona saying, "I just got off the phone with the headmistress at the school, "and she needs your birth certificate in order to register you."

"I thought when we talked about it yesterday that money would be an issue," said Brenda. "I will not steal Noel's legacy."

"Brenda, I can see that you are adamant, so let's look at the money as a loan. At some point before he needs it, you can pay it back," said Fiona. "And because there's no time like the present, I signed you up. There is space for you in the fall term."

"And the money?"

"You let me worry about the money. I don't suppose you brought a birth certificate with you?"

"No. There was an envelope with forms in it that the hospital gave me to authorize the travel and so on, but I think that if it's anywhere, my birth certificate would be in that wooden box of Mum and Dad's things we had shipped here after the funeral."

"And that ended up where?"

"I put it up in the loft in the boat shed."

"Have you gone through it yet?"

"No. I'm not really interested in their things," she said and then sighed deeply. "But I'll go and look and see what I can find."

Up in the loft, the wooden box was where she had left it. On top of it sat the parcel from the suitcase that Uncle Michael had brought her at Christmas. She put it aside, opened the box, and picked out a photo album of family snaps. She sat on the bench and starting with a faded old sepia image of her father as a young boy, she flipped slowly through the pages. There was one of him in his firefighter's uniform and one of him and Dorothy in their wedding finery. Spread over two pages was a series of photos of him with his crew, proudly standing in front of various pieces of fire equipment. Brenda then recognized her mother as a young graduate posing in front of the hospital with a group of nurses. Next came a photo of her mother, herself, and her brother at the zoo. She couldn't tell from the photo what was in the cage behind them, but she remembered the day. It had been wet and cool, and despite the weather the whole family had enjoyed themselves. Dorothy had made a packed lunch, and Brenda and Lawrey had spent the day moving among the exhibits playing "Did you know", based on information displayed on little bronze plaques beside each cage.

Brenda's breathing became quick and shallow; her throat tightened. It took her several minutes to find her equilibrium again. Outside a piece of driftwood knocked on the rocks to the tune of the waves lapping the shore. She wiped tears away with her sleeve, then closed the album, placing it at her feet with the intention of taking it up to her bedroom. Small cardboard boxes she found inside the wood crate were filled with old letters and newspaper clippings. Those she moved aside. Then came a large manila envelope marked "Papers." Inside was her parents' marriage license, official-looking professional certifications of nursing and firefighting, a copy of the lease for the flat they had rented in Bethnal Green, and four birth certificates. Her father's birth was listed as 1899 and her mother's was dated 1902. So long ago, she thought. She picked up her own and examined the script. Of course she knew her own birthdate, but it sent a frisson of satisfaction through her to see it officially documented. Lawrey's record of birth was also there, and she wondered where his death certificate might be found. Brenda went through the contents a second time but could not locate the document.

After replacing all but the photo album and her birth certificate, Brenda closed the box, placed her father's bound parcel back on top of it, and then paused. Curious now, she eyed the large parcel. Perhaps her father had put Lawrey's certificate in with his own documents. The string was tightly bound over the paper and did not yield to her efforts to snap it. She dashed down the stairs and grabbed a pair of secateurs from the rack of garden tools.

It was then that she heard Fiona calling her name. The voice was strained and urgent. Brenda trotted up to the house where she found her aunt standing at the back door, dangling Noels burping cloth from her right hand.

"I just nursed and burped him, and look, blood!"

Brenda took the rag from her and examined it. Where Noel had spit up, the milky wetness was tainted with red. "What does that mean?"

"Oh Bren, I don't know, but it can't be good.

8

Doctor Malcolm looked up from completing a thorough examination of Noel who laid sprawled naked on the kitchen table. He spastically kicked his legs and arms, and in his excitement, smacked himself in the face. At the impact, his face suddenly soured.

"Young Noel is in fine fettle. Healthy as they come."

"But the blood…" said Fiona.

"He nurses right well, I'll wager. Look at his rolls," he said and patted the well fatted tummy.

"That he does. To my discomfort, I'll admit"

"Could you shed your top please Missus? I'd like to take a look, if I may."

Brenda scooped up Noel as Fiona turned away and shed her top and undergarments. She turned to face Doctor Malcolm; a tinge of red lit her cheeks.

Malcolm, put on his reading spectacles and approached his patient, bending down to zero on her naked breasts. "Aye, just as I thought. No wonder they are sore. Badly cracked they are—the nipples. That is the source of the blood." His mouth twisted with indignation. "Daisy should have given you cream to keep them from chapping."

He rooted around in his bag and came up with a small vial. "You'll need to go and get this refilled from the Chemists, but this will last a day or two. Tend to them well, and you'll be right as rain." He gave her instructions on its application, packed his bag and then went on his way.

"Well you sure gave us a start, young master Noel," said Brenda as she passed her nephew to his mother. "I'm just going to dash down to the shed and retrieve those papers. I will be back in two shakes."

"Why were we living in a rented two-bedroom flat in Bethnal Green when my father had that pile of money at his disposal?" asked Brenda as she sat looking at the stacks of bank notes on the kitchen table.

"I honestly cannot imagine," Fiona replied. "Where, when, or how could he have gotten his hands on such a trove?"

Brenda just shook her head in wonderment and then said, "Cards or horses probably. He loved a flutter on the ponies." She paused as another thought came to her. "Then again, it might have something to do with being a firefighter. Maybe it fell into his pocket at a bomb site. It does seem kind of illicit the way he was hiding it," she said. A grim look spread across her face. "What should we do with it?"

Fiona thought for a few moments, then said, "I suggest we engage the solicitor in Lancaster that dealt with my mother's holdings. You'll have to claim this money as part of your father's estate, and then His Majesty's Inland Revenue will want to take a piece. But then with their official stamp you can bank the remainder," she said and shifted Noel into his bassinet as he began to fuss. "I suspect the solicitor will require a trust to be set up to manage all this, as you are underage. But just think, Bren, you are set for school in the fall and eventually your pick of university," she said and gleefully clapped her hands.

13

Arlene, one of the hospice nurses, came into Brenda's room and gave Lacey a quick pat. Her eyes opened, but otherwise she lay inert on the quilt.

"I'm afraid I'm going to have to interrupt your visit," she said. "We have to do a little procedure for Brenda."

"No problem," I said, coming to a stand. "We'll leave you to it." I reached for the dog and lifted her to the floor. She shook to settle her fur, still looking a bit drowsy.

"It turns out my bowels are a bit constipated from the morphine," said Brenda. "They have a plan to unblock me."

"That happens a lot around here. Lacey and I can pop down the hall and visit someone else. I'll see you another time."

"No, please don't go. Come back in a few minutes when we are done here and then I can drone on a little more. At least until I get myself out of England. We're almost to the good part."

"I tell you what; Lacey and I will visit down the hall, and when that visit is over, if you're ready to continue at that point we'll come back for the next bit."

Brenda's hopeful expression bloomed into a wide smile and the deal was struck.

It turned out the elderly South Asian lady in room 120 spoke only Urdu and didn't like dogs, so I grabbed the notebook from the nursing station, moved to the sofa in the hallway, and began to jot down summaries of my visits for the day. As Lacey and I sat there, a young woman approached us. Her gait was stilted and awkward—cerebral palsy, I thought. She too was South Asian and introduced herself as Piya, the granddaughter of the resident we had just left.

She knelt and asked whether she could pet my dog. With only the slightest invitation, Lacey will freely offer herself up for attention to anyone and spotting an obvious opportunity, she quickly sprawled at the woman's feet.

Even the artificial light of the ceiling fixtures did little to diminish the gleam of the young woman's long, coal-black hair. Her face was exquisitely formed, and her dark, flawless skin highlighted her deep-brown eyes, which were framed by high-arching brows. Clearly an animal lover, Piya pampered Lacey with such ardor that with her eyes focused only on Lacey, I was free to indulge myself in her smile. A smile like that can cut through fog. It can bring back memories.

We said our goodbyes and then as I watched Piya head down the hall towards her dying grandmother, her spastic, inelegant steps carrying her away, I could feel it coming. My hands began to shake, and my throat tightened. I wanted to scream out to her that I had such a vast, empty space inside me now that could take as much of her pain as she might wish to give. Maybe that's why my wife's death has eviscerated me: it has turned me into a vessel for others to fill with their anguish. I would willingly take this young woman's pain and give her legs that dance, legs that swim, or legs that clasp a lover's groin to her own, for my emptiness is endless. I know there is no limit, for when I receive phrases of condolence from friends and relatives, I feel nothing, absolutely nothing…except maybe the burden of shouldering their pity.

Arlene came and laid a hand on my shoulder, then passed me a tissue to daub at my tears. "Are you sure that you're up to going back in?"

"Give me a minute," I said and headed for the visitors' washroom to compose myself. Lacey stayed at the nursing station.

I splashed water on my face, stared at myself in the mirror, and then admonished myself for such grand self-indulgence.

Sometimes I purposely dive into the gloomy pond of self-pity. Its almost like I do not want to let go of the grief. I know that there is a difference between wallowing in grief and simply letting yourself experience it. I have been doing the self-pity thing a lot less lately and it was time to give it up altogether.

Counselling has taught me that I will get over the grief and that I must go through it and not around it or deny it, but I also know that the day she died, my life changed and that I will never get over the loss. One lady in the walking group described grief as akin to having a leg amputated. For the first while, you are always falling down, losing your balance and unable to function. Eventually, with support and time you learn to walk, but the leg will always be missing, and you will never run the way you used to do before the axe fell.

A light fecal pong hung in the air when Lacey and I re-entered Brenda's room. It was a smell common to care facilities, and we had become quite accustomed to a wide range of odours. I remember one lady who would apologize profusely each time a person entered her room, so keenly aware was she, that well before her taking a last breath, her body was already in a state of advanced decay.

We settled into our roles, and I asked Brenda how school had turned out.

She replied, "On the whole, I think it was a bit of a float. Certainly, the course material wasn't problematic. There was one girl, though, who delighted in giving me a hard time about my diminutive stature or my hair or the clothes I wore. She was one of those rich, prissy types that gathered a group of minions around her to puff up her own ego constantly, and she reveled in crushing the self-esteem of others."

Brenda frowned, met my gaze, and with a special sparkle in her eyes continued, "So one day near the end of term I got even. On the inside cover of each textbook was a number stamped in black ink, and that number was recorded when the book was issued to the student at the start of term. Of course, the teachers went through each book at term's end so they could dock you if there were pages missing or crib notes in the margins. So, without the girl noticing, I swapped out her history book for mine, and on the weekend, I took it home. On the very last page, I indulged my artistic passion and copied an anatomically correct and extremely detailed image of male genitalia from my uncle's *Gray's Anatomy* text. Then I swapped her book back on the day we were to hand them in. It worked a charm!" Brenda laughed heartily till she coughed up a little blood. I handed her a tissue and waited for to her continue.

"Of course, the big issue wasn't that the book was defaced. It was the fact that she had apparently drawn the offending male part with such accuracy, that it strongly suggested intimate and long-lasting contact with the real thing. Parents were called, and suddenly Primula was no longer at the school. Big scandal, that."

"Did you ever come to regret your part in that episode."

"Oh, I suppose so…well to be honest Colin, and I promise to always be completely honest with you, not really. I despise bullies."

14

April 1942

"What have you done to that old knapsack, Bren?"

"Just a few modifications. You said the bus driver can't or won't allow you to take the pram on board, and we have to take young Master Noel with us to Sterness, so I've made holes in the canvas for his legs and his arms. If it rains, you can just flip the flap over his head and he'll be snug as a bug. Here, give it a try."

"Are you serious? Everyone will laugh, surely."

"Well, he's getting bigger and your arms will give out after a short while. Do you have any other suggestions?"

"No, but honestly, Brenda."

"Just give it a try, Auntie Fi."

Fiona slung the pack onto her back while Brenda lifted her cousin into the air and guided his dangling legs into the satchel and out through the openings. He settled in nicely and to test it out, Fiona took a few tentative steps around the kitchen. Noel gurgled enthusiastically, and with that endorsement his mother stepped out into the garden and walked about. A few minutes later, she returned wearing a triumphant look. "It's brilliant!"

Once into town, they headed for the bakery but were brought up short by the sudden appearance of a police officer blocking their path. His uniform was ill-fitting on his thin tall frame, and he was distinguished by a significant under-bite that displayed his yellowed and mangled teeth when he spoke.

"Hello, Miss Corium," said the constable curtly. "Who's that then?" He stared at Brenda and gave her the up and down as might a butcher deciding where to cut first. "And what's that you've grown on your back? A hump?"

"Actually, I'm Mrs. Leamington, constable, have been for some years now; you may wish to keep up with the times. This is my niece, Brenda Leamington, and on my back is my two-and-a-half-year-old son," she said and stepped up to within two feet of the officer, her eyes hard and cold. "I'm sure you have better things to do than chatting up young women, so we'll bid you good day."

Fiona stepped around the man and accompanied by her son and Brenda, strode down the cobbles and entered the bakery.

"What was all that about?" asked Brenda as the door closed with a tinkle behind them.

"Constable Tilbury is related by marriage to the partner who arranged the pilfering of my father's estate, and he is a cad of the worst order. There is no love lost between us, and I urge you to have as little to do with that man as you can possibly manage. He has his fingers in every dirty pie in the district and is not the paragon of virtue that one would expect in an officer of the law."

"He gave me the creeps. Why hasn't he been replaced?"

"Every healthy, intelligent, and honest young man with integrity is otherwise engaged in the war serving his king. That leaves us with the likes of Constable Tilbury, the dregs."

With no further unpleasant encounters, the trio enjoyed the rest of their outing. The baker, chemist and the butcher all commented positively on the innovative baby carrier and Noel sopped up the attention. He was especially delighted with his first experience eating a shortbread cookie.

"It looks like it will be nice weather tomorrow Bren," said Fiona, as they climbed on the bus for the ride home. "You should take out the Swan. I'll help you get it in the water."

It was the first outing of the season. On this Spring morning, as Brenda let out the mainsail to fall onto a beam reach, the little sailboat surged ahead and sped Brenda and her one crewmember up the lake. Nelson was settled forward on a blanket, his head between his forelegs, eyes closed and oblivious to the surging and slapping of water against the hull.

"As the locals would say, Nelson, 'There be a glisky sheen to the water,'" said Brenda as she squinted into the blinding glare reflecting from the wave tops. Unlike his namesake, Nelson took little interest in the sailing conditions; he continued to doze.

The wind increased as the morning waned, and ahead lay Beddall Holme, a small, crescent-shaped islet perhaps one football pitch in width and two in length. It was treed on its low crest, and the bay side was shallow and filled with reeds. The outside arc was formed of granite that had been smoothed by glaciers in ages past. Given the wind direction on this day, the lee side of the island was also the sunny side, so Brenda dropped the mainsail and, using the heavy oars, made her way to a natural indentation in the rock that allowed her to direct the craft right up to the shore. Roused by the activity, Nelson bounced in the bows, eager to leap ashore. He claimed first landing rights, and she followed him onto the dry stone and tied the long painter to a low shrub that desperately held itself in the grips of a crevice. The dog bounded about, wildly sniffing bushes, a sun-bleached old log, and then the high-water line. Brenda clambered up the rock and sat in the sun, which held the first stirrings of the summer warmth to come. The air quietly shifted the high branches of the trees that were slowly coming out of bud.

She lay back and enjoyed the sun for a while; it felt good on her face. With eyes closed, she idly traced the line of the burn scar on her neck and softly murmured her hymn. After a few minutes, Nelson returned to her side and then sniffed at her knapsack, pawed at it a few times, and turned to glare at her.

"Me too, Your Lordship. I could use a bite as well."

Brenda withdrew a thermos of tea, a sandwich, and a scone. She shared her lamb and mint jelly sandwich with the dog but saved the scone for herself. Despite the sun, she did feel a bit cool, so the hot beverage fit the bill nicely.

"Right, then, let's explore a bit."

Brenda checked that the boat was secure and together they followed a little trail up the spine of the holme. At the trail side, small, delicate bluebells were just coming into bloom. She knelt and gently inspected the dark blue blossoms, which bobbed their heads in the light breeze. Nelson gave the flowers a perfunctory sniff as Brenda moved up the trail. At the crest, she stopped in her tracks. Through the trees to the bay she could see a man in a rowboat using an oar to pole his way through the reeds. He was a bulky man with upper arms bigger than her thighs. She squatted to watch as he made his way to a mat of rushes defended by a pair of Canada geese. As the boat neared the nest, the gander began honking frantically, then he raised himself on flapping wings and attacked the boat. As the bird launched his assault, the man countered with a single swing of the oar, striking the gander in the head and knocking him senseless. The man grabbed the bird from the water, wrung its neck and tossed it into the bows. Still defending her clutch of eggs, the goose shifted uneasily on her nest, having seen her mate go down. But with an invader within feet of the nest, she finally struck out at the aggressor and in short order joined her mate in the bow of the boat. The man then lifted the eggs from the nest to be candled later for selection and then sale on the black market.

As the figure stood up to pole back out into the bay, Nelson barked and then trotted assertively toward the water's edge. Brenda lurched forward to grab at the dog by his collar just as the man looked over and saw her silhouetted against the sky. He shouted something at her, loud and discordant.

"Nelson!" she hissed. "Come. Come!"

The dog looked over his shoulder and saw that his mistress was walking quickly back up the trail, and he raced to join her. They scrambled back to the lee side of the holme, and Brenda hastily freed the painter from the branch, lifted Nelson into the sailboat, and pushed off. She struggled to drop the oars in the locks and then swiftly rowed out into the wind to set sail for home. As the breeze filled the mainsail, she felt a wave of relief, secure in the knowledge that the man in the rowboat was no match for her little craft. In the distance, Brenda could see the man pulling for the far lakeshore; the whole while she knew his eyes were fixed on her little craft as it slipped away for the safety of Elterwater.

Two weeks later found Fiona, Brenda, and Noel in Sterness. It was a day of high, thin cloud, bright but cool. They had just exited the post office and nearly collided with the large man from Beddall Holme. He stopped and eyed Brenda suspiciously, unsure how to respond, if indeed this was the young female witness to his poaching. Brenda voiced a hushed, "Excuse us," and grabbed at Fiona's hand. She was relieved to see the form of Constable Tilbury stride up behind the man. The policeman slapped his hand on the shoulder of the bulky giant, who turned and, seeing the uniform, said, "John, you are looking uglier by the day."

"And you're looking fatter, Reed," replied the cop, and together they joined in a laugh.

"This little lasso trying to peddle her skirt? I'll run her in if she's after you for a tumble."

Not to be cowed, Fiona stared at Tilbury and said, "We all know that poaching game for the black market is highly illegal. So, Constable, is it to you that one would report a case of goose poaching out on one of the holmes?"

Tilbury's eyes turned to a squint. Fiona continued, "Say for instance, if someone was out sailing recently and came across someone throttling Canada geese and stealing their eggs, would it be you that should be notified?"

"It would be me, yes," he said. His brows screwed up into dark challenging arcs.

Undeterred, Fiona added, "And if the perpetrator were to be well known to the local constabulary on, say, an amicable basis, would it then be wiser to report the issue to a higher authority instead?"

Brenda glanced at the hulk standing beside the officer and watched as the knuckles on his sledgehammer fists turned white.

"Well, lasso, for starters I doubt whether an off-comer from London would know her arse from a goose. Secondly, and this is where you should take heed, I would caution that someone, whoever she might be, to be very sure about reporting what to whomever. Sometimes things don't resolve themselves as one might hope. Long-term consequences and the like."

"So what you are saying is that a poaching incident is best left unreported?"

"Well, if the person reporting the incident is a child," he said and shrugged. "Who is to believe what comes out of the mouths of babes?"

"I'm seventeen and fully capable of identifying a goose and the man who strangled it," Brenda said and turned to glare at the hulk standing shoulder to shoulder with Tilbury.

In return Reed leered at Brenda and said, "Oh are you now? Just coming up ripe then?"

"Enough!" snapped Fiona and turning, she guided her family away from the two men.

"I thought you wanted to steer clear of the constable, Auntie Fi. It probably wasn't a good idea on my part to even tell you about the geese."

"No, Bren, it's my fault. Sometimes I just can't help myself. That man Reed is a beast. He is known in Sterness to be a bully and worse. To their shame, a number of local girls have regretted ever finding themselves being alone with him."

"Couldn't they have reported him? Have him arrested."

A frown came to Fiona's lips. "The reality is that even in this day and age, the deck is observably and irrevocably tilted in the man's favour, especially with the police being populated with the likes of Tilbury. The only hope for a woman is to stay clear from the likes of Reed."

15

July 1943

As was her habit on hot summer Saturdays, Brenda loaded Nelson, a picnic lunch, and a beach blanket into the Swan. Noel was down for his nap and her aunt was puttering in the victory garden, pulling weeds and harvesting peas, carrots, and scarlet runner beans for dinner. It was late morning and a breeze blew down the lake, pushing ripples into wavelets that soon would be at least a foot high. The wind would drive the little craft up the lake and back, a magical, natural force that never ceased to impress her. It had been hot this past week, and to battle the heat she wore her bathing suit. This was to be the hottest day yet, but in the distance, clouds were piling high above the hills; a change was coming.

Brenda locked the dagger board in place, set the sail, and headed off up the lake, tacking back and forth into the wind. She loved the process of harvesting the free energy from the air and the feeling of control it gave her to determine the speed and direction of the little craft. On her starboard side was the temple folly at Storr's Hall. The octagonal stonework structure stood at the end of a narrow stone pier that jutted out into the lake from the well-treed grounds of the hotel estate. A young boy stood inside the little tower, leaned out through the arched front casement, and waved at Brenda. Though his head was topped with ginger-red hair, he was the right age to be Lawrey. Brenda returned his wave but had to quickly avert her gaze.

As they made way, from up the lake came the roar of powerful engines. Far away she could see a wide shape skimming the surface of the lake, and with each second that passed it grew in both size and volume. The shape shifted into a massive Sunderland flying boat on its maiden flight from the factory up the lake at Calgarth Estate. At over eighty-five feet in length and with a wingspan of more than 110 feet, the behemoth dwarfed her little ship as it became airborne a quarter mile from her position along the shore. Nelson cowered in the bows as the deafening sound of the four massive Bristol Pegasus engines buffeted them. As the aeroplane disappeared into a mass of distant dark clouds, its drone fading, Brenda said to Nelson, "How is it possible that something that big and heavy can fly? It just doesn't seem possible; but physics is physics I suppose." She stared at the clouds where it had flown. "There must be some books about that."

Wray Castle, in all its neo-Gothic splendour replete with turrets and sham arrow slits, stood stony grey and dominant atop the slope that led down to the lakeshore. At some point in time, large stones from along the rocky beach had been arranged in a ragged line that poked out into the lake. In the lee of the bay, the wind and waves were muted, allowing Brenda to lift up the dagger board and easily slip the boat up beside the stones.

Freed from the confines of the bows, Nelson leapt to freedom and then incautiously slid off the slippery wetness into the water. Undeterred, he swam to the shore, shook wildly, and then bounded back and forth as Brenda made the boat fast to the stones. Rather than risking the slimy pathway, she simply stepped into the knee-deep water and joined Nelson on the secluded beach, which was mostly gravel with intermittent patches of coarse sand.

Eager for exercise, Nelson continued to bounce and dash about, so Brenda picked up a stick floating at the shore. It was the length of her arm, hefty and free of bark. She heaved it along the waterline, and Nelson dashed along the beach and returned to drop it at her feet. Picking it up, she paused and then tossed it into the water about twenty feet from shore. The dog plunged into the water but only up to his chest; he began to whine.

"Oh come on! Go get it."

Nelson looked back over his shoulder at his companion and gave her a desperate look.

"Get the stick, Nelson. Get it."

After a long minute of urging and cajoling with no progress, Brenda strode into the water past Nelson and swam out to the stick. She was not a strong swimmer, but her aunt had taught her the basics in their first summer together, and on this hot day it felt exquisite to cool down.

She turned and treaded water. "C'mon, Nelson. You are supposed to be a water dog. Come get it." She splashed the stick for encouragement.

Nelson began an even more desperate dance, his whining reaching a frantic, discordant pitch.

Then, from a figure emerging from the undergrowth along the shore, "You come and get it, baby girl." A sneer was smeared across his face. "I see that you are a whole year riper."

It was the big man, Reed the poacher, now standing at the shore's edge with a brace of rabbits hanging from snares that dangled from his hands. His dark brows formed a threatening complete line above his squinted eyes, and a long-sheathed knife hung from his belt.

"I said come and get some of this," he shouted and grabbed at his crotch.

Brenda continued to silently tread water, but while her eyes were fixed and steady, her mind spun wildly, searching for a response. Her breathing came shorter and faster.

"It would be a shame if your little dog were to drown, don't you think—him not being a good swimmer and all."

The man dropped his catch, took several steps out into the water, and grabbed Nelson by the collar. He pushed the dog's head under for a few moments. Nelson came up frenetically thrashing his paws and frantic to get to the shore. He twisted, turned, and was suddenly liberated when his collar pulled over his ears and free from his head.

"Not a good swimmer at all," Reed said as the dog bounded away.

Brenda slowly swam forward till she could feel the rocky bottom under her feet and carefully made her way towards the shore. When the water was at her waist, she stopped and sought an escape, from both the disgusting beast of a man and the familiar cresting tsunami of terror he had triggered. Now only ten feet from him, her eyes locked on his and immediately she felt her limbs begin to shake. A dizzying whirring sound rushed through her head.

Think.... How do you think?... Think!

Brenda sneered and then spat.

"Oh, you little bitch!" he said and lunged at her, splashing forward into the water.

As he drew near, Brenda offered her left arm for him to grab. With both hands he reached for her outstretched limb. Just as he made contact with her wrist, she lifted and swung Nelson's stick in one smooth, violent motion with her free hand. The piece of wood met the left side of his head with a resounding thunk, as might a fist knocking heavily on a ripe melon. Reed wavered and then stumbled past Brenda and collapsed face first into the water. Momentum carried his body out and away from her and the shallows.

She had held her breath while she struck the blow, and now Brenda gasped for air as she waded desperately for the shore. As though seeing down a tunnel, she noticed the weapon was still in her hand and she flung it as far as she could out into the lake. Nelson greeted her with oblivious enthusiasm and eagerly danced about as he followed her to the rocks, where she picked him up and dropped him into the bow of the Swan. As she freed the boat, the floating figure began to move and then thrash. Blood swirled in dark clouds around his head, which did not rise free of the water for a breath. Her hands were shaking wildly, and it took Brenda several attempts to drop the heavy and cumbersome oars into their locks. At last she sat and began stroking madly away into the bay, all the while

CRAIG MICHAEL SMITH   154

focusing her gaze on the writhing hulk in the water. After some moments, the struggles became subdued, till finally the only movement was the wavelets slapping into the back of his head and shoulders, which slowly sank out of sight.

With the sail up and making way, the sun blinked out behind the mass of clouds building along the hillsides. The surface of the water took on a steely grey sheen. The wind strengthened as it hurled the little craft homeward on a beam reach, and they tore along through the wave tops. Scrambled thoughts filled Brenda's mind and she struggled to organize and process the whirlwind: to tell Fiona or not, to tell the authorities or not, to do something or not. She screamed into the wind.

As the air cooled, Brenda managed to work her way into a cardigan, all the while keeping one hand on the tiller. After some time, Sterness appeared on her left and then later the folly at Storrs. It was half five when she tied up at Elterwater.

"Oh my goodness, didn't you get some colour today," said Fiona as her niece entered the kitchen. "You should put some cream on that, sweetie."

"Part of it is wind burn, I think, but it was bright and sunny in the morning. What can I do to help with the meal?"

"Not much; things are coming along nicely. What say you entertain his nibs while I get the plates out?"

Is that it? Brenda thought. Is that all she can see is a sunburn? Shouldn't there be some obvious sign or expression that she can read? She felt lightheaded.

"What did you see out there today?"

Brenda dropped her shoulders, let her tongue soften, and released a deep breath before she spoke. It felt like her brain was sparkling, vibrant, and capable of the most challenging calculations or crossword. Ideas blurred by at tremendous speed.

"A Sunderland took off not too long after we got underway," she said and took Noel into her lap. "It just doesn't seem real that not long after my father was born, airplanes were just taking to the sky and were hard-pressed to lift a man. Now they can carry tons of bombs, or trucks, or whatever payload you'd want. A sail is just a wing pointing upwards, you know. Lift coefficients essentially based on the same principles. I'd like to find a book on aeronautics; the mathematics must be amazing."

With her lips carrying a broad smile, Fiona turned to look at her niece and shook her head. "Good on you," she said.

Later in bed, Brenda tossed about through the wee hours, unable to disengage her frantic brain and blank out the day's events. The sheets insisted on twisting around her legs, and she couldn't count the number of times she had turned from side to side. Her pillow had taken several beatings but finally, not long before the dawn diluted the blackness of the night, she finally fell into a restless sleep. The dream settled on her with smothering dead weight, and Brenda found herself naked in the lake. The man was also there and naked, but his face, torso, and massive arms were covered in lake slime as he stood on the shore. In his left hand hung wire snares, and his massive thighs held him in a defiant stance. Unlike the familiar illustrations in her anatomy text, the man's phallus was a knotted mass that suddenly uncoiled and wavered before him like a snake eager to slither between her thighs.

"Come and get this!" he said and beckoned with his right hand.

As though pulled to him by an invisible cord, Brenda found herself moving towards the man, unable to squelch the force driving her forward. As the distance between them narrowed, the only thing that held her attention was the snake. The figure of the man seemed to fade as though in mist, and Brenda held out her hand to feel the snake. Just to touch it. Initially, the skin felt smooth and cold as stone, then she grabbed it with both hands and pulled it free. The man screamed, fell into the water, and in a swirl of eddies sank from view, but the snake continued to writhe in her grip, pulsing and muscular, warming in her hands. It took the strength of her whole being to control the movement of the snake, and the more tightly she held it the more intensely it resisted. As she squeezed and pressed the now hot reptile to her body, a pulsing heat transferred to her own groin. She called out as a spastic eruption swept through her body and yanked her awake.

Brenda heard the footsteps and then Fiona swung the door open. "Are you okay? I heard you shout. Are you dreaming again?"

Brenda took a moment to find her bearings. After a pause she said, "Yes, but not a Lawrey dream. I must have been...calling Nelson or something."

Relieved, Fiona said, "Okay good." She entered the room and looked down at her niece. "Do you need to come back to bed with Noel and me?"

"No. No. I'm fine. You go back to sleep." Fiona kissed Brenda on her forehead and quietly closed the bedroom door.

The next nights were rampant with dreams—dreams in which Reed held her, not Nelson, under the water. And there were dreams where she swung the stick but the man grabbed it and struck her instead. There were no more dreams of phallic snakes but dreams where the man grabbed her and throttled her as he might a goose. One night after a particularly violent episode, Brenda left her room and climbed into bed with Fiona and Noel. She quickly fell asleep and did not dream.

Fiona had just poured boiling water into the pot for a mid-morning cup of tea when the door knocker echoed down the hall. She made her way to the front entrance and was met by a gentleman in a well-worn suit. He was accompanied by the despised local constable.

"Hello. I'm Inspector Meridith with the Cumberland and Westmorland Constabulary, and this is Constable Tilbury, with whom you may already be familiar. We are investigating the circumstances around the death of a local resident. May we come in?"

The man was stiff and tweedy. Fiona's jaw tightened but she welcomed the men into the library, where Brenda was on the floor with Noel playing with little wooden blocks. Introductions were made and offers of tea were declined. Fiona asked, "So what is this all about?"

"Well, Mrs. Leamington, it's about a local man, Kevin Reed. His body was found up lake at High Wray two days ago, but we think his death preceded that by some days. I'll have to be a little indelicate here, but it looks like he had been in the water about a week. We are asking locals if and when they might have last seen Mister Reed."

Fiona nodded and paused while she contemplated her response.

"Not recently, but we did see him back in the springtime. It was the beginning of May, I should think. Wouldn't you agree, constable?" said Fiona and glared at the officer.

Meridith turned to eye Tilbury, who rubbed the flats of his palms on his thighs. He sat perched on the edge of a chair as though set to sprint for the door.

"I ran into Reed and the two young ladies outside the post office at Sterness. And yes, I believe it was early May."

"There was some discussion about poaching, if I recall," said Fiona.

"Poaching?" asked Meridith.

"Yes, sir. As you know, Reed worked at the factory at Calgarth, but he was well known in these parts for feeding the black market with waterfowl, rabbit, and venison," said Tilbury, whose voice took on a higher, tense pitch.

The inspector's jaw twitched in frustration as redness came to his cheeks. He would have Tilbury's bollocks for holding back that information.

"Especially geese," added Brenda.

"May we ask how he died, inspector?" asked Fiona.

"He drowned, but there was also evidence of a blow to the head. Perhaps from a fall. Were either of you up that way, say around the last few days of July or the first few of this month? Possibly seen him or anything untoward?"

Fiona shrugged and shook her head and then turned to Brenda, who pursed her lips as though in thought to review the dates.

Brenda felt as much as saw the intensity of the inspector's gaze. He knew something.

"July thirty-first," she said finally. She turned her attention to Noel, who had just knocked over a stack of blocks. "Nelson and I were out on the Swan, though I don't remember seeing anyone else on the water."

"Nelson is...?" asked the inspector; his heavy brows formed a high arch.

"Oh. He's my dog. Sorry," Brenda said and turning to meet the inspector's gaze, she eased a meek smile across her lips.

"We did have a report of a small sailing vessel that day near Belle Grange. Could that have been you?"

There it was then; he had known she had been out on the lake.

"Yes, quite possibly."

"You know, inspector," began Fiona, "Kevin was known to be a bit of a ruffian, and if there was foul play involved in his demise, in all likelihood it would be at the hands of his close associates. If it was me leading the investigation—and of course, how many women have a chance to do that?—I would pay particular attention to anyone who was on a friendly basis with the man."

Tilbury swallowed and glared at her.

"So the last time either of you saw Reed was back in May. Am I correct in saying that? Nothing since?" asked Meridith.

"No," said Fiona. "And I must say I'm glad for that. He was a beast of a man, and it must have taken someone equally big and mean to take him on, wouldn't you agree, constable? He was, after all, your friend so I imagine you would be familiar with all his chums, yeah?"

All eyes turned to Tilbury, who managed only a slight nod of agreement.

"We'll put on our thinking caps and let you know about any little thing, inspector," Fiona said and came to a stand. Seeing that their hostess wished to complete the meeting and that they had exhausted their line of enquiry, the men also stood.

"Well, thank you for your time, ladies. If you think of something else, perhaps you would call me directly rather than the constable," said Meridith and handed Fiona his card.

Oh oh, thought Fiona and glanced at Tilbury. It'll be a nasty ride back to Sterness for you.

The rumble of the departing police car faded in the distance as Fiona stood in the doorway, Noel on her hip and a broad smile on her face. Brenda came to stand beside her and said, "Aunt Fiona, I have something I need to tell you."

That afternoon found Brenda energetically splitting firewood in a desperate attempt to exhaust herself. What with the police visit earlier, she knew that a full night's sleep would not come without the impetus of fatigue. Unfortunately, rather than divert her attention from Reed's death, each contact of the axe with a log echoed the sound of the blow to the man's skull. Nevertheless, she split a full cord before coming in for the last meal of the day.

16

August 1943

Having washed and dried the dinner dishes, Brenda hung up the dish towel and sighed deeply. She could hear her aunt upstairs chattering at Noel as she put him down for the night. The windows were open to the warmth of the evening, and she could hear the birds outside chirping happily, not at all in keeping with the crushing torpor she felt. She made her way to the library and collapsed on the sofa. Brenda eyed the volume of *Britannica* she had been reading earlier but couldn't generate the interest to pick it up.

Fiona swept into the room, and when she spotted the slumping form of her niece said, "You might think about having a sherry before you go to bed tonight, Bren. Ease your nerves. Even better, the other day I found a half-full bottle of Glenkinchie that Michael left behind on a previous trip."

Brenda managed to bounce her shoulders in the smallest of shrugs. Fiona chose to interpret the movement as an assent and returned moments later with the bottle and two crystal glasses.

"I'm not much of a scotch drinker but I will join you. Rather than bedtime, let's have a bit of a tipple now. Couldn't hurt, yeah?" She poured several healthy fingers for each of them and settled beside her niece.

"You know in your heart of hearts you did what you had to do, Bren. If you hadn't acted, he'd have raped you or worse. If there is a worse."

"I know. But the way I'm feeling physically doesn't seem to have any relation to my understanding of the circumstances. I just want to turn the feeling off, make it not to have happened. Nelson and I were having such a nice day until then." She took a sip and made a face. "This is awful. People drink this on purpose?"

"It's an acquired taste. Keep at it," Fiona said and winced as she swallowed a dose from her own glass.

"We can't ever give them the slightest hint of your involvement in that man's death," Fiona said, avoiding his name. "The police don't like women, especially women who are independent and don't cower in their presence. They'll try and make you out to be a harlot and drag you by the hair through the muck if they get half a chance. Especially Constable Tilbury." She took in another mouthful.

"Well, I don't think of Tilbury as a mental giant. I think there's more to fear from that detective. He has a lot of experience and plays his game very shrewdly. Meridith knew that I had been seen in that part of the lake and thought he might catch me out in a lie. Though I don't think for a minute he thought it was me that put Reed down." Brenda looked down into the amber liquor and gave it a swirl before choking down another draught. She could feel the pulse of warmth beginning to glow deep inside her.

"I wish it had been me and not you alone on that beach," said Fiona. "It makes my blood boil to think of you there by yourself with him. Men are allowed to tramp around by themselves wherever they wish, but we women have to be circumspect in everything we do. It's not fair."

Brenda snorted a little laugh. "Whenever Lawrey and I said that, my dad would come back with, 'Fair! You want fair? Most of the world is starving to death or being blown to smithereens so join that club if you want fair.' There's a lot to be said for that point of view, I suppose. Perspective can be relative."

Fiona looked at her niece and smiled. "Well, my perspective is that you are a fine relative and I love you. We'll make our way through this, don't you worry."

They spent the next hour chatting about Noel and politics and just about anything other than the obvious. The contents of the whiskey bottle shrank until finally Brenda waved away the offer of more, saying, "I think I'll have a soak in the tub before I go to bed." She stood, wavered a little, and headed down the hall.

At some point later, Fiona heard Brenda move to her bedroom. Fiona stayed on the sofa and through the golden filter of her benign intoxication she listened to the sounds of the house and the utterances of the night sighing through the window. She thought of Michael and hoped he was safe and well. She thought of Noel sleeping upstairs and felt a physical ache sweep through her. Then, she remembered partners past and imagined partners future. Finally, with the darkness now well settled, Fiona slowly navigated her way through the house and thought she might check in on Brenda before she herself found sleep.

The bedroom door opened soundlessly to her hand, and by the moonlight filtering through the curtains she was able to see a naked form sprawled on the bed. Brenda had succumbed to the alcohol, fatigue, and the soporific heat of the bathwater, and she lay on her front, her head to one side as though whispering to her left hand. Her left leg was crooked upward, her right was straight out. Brenda's skin glimmered as might alabaster in the dimness, and Fiona was reminded of the Florentine sculptures she had long ago delicately caressed to absorb the feel of the curves before sketching the muscles, breasts, and hips. She stared at the diminutive nude figure for some minutes, suddenly awash with unbidden hunger. The languid curvature of the spine formed an arrow that drew her gaze to the translucent skin along the smooth flesh of the haunches, along the line of the thigh and the bow of the calf. Fiona's legs began to tremble, and she suddenly became aware that her fingernails were digging deeply into her palms.

She stepped close to the bed and saw that Brenda's breathing was deep, regular, and innocent of strain. Fiona reached out her right hand and saw that it was shaking. She lowered it to the foot of the bed, straightened the snarled bedclothes and pulled them over the sleeping figure beneath her. Deep in a quiet slumber, Brenda did not hear the click of the latch as Fiona left the room.

The next morning found Inspector Meridith at the front door. This time it was Brenda who answered.

"I have a few more questions, miss, if you don't mind."

Hearing the man's voice, Fiona briskly strode to the front door with Nelson by her side. The dog stood stiff-legged with his nose twitching, quietly alert to the cautious posture of his masters.

"I was just telling your niece that I had a few more questions for you both. May I come in?"

Fiona flashed a high-beam smile and then gestured for Nelson to lie on the mat and stay. She invited the officer into the library, where they seated themselves.

"Noel is just down for his nap," she said brightly and then added, "Constable Tilbury not with you today, inspector?"

"He's pursuing other lines of inquiry," Meridith said curtly, and then he reached into his jacket pocket. With a flourish he pulled out Nelson's collar. "Is this at all familiar?" he asked while quickly turning his head to gauge the responses of both Brenda and Fiona.

"I'll guess it's a dog collar, but it might be a piece of martingale or harness," offered Brenda with a deep look of concentration on her face.

"May I have a closer look, inspector?" asked Fiona. He stood and passed it to her. "You may know that my father owned a leather goods company, and it would not surprise me if such an item was in his catalogue. Why do you ask?"

"It was found in the water near where the deceased was discovered. Its provenance may be germane to the inquiry."

"Well, I'm sorry, but my family is no longer associated with the company. If you need to track down the potential purchasers of such a piece of leatherwork—of which I suspect there are many—you'd have to speak to the current owners, I'm afraid," said Fiona.

Brenda watched the man's face and waited for what she knew was coming.

"Does your dog wear a collar?" he asked and fixed his gaze on Brenda.

"He does, yes. Nelson!"

The spaniel bounded into the room upon hearing his summons and rubbed up against Brenda. "He wears this sailor's knot affair that my uncle fashioned for him last year. It's made of Egyptian cotton twist. You see, it even has a stainless-steel ring on it for when he needs to go on leash."

She rubbed his ears and the dog began to quietly grunt and murmur his appreciation.

"Did you go ashore at any point in your outing that day?" asked the inspector. His tone was mild and conversational.

"We did. Went for a swim."

"And you saw no one," asked Meridith.

"Correct. Not a soul. My aunt is always on about looking out for strangers, so I'm pretty careful about putting myself at risk."

"Do you remember where you went ashore?"

"Not really. Up the far end of the lake somewhere. I'd not been up that far before, so it was all new and unfamiliar. I did see a plane take off from the lake, if that's any help," she said, knowing full well it wasn't.

A memory suddenly came to her. "Oh, I did see a boy wave to me at the folly, so I stand corrected. I did see someone!" she said, her voice brightening. There it was, she thought; he was the witness that Meridith had in his pocket, confirming the where and the when of her presence on the lake that day. Nobody could place her anywhere near the scene of Reed's death. A wave of joy flooded through her.

"One last thing, if I may?" he asked and scanned their faces as he spoke. "To assist me in my inquiries, I would ask that I have a quick look at your little sailing vessel."

"Of course, inspector," said Fiona and jumped to a stand. "Let me lead the way."

At the dock, the Swan bobbed in the wavelets that mildly slapped the gunwales of the little white boat. The sun was warming to their faces despite the gentle breeze.

Meridith bent to one knee and lifted the oar closest to him, carefully scanning its surface. Then he turned and offered it to Brenda.

"Could you hold that please?"

The young woman obliged and took the long piece of hardwood into her arms, then because of the weight she let the blade end ease to the dock with a light thunk. "Heavy," she said. "Uncle Michael has promised to make a set out of yellow cedar and mahogany for me. They'll be ever so much lighter and easier to use."

Meridith reached across the seat to the far side and grabbed the other oar, which he examined with concentration equal to the first. He could see that the oars would be difficult for the tiny young woman to wield as some kind of weapon. Satisfied that there were no traces of blood or hair on the lacquered wooden surfaces, the inspector pushed himself to a stand. Tilbury's thesis that these women were somehow involved in Reed's death was now, in retrospect, preposterous beyond imagining. More than likely the culprit would be found in Reed's black-market acquaintances.

"I'm sorry to have taken up so much of your time, ladies. If anything were to come to your attention or remembrance about this matter, I would be very obliged to hear from you. Good day," he said and strode off the dock and up across the garden.

Fiona looked at her niece and smiled. Brenda shipped the oars back into the Swan and then, to the sound of the retreating police car, they hugged and then bounced up and down, giggling the while.

As they headed in for tea, Fiona asked, "Where did you get that collar for Nelson?"

Brenda shrugged. "Is that what it is, a collar? I just found the thing hanging on a nail in the boathouse the other day. I thought it was some sort of maritime contrivance. A bit moldy, but it fit him."

17

The volunteer pushing the tea cart gave the door a sharp rap and announced her arrival before rolling in and offering us tea and cookies. Lacey's nose caught a whiff, and, in a flash, she pushed herself up to a sit, ready for offerings. Alicia served us with fine bone china—donations from the estates of residents long gone—then headed off to the next room.

"Is Lacey allowed a little piece?" asked Brenda.

"Well, she has a host of food allergies. They give her little itchy spots, which get infected if we don't keep on top of them; sorry, if *I* don't keep on top of them. So, for situations just like this, I keep some vet-approved snacks in my pocket. Here," I said and passed her two little bits, which Lacey then wolfed down.

Brenda looked at me, seeking to mine the expression on my face. "Have I shocked you?" she asked. "A murderess in your midst. Would you denounce me?"

I thought for a few moments and then said, "It's not up to me to make moral pronouncements. I find that far too many people are willing to take the opportunity to castigate someone they feel has a moral shortcoming." I sipped my tea and then added, "In my experience, the louder they proclaim, the higher the degree of hypocrisy. Besides, in your case I would rule it a blow well struck in self-defence."

"That's what Aunt Fiona and I decided. Even today, a woman does not fare well in the courts when defending her honour, and with Tilbury on the wrong end of things, it was guaranteed not to go well had I reported the death."

"Well with so many good men dying in the war, I really don't think it likely that Reed would have been missed for any decent reason."

"Still, with that hanging over my head and nightmares from the bombings—it was a stressful time."

"I've read about the war and the bombings. My father was a radio operator on a Lancaster bomber and he told me some tales, but I cannot imagine what it was like to actually live in a war zone. It must have been an incredible relief when it all ended."

"There were so many people traumatized by the time the war was over. We were all shell-shocked, I think. Nowadays they call it post-traumatic stress disorder. Can you imagine having so many citizens as well as armed forces personnel suffering from PTSD? After the joy died down a week after the armistice, it was like the whole nation went into a coma."

Brenda's fingers found Lacey's ears, but she continued talking.

"The economy was in tatters, and all the boys came home to find there was no work, so the government initiated the Assisted

Passage Migration Scheme. For a ten-pound fee, one could emigrate to Commonwealth countries like Australia, New Zealand, and Canada. More than a million 'ten-pound pommies' took up the challenge. I was one of them. Of course, I had money, so I didn't need to leave for financial reasons, but with no real parents or siblings, and blood on my hands, I was eager to leave."

"How did your aunt take it? You two had been through a lot together."

"She was torn. Like any mother—and she really did think of me as her daughter—she was proud that I was heading off to start my own life. But she also had relied on me. Well, truth be told, we relied on each other to get through the war years, and she was loath to see me go. In the end, I was going off to a university anyway and wouldn't have been coming back to Windermere to live even if my life plans had worked out in England. She and Noel moved to London. Uncle Michael stayed in the navy; surprisingly, they never did divorce, even though years later it became so much easier to do that. They stayed great friends but simply continued to live separate, happy lives."

"And the dead poacher issue?"

"On that side of the Atlantic, he never raised his head again, so to speak. I did have a resurgence of nightmares for a while, but it was strange; they were never about his death. They were always about the Swan sinking in a great storm and me being alone out in the middle of the lake and unable to even see the shore. I'd wake up thrashing in the sheets, trying to swim to safety. His death just sat there in some dark corridor, a poisonous toad in the garden of my mind till I landed in Canada."

"It all changed when you left England?"

"Totally. When I washed up at the University of Toronto, it was as if all the deaths I had experienced became distant in both time and space. As I've told you, I'm not a religious person, but I think I know how those born-again Christians feel after they've been dunked and re-christened. It wasn't that I ever forgot those deaths— I can recall those moments in explicit detail—it's just that they ceased to have a hold on me. I was renewed. Much later, Reed's death did come back to bite me, though not as you might expect."

Her expression was the antithesis of renewal; exhaustion was writ large across her features now. I stood to leave. "This seems like a good spot to stop for today. It turns out that there is a training session here for us volunteers on Monday evening. If you would like, I'll pop in after the session and join you in a cuppa."

"Good," she said. "Then I'll be able tell you about my daughter."

The next day, I took Lacey for a walk down to Steveston Village by the water. We stopped in at a café and I ordered a cup of Earl Grey. The sun was shining, and we sat at a table beside a purple Japanese maple tree to give the dog the benefit of shade; at her age, the sun heats her up terribly. A young woman had settled across the patio from us; with matted hair, dirty, tired jeans, and a knapsack bulging with what looked to be her life's belongings, she appeared to be homeless. She did have a cup of coffee though. I suspected the funds had probably come from panhandling. A grimy looking line sullied the skin of her neck where a silvery necklace disappeared into her shirt top. My daughters would not have called it a blouse; it appeared to be a well-worn man's work shirt. She was diligently shifting small pieces of paper around on the tabletop, but I couldn't see the result of her efforts from where I sat.

It took me some time to work out a plan of action; getting the wording right was critical. I did not want to seem like a dirty old man trying to pick up or take advantage of a young woman in distress, and I didn't want to embarrass her by bringing her plight to the attention of the other patrons. Had she been begging on the street corner, I would have dropped her a twenty. If she had been a guy, probably not.

"Hello," I said. "You look like you might have an interesting story to tell. Can I get you a sandwich?"

Her head popped up as I was hit by the acidic smell of sweat, urine, and mildew. From the intensity of her glare I knew it was not going to go well; I had seen that wild look in a woman's eyes before. I had lived with it.

"That's inappropriate, man! So inappropriate. Can't you see I'm working here? That's just so inappropriate."

"I was just trying to help. I thought maybe you could use a bite to eat."

It was then that I looked down at her table. On it was a sloppy pile of individual words clipped from newspapers as though she was putting together a ransom note or a weird coded collage. It appeared that she had not made a lot of headway. When she tracked my eyes to the mess of variously coloured words, she quickly covered them with her hands.

"So inappropriate. I need you to leave. No one can see this!"

Patrons at other tables turned to witness and enjoy the melodrama being played out.

"Okay, okay. I'll leave you to it," I said and left the patio with my ears burning with embarrassment.

As my wife's illness progressed, she became less and less the person I had known. Her caring, happy countenance fell away, and she slowly slipped into a world of irascibility and dissolution till there came a point in her disease when hope changed. It shifted from my hope of a miracle recovery to the hope for a quick and painless death. The day that hope changed was the worst day of my life.

It was in the morning; Lacey was in bed beside her. I had come up from the kitchen with a nice hot latte. She looked at me as I entered the room and she tapped her chest with her pointer finger and, struggling to form the word, said, "Don." I met her gaze with a kind of stunned look on my face and said, "No I'm Colin. Colin. Your husband."

From her mouth came a sound that I will never forget. It was somewhere between a gasp and a wail. It wasn't till later that I realized that she was trying to say, "I'm done"— That she wanted to die. By the end of that week, she could no longer talk. Blessed with cancer that had metastasized to the brain, she was no longer my wife. I said goodbye to the true love of my life well before she died, but I looked after the shell of her to the end.

The hospice chaplain said to me the other day that God works in mysterious ways, so I am left to wonder how my love's death would be different or if she would still be alive and healthy if there were no God.

"So the last thing I'd like us to do this evening," said the counselling psychologist, "is have you share with the group any self-care processes you engage in to deal with issues that may arise for you when volunteering here at the hospice."

She was young and vibrant, yet an aura of calm hung about her as she scanned the twenty occupied chairs that formed a tight circle. Eyes were suddenly averted, and heads tilted toward fingernails. There was always reticence about being the first to speak. The group was mostly elderly women, but there were a few men.

"It could be something as simple as writing your feelings in a diary or talking in general terms to a loved one about some feelings you are experiencing," she prompted.

Finally, a grey-haired woman broke the silence and said, "When I arrive at the hospice, I always check in with Marnie, the volunteer coordinator, to prepare myself for who has died since my last visit. And then again when I leave, I let her know how my visits went. I find it's always the toughest when someone I have spent a lot of time with is no longer able to communicate with me or has died. It feels good to just sit down and talk about the times we had spent together. I feel I'm honouring their memory, and when I've done that, I can leave the sensation of loss in her office."

"Good. Thank you for sharing that. I heard the word 'feel' a couple of times in your answer, and it's feelings that can become problematic when dealing with death unless we find a way to let them go."

A woman stuck up her hand. The counsellor nodded and said, "Yes, go ahead."

"I've found a way of releasing those feelings is to write down what I'm feeling in great detail on a piece of paper. Well actually, I type it on my computer and then print it out. I'm hard-pressed to read my own writing, so its technology to the rescue." The group broke into chuckles and smiles. "So, then I read it aloud and then burn the paper in my fireplace. That's how I let it go."

"I like that. You've found something that works for you. Remember that letting go does not mean forgetting. Those memories and experiences are to some extent the reason why you volunteer. You wouldn't do this if you found no value in it."

More people ended up sharing after that, so I didn't pipe in. Normally I just talk to Lacey on the way home if something has been bothering me. She's a very good listener, even if she is almost as deaf as a post.

The meeting concluded and Lacey followed me down the hall, lured by the smell of fresh chocolate cookies nestled on the saucers of two cups of tea. With full hands, I could only lightly tap Brenda's door with the tip of my shoe.

"Yes?" came her voice. It sounded even more frail than on our Thursday visit.

"I took a rather inelegant trip across the Atlantic in a converted troop ship that landed in Québec, then I moved on by train to Toronto. Even at the beginning of the war, the Faculty of

Engineering and Applied Science had twelve women in the fold, so it wasn't as if I was breaking down any gender barriers. Still, among some of the male faculty and most of the male student body, there was a certain degree of disbelief that we women could hold our own against the self-proclaimed towering intellects of the men."

Seated in the recliner chair, I had settled in nicely with my tea, and Lacey lay on the bed.

"In the thirty years I spent at UBC, there was a real sea change in the academic role of women there," I said. "I think now thirty percent of the student body in the Faculty of Applied Science are women, and they've actually set a goal of parity for the beginning of the next decade. Having said that, bias doesn't just disappear, but it certainly is a more inclusive environment than when I went there as student. Not in engineering, mind you; it was physiology for me. I did medical research when I finished school."

In the last several days, Brenda's skin had turned a darker yellow, as if her whole body was a recovering bruise. It was obvious that her liver was pretty much done.

"It was great fun really at U of T," began Brenda. "The boys were given financial aid and bursaries after they were de-mobbed, and for so many of them it was just a relief to have made it through the war. Classes were overflowing, and there were lots of dances and social gatherings; it was so vibrant and forward looking."

She paused in thought and perhaps to catch her breath.

"In contrast, England was numb and directionless, still picking itself up out of the rubble while battling with societal change. Just after the war ended, Winston Churchill, the man who led Britain through its darkest hour and on to victory, was tossed out on his arse by the proletariat and the Labour Party."

I wasn't sure whether it was from weakness or excitement that her hands were shaking as she took a sip of tea, but I was a little concerned that she might spill the hot liquid on herself. I shifted to get up, but she managed the task before waving me away.

"Fickle and spiteful, yes. But people were tired of war and having lords and ladies running the show. Just like me, they wanted a new beginning. Canada seemed so much less class conscious and as I said before, I was pretty much able to put my family's deaths behind me; it had been five years, after all."

"Dead brother, dead parents, dead rapist, all behind you?"

Brenda sighed heavily. "No. In truth? No. But at least I was functional and moving forward." She sighed heavily, then added, "The mystery money put me through university and allowed me to live comfortably; I was never a big spender. Eventually, the last of it went into buying a farm and starting a new life."

A motion-activated light flicked on outside, momentarily turning my attention to the back garden. Curious, I glanced through the sliding glass door as a raccoon waddled its way across the lawn, unperturbed by the flood of light.

"He comes most nights, though usually not this early," Brenda said. "I don't get many long stretches of sleep at night now, so sometimes I'll catch him marching around out there at three in the morning." She turned to look at me. "Where was I?"

"U of T."

"Oh yes. I finished my degree in 1951, and though it took a while, almost a year later I got a job at the National Research Council in Ottawa, testing airplane designs at the wind tunnel facilities. Not long after, the project of a lifetime landed in our laps. The first models of what would become the supersonic Avro Arrow came for testing in September of '53."

Brenda coughed and used a tissue to wipe away her bloody sputum.

"The designers were breaking new ground in aeronautics. It was all very exciting. For instance, the air conditioning system required to dissipate the heat from the friction of air rubbing against the fuselage at supersonic speeds had the capacity to make the equivalent of twenty tons of ice a day. The control systems were all intended to be automatic; the pilot was there just in case of emergency. They wanted the plane to fly itself."

"So not like *Top Gun* then?" I said.

Brenda snorted. "At supersonic speeds, human reactions to engage an enemy are impossibly slow. You can't see an enemy aircraft flying at you at those speeds. Say you're both flying at each other at twice the speed of sound and you manage to see each other when you're about a mile apart. Literally in the time it takes to blink, either you've crashed into each other or he's passed you. No, at those speeds, interceptor fighters are all about electronics."

She took a sip of tea to moisten her throat. "I met my husband in the fall of '55."

18

Ottawa 1955

Brenda sat at her drafting table with a slide rule in her hand. She was crunching numbers from a recent test that would help to determine the surface area anomalies of the innovative delta wings. Lost in the mass of calculations, Brenda did not notice the approach of her boss with a young man at his side.

"Miss Leamington, this young chap is Morris Senda. He is visiting us from the Arrow design team, and I'd like you to go through the initial subsonic stability and control findings with him, if you'd be so kind. Of course, he has full security clearance, so no holding back on that account. Just walk him through the results. Not up to you to make recommendations, mind."

Brenda shook hands with a good-looking man sporting short military-cut blonde hair. Unobserved by the older man, he bobbed his eyebrows at the last comment.

"Have a seat," she said and pointed at a stool several feet away as her supervisor excused himself and departed. "What specific part are you designing?"

"The internal missile support assembly in the undercarriage," Morris replied. "I need some guidance on placement and strut profile, but from what your boss just said, apparently he doesn't believe you're qualified to advise on such matters."

"Qualification and authorization are two different things, Mister Senda. Also, it may well be that Mister Kilburn wants to find out what kind of answer you can come up with of your own accord. If I just lay out the results, he'll then see if you're capable of pulling the conclusion rabbit out of the hat—a test of your competence, not of mine."

Senda laughed, and Brenda felt a pulse of heat burst in the pit of her stomach.

"Do you really think that's what he was on about?" he asked.

"Absolutely not. He thinks I'm just a precocious little girl dallying about until I can snag a husband. To him, I'm a temperamental calculating machine foisted on him by a bureaucracy bent on sabotaging the program. Easily replaceable."

"When in fact you're a....?"

She met his gaze, searching for just the slightest hint of glibness or mockery, and found none. "I'm an engineer," she said and flipped open the book of calculations.

Later, at the canteen, they continued their conversation over lunch.

"So you work at the facility at Malton. Just here for a quick peek?"

"Yes, they hired me on there as a structural engineer. Metal stress and fatigue is my area of expertise. They sent me along to review the latest tunnel test results to help my deliberations, although fluid dynamics is not really my bailiwick."

"Are you familiar with the Whitcomb Area Rule?" Brenda asked.

"Refresh me," Morris said in ambiguous response.

"Basically, as an object approaches and passes through and above the speed of sound, wave drag forces become so significant that they reduce the design efficiency and power. The aeroplane becomes too unstable, drag heavy, and power hungry to fly at supersonic speed. At these speeds, air doesn't act as a simple fluid flowing over the skin of the fuselage. So the solution to the problem is based on narrowing the cross-sectional area at crucial points. Sort of like turning the wiener-shaped fuselage into a Coca-Cola bottle with wings."

"So if we're building a supersonic interceptor to shoot down bad guys," he said, "we have to make sure the missile delivery systems don't mess with the drag forces."

"Oh, they'll alter the drag forces sure enough, but it all has to do with the correct placement of those drag forces in relation to the cross-sectional area at critical locations on the fuselage."

Morris was quiet for a few moments before he asked, "Are you aware of any drag forces that would prevent you from coming out to dinner with me on Saturday night?"

Brenda smiled and looked directly into his wide blue eyes, "None that come to mind."

ϐ

Brenda spun in front of her full-length mirror. She declared herself pleased with the flow of the floral print material. Her recent purchase was an A-line dress, highlighted with a Peter-pan collar and a bow. She went to the bedroom window and looked down as a cab pulled up at the curb. Morris stepped out, walked to the house, and rang the bell.

At the door she said, "Hello Morris," while meeting his gaze.

"Shouldn't you doddle or something? You know, to make me wait."

"Feminine guile is not my strong suit, I'm afraid."

"Well I am glad not to have to wait to see you. You look beautiful."

A blush flooded her cheeks, "Why thank you Mister Senda."

"Our pumpkin awaits," Morris said and with a flourish, led her down the walk.

He opened the back-passenger door on the taxi, a Hillman Minx, guided Brenda into her seat, gave the driver the Rideau Street address, and then settled in beside her. "That's a nice house you're in," he said.

"Yes, I'm renting the top floor. It's a short drive to the NRC and to downtown, and it's a quiet neighbourhood. I like quiet."

"I thought we might try the Del Mar," he said. "I heard it opened back in May, so they should have the bugs worked out by now."

The driver dropped them in front of Freiman's department store, and they crossed the street and stepped inside the restaurant. They were guided to a table in the Bar-B-Q room at the rear, where a wagon-wheel chandelier festooned with lanterns hung from the ceiling. The walls were finished with knotty pine.

"It looks like the Wild West," said Brenda.

"The Wild West of Chile, apparently. It's named after a place there."

"Ándele, ándele, amigo."

"Pardon me?" asked Morris.

"Oh, it means 'Let's go' in Spanish. And that's about the extent of my Spanish vocabulary, I'm afraid. There was a Swiss chap in my structural analysis class who was fluent in four languages. Imagine being able to converse pretty much anywhere in the world. I used to tease him that if he spent a week in China, he'd be fluent in that too."

"And he taught you the Spanish?" Morris said, his voice hardening slightly.

"Taught is hardly the word. I picked it up from him, I guess." She quickly turned her attention to the menu. "I think I'll have the barbecued chicken."

After the waiter had taken their orders, there was an awkward pause in the conversation. To move things along Brenda said, "Senda is an unusual last name. Do you know its origin?"

Morris took a few moments before nodding. "Yes. Lost in the mists of time, someone emigrated from Japan to Canberra, and then several mixed generations ago an ancestor emigrated here from Australia. Not a lot of us about really. What about you? Leamington?"

"Back to Saxon days apparently. Though, our little twig of the family tree is probably quite traceable, I've never bothered. Past is past. I don't dwell on it."

"Who knows, you could turn out to be a princess or something," he said, and gave her a wink.

"Oh no, that would be my worst nightmare. I would not ever want to have a royal tag on my collar. Horrid. Besides, given family recent history, it's more likely to be something far less auspicious." Brenda smiled broadly and said, "I am trying to focus on the future and leave the UK behind me."

"Well, don't leave your accent behind you; I must admit to finding it very alluring."

Just then, the waiter arrived with their beer and not too long after, their meals. Morris led the conversation, focusing on his career and plans to one day command his own engineering firm.

"I'm impressed that you have things so well plotted out," said Brenda. "I, on the other hand, am still figuring out my own path forward. It must be nice to have that confidence; to feel that assurance."

"It's not cast in stone or anything. I'm very open to additions and improvements," said Morris. He carefully placed his knife onto his plate and laid his hand on her wrist.

The couple spent the remainder of evening chatting about aeronautics, university experiences and the latest films they had seen. Laughter came easily to them and Brenda relaxed into the cozy atmosphere of the restaurant and the warmth of Morris's charm.

At the end of the evening, he walked her from the cab to her door.

"I'd very much like to see you again, Brenda. As you know, I don't have much free time right now; I'm into it well above my ears for the next several weeks. But I'll do my best to come back to Ottawa as soon as I can get away."

"I'd like that."

Ever the gentleman, he bent to give her a chaste kiss on the cheek and watched as she entered her home.

For the next while, he would phone her almost daily from the Avro design office at Malton, ostensibly to discuss air tunnel results but primarily just to hear her voice. He suggested a hike and picnic outing in the Gatineau Hills in three weeks' time.

"We'll take my car if you like," she said. "You can drive."

They had agreed she would pick him up at his hotel on the Saturday morning, as his train would get into the Sparks Street station no earlier than ten Friday evening. A big smile broke across his face as he caught sight of her in the lobby. Brenda was wearing a sweater and blouse combination with a pair of Capri pants and loafers. She carried a warm jacket over her forearm in case the cool autumn air became too chilling. True to her word, she handed him the keys to her new red Chevrolet Styleline sports coupe.

"Wow," he said as he settled into the driver's seat. "Fluid dynamics engineering must pay better than junior structural engineering."

"I liked the style and the lines," she said.

"Ditto, he said, boldly eyeing her. She tossed her head back in a laugh, as Senda put the car in gear. They crossed into Quebec and followed the Ottawa River into the countryside, all the while chatting about their lives and questionable bosses at work. The flat farmland soon gave way to the Eardley Escarpment, a tall stony mass of the Canadian Shield. They consulted a map and followed a side road to a trailhead. It took the pair a good part of the morning to climb up through the reds, oranges, and yellows of the deciduous forest to reach what turned out to be a spectacular viewpoint.

The Ottawa River Valley lay spread out before them as they sat on the sun-warmed rocks and tucked into their food.

"This reminds me a lot of Windermere. The high prominences and the farmland below, and of course the water."

"Do you miss it?"

"Yes, I do. I loved the sailing. And I miss my aunt and my little cousin. Elterwater Cottage was a haven during the war."

"Elterwater?"

"Oh, it means Swan Lake in old Norse."

"Would you ever go back?"

Brenda thought for several moments. "Not to live there. I don't think you can ever go back. It just wouldn't be the same, but that's probably a good thing. I can hang on to the good memories and enjoy them for what they are."

"I imagine the bombing was terrifying."

"Terrifying is just a word. The feeling of being bombed every day and fearing that you'll be blown up is beyond words," she said and raised her hand to her throat. "That's where I got this," and she turned her head and arched her neck to display the angry line of her scar.

He leaned forward as if to inspect her wound but instead gently laid his lips on her throat.

A Saturday in January found them on the Rideau Canal. He had given her a pair of ice skates for Christmas, and she sat on a bench in a warming hut while he laced them up for the first time.

"This is not going to go well," she said dully as skaters flew by, somehow balanced on thin steel blades while carving graceful arcs in the ice.

"Just hang on to me and you'll be fine. I've been on skates ever since I could walk." He finished, blew on his fingers, and put his gloves back on. "Okay, here we go," and lifted her to a stand.

She was bent at her waist and gripped his arm in desperation.

"Okay, first off, you need to stand tall. Use your core muscles to keep you upright, and bend your knees to keep the centre of balance over your skates."

"Considering I'm barely five feet in height, standing tall will be a bit of a challenge."

"You know what I mean, Brenda. You look like you're melting. It's just physics, right? Think of keeping your body mass centered so that any applied force doesn't cause forward rotation of your upper body. Otherwise, boom, down you'll go."

Brenda took a few tentative steps and he pulled her along the ice.

"Remember, we're not walking. Think vectors. What force must be applied to move you forward? You have to angle your foot and push off to give you forward momentum."

It took some time, but eventually with Morris's assistance she was able to push and glide, push and glide. At such low speed, she persisted in flailing her free arm in the air for balance, but only once did she drag them both down to the ice in a giggling heap.

"I think I'm done," she said. "My toes and fingers are frozen."

He guided her to their bench and knelt to take off her skates, then slide her feet into her warm boots. Task accomplished, he reached into his pocket for a small jewelry box.

"While I'm down here on my knees, Brenda, I want to ask if you'd make me the happiest man in Ottawa. Will you marry me?"

In late spring, they went together to apply for a wedding license. The clerk filling out the form asked, "And will your wife be taking your last name?"

"Of course," said Morris.

"No," said Brenda. "I'll be keeping Leamington."

Morris stared at her in disbelief. "Of course you'll take my last name. What wife doesn't take her husband's last name?"

"Morris, I will not become Brenda Senda. Surely you can see that's a problem. And besides, I am Brenda Margaret Leamington. It's who I am. It's my professional identity."

He looked at the clerk and said, "We'll have to come back later after we've straightened this out."

Morris sat in the driver's seat, gripping the steering wheel while Brenda's car idled quietly at the curb. His knuckles were white; his face was red. Brenda sat huddled beside him. While sobbing, she managed to choke out, "Morris, you have to understand that my father is gone, my mother is gone, my brother is gone. The only remaining thing I have left of my family is my name." Tears spilled down her cheeks, "I cannot give that up as well. I just can't."

Morris inhaled slowly and noisily through his nose before loudly stating, 'If I permit you to keep your name, you have to agree that our children will be Sendas. None of that British double-barreled nonsense. They will be Sendas and Sendas alone."

His clenched jaw and narrowed eyes demanded the right answer.

"Of course, Morris. Of course. Our children will have your name."

19

1956

"Did you know that now, in the month of June, when the days are longest, that the traverse of the moon is always very low in the sky and because of that, it takes on a yellowy hue? Hence the word honeymoon."

Brenda lay sprawled naked on the bed, the morning sun streaming through the window of the cabin, with the view of the lake only partially obscured by trees. The bathroom door was slightly ajar, but no response came. She stretched luxuriously and then watched as a goldfinch in its sartorial yellow and black flitted amongst the greenery.

Morris abruptly emerged from the bathroom, wearing a bathrobe and a humourless look. He had been holed up in the bathroom for some time, and Brenda had thought he had been conducting some arcane male toiletry or at the very least shaving, but now she could see that she had been mistaken. She felt a stab of foreboding as he sat on the edge of the bed; his eyes were red and squinty.

"I'm not the first, am I?" His voice was contorted with disgust.

Brenda stared at him, speechless.

"You've been with a man before, haven't you?" he continued. "Often. You're too comfortable with it for it to be anything other than experience."

"It? It? Does it matter?"

"Of course it bloody matters!"

Brenda felt fury flash up her throat; her scar pulsed. Through clenched teeth, she said one word, "Why?"

Morris slammed his right hand down on the bed, "Because it does. Because you were supposed to be a virgin. Because you've been sullied by another man. How can I have sex with you ever again? Every time, I'll be thinking that someone else has already had you and maybe you'll be thinking of him or comparing him to me when we do it."

"Are you telling me that you were a virgin before last night, that you'd never had sex before?"

Morris sneered at her, "That's not the point. It's different for men. We have needs!"

"What, and I don't?"

His eyes widened. "You're not supposed to act on them. You're a woman!"

Brenda squeezed her hands into fists and then forced herself to splay her fingers flat on the bed sheet. "So what you're saying is that I am now suddenly without virtue. In your eyes, I'm some kind of violated succubus." She glared at him. "Damaged sexually beyond redemption. Is that it?"

"Yes, damn you!"

"You do remember that our vows just said, 'to have and to hold.' I do not remember declaring any phrases about nullifying nuptials because of premarital sexual activity. I married you in good faith." Her voice had turned sharp and cold.

"Good faith! You didn't even take my name!"

"In the end, you said you were fine with me keeping my name, that it didn't really matter."

"Well, that was just something I said."

"I wanted a longer engagement so that I could finish my work on the Avro before I quit and became your doting wife, but you wanted to get married sooner. So, me not quitting my job right away, was that also something you 'just' said? That was what, just hot air?"

"I am a man, and I don't want my wife to work. It reflects poorly on me. It's my job to provide."

"Why is this all coming up now? You gave completely different answers about these questions before we got married."

"Well, it's not at all worked out the way I wanted."

"Well, I guess that's the price for not asking the right questions or not saying what you really mean."

"And I didn't mean until death do us part, as it turns out. I want an annulment." He stood, strode to the bathroom, and slammed the door.

Brenda snorted a laugh and then raised her voice enough to ensure she would be heard. "You realize, of course, how ironic that will be. To be given an annulment, you'll have to claim we didn't consummate our marriage. Then when the wedding registrar has erased our vows, I'll be a certified virgin!"

It was difficult at work. She had returned the wedding presents and suffered the ignominy of pity from the female staff. The male staff treated her pretty much as before, with distance and condescension, but perhaps with a little more disdain than previously, as though she carried some communicable social illness. Alone in bed at night, while clawing for the relief of sleep, her mental safe haven of engineering calculations was inevitably overrun by thoughts of her failed marriage. Countless times, Brenda worked through every frame of her relationship that she'd had with Morris, evaluating every nuance and misstep, from the moment of their first meeting, to the signing of the legal papers that made their wedding an absurdity. Not as a bolt from the blue, but more from a growing realization, a crystallization of her new adult self, it came to Brenda that never again would she let a man set the boundaries of what her life would be.

Still, the work continued, and with time and technical challenges taking up her mind, the sting of her failed marriage became just a heavy cloak and no longer a crushing weight.

Work reached fever pitch toward the end of March 1958, and early on the morning of the twenty-fifth, a group of technical experts from the NRC, including Brenda, flew to Malton airfield to witness the first flight of the Arrow.

Outside the Avro hangar, her co-workers were huddled in conversations with the engineers, and all the staff who had taken part in the design and construction of this innovative and groundbreaking aircraft stood in groups that buzzed with anticipation. She had not seen or even talked to Morris in more than two years, and suddenly there he was, chatting with his co-workers. He looked up and saw her standing alone, a tiny figure silhouetted against the bulk of the hangar. Expressionless, he turned his back as a cheer and then clapping erupted. Along with the crowd, Brenda's gaze snapped to the test pilot, Janusz Zurakowski, striding across the tarmac, followed by the ground crew. He climbed a ladder and dropped into the cockpit as his crew strapped him in and gave him a last slap on his shoulder for luck. The clamshell cockpit hatch snapped closed, and after the pre-flight checklist had been completed, the jet engines exploded into life. For the first time, the cutting edge of supersonic flight, the culmination of countless hours of planning, design, and construction, taxied onto the runway and leapt into the sky.

Three hundred and thirty-two days later, the prime minister of Canada rose in the House of Commons and, citing costs and a changing defense environment, announced the termination of the CF-105 program. Orders were given to destroy all the aircraft, prototypes, designs, and records, leaving the industry gutted and in disarray. Many of the Canadian designers and engineers fled south to join the fledgling space race; Brenda went west.

20

1960

"Historically, the greatest primary fault when looking at system failures has been an inadequate understanding of the real loads and forces on the structural components," said Darryl Saunders from behind his immaculate steel desk. His office reflected the state of the man's mind: efficient, utilitarian, and uncluttered. Brenda was wearing a conservative grey pantsuit to the interview. With her résumé to back her, their meeting had gone well.

"And in December, the Royal Commission into the mid-construction collapse of the Second Narrows Bridge found just that—negligence resulting from improper design and construction not in conformity with the contract specifications. Of course, faulty erection procedures and bad construction are often contributory elements, but most of the time it comes down to not getting the engineering right. So, before we go much further, we go back to the beginning. Among other things, we're redoing all the calculations on everything to do with this bridge, including the wind effects data for this structure. That's where you come in, Miss Leamington."

"I look forward to working with you, Mister Saunders," said Brenda.

"Yours will be a contract position, of course. For our ongoing hires, we prefer to take on men with families to feed."

Brenda had expected as much, and though it rankled, she simply nodded. 'Twas ever thus, she thought. She had been told by her colleagues in Ottawa that for a woman, just getting an interview here could be seen as a victory. Quite surprisingly to her, Brenda's boss had written a glowing evaluation of her skills. That, plus the issue of immediacy and the lack of any other aeronautical engineers willing to take on a short-term post, had secured the job. Rather than embracing gender diversity in his office, it seemed to Brenda that Saunders was simply ignoring the fact.

"It turns out we have a bit of a time window. You may or may not know that the bridge workers are currently out on strike. The conciliation board has recommended a forty-four-cent increase over something like two years, but the union isn't biting. I think the average wage now is two-sixty-two an hour."

"Well I guess considering twenty-three men died building the bridge, it must be tough settling on a wage that can compensate for that kind of risk," she said and met Saunders' gaze.

"Thankfully, that's not a task you and I have to resolve. Our job is to eliminate the risk of another structural failure. Welcome to Vancouver, Miss Leamington."

The job was intense, and the project timelines required Brenda to work twelve-hour days, and often, six or seven days a week. Following completion of the new airstream assessments,

Saunders tasked Brenda with double-checking every calculation made by the construction engineers. It did not make her popular. Her life consisted of work and sleep; she had no social life.

Brenda had moved into a flat on the Fairview slopes, on West Third Avenue near Arbutus Street. It was a newly constructed three-story apartment complex, and she quickly fell into the rhythm of the neighbourhood. It had a bohemian feel that called to her, and she enjoyed treating herself to breakfast on every free Sunday morning at a café just around the corner. On this particular occasion, the café was packed, and it buzzed with conversation. Denied a spot, she turned to leave but a young woman at a table by the door said, "Don't go. Come sit with us."

She had long, straight, brown hair highlighted with sun-bleached wisps, well past her shoulders. Her companions, two young men, smiled in welcome. Brenda paused, but reflexively declined their invitation to sit at the only open seat in the restaurant.

The woman reached out her hand to Brenda. "Please? All these guys talk about is Marx and Jack Kerouac, and I would really enjoy your company."

Overwhelmed by the smell of good food on an empty stomach, Brenda acquiesced and sat in the empty chair. "I'd ask 'Who is Jack Kerouac?' but I know it would start another round of discussion you'd rather avoid. I'm Brenda."

"Cindy," said the girl. "And this is Randall."

The young man simply raised his eyebrows and flashed the smallest of waves with the fingers on his left hand.

"And this is Will. He's a Jack London fan."

Brenda smiled at the curly-red-haired stranger across the table holding a tattered copy of *White Fang*. His face was freckled, and his smile radiated warmth and ease—not at all lupine, although his teeth were white and straight.

"So, you're a literary group then? Critics?"

"No, not literary, but I'd say we're critical," replied Randall. "We're pursuing a route out of the bourgeois construct of class structure. Analysis of societal alternative paradigms is just the start to dismantling the existing framework."

Brenda couldn't suppress a smile from arching her lips.

"He loves to spew the unintelligible party line to a captive audience," said Will, seeing the smile. "But as pretentious as that sounds, we really do believe there's an alternative way."

"To what, exactly?" she said and reached for the menu.

"To a new kind of society. As we watch, the world is tramping wildly ahead into a maelstrom of greed and environmental destruction. It's a malevolent sign that love and respect for each other and the world have become laughable ideals."

"You are students then, out at UBC?" asked Brenda as the waiter came to take her order. She chose the French toast.

"Not anymore. We've just graduated," said Cindy. "I did an M.A. in fine arts. Randall sat his doctorate in philosophy, and Will recently defended his doctoral thesis in sociology. What about you? Are you a student?"

Brenda laughed. "Hardly. I'll be thirty-five this year. I did an engineering degree some years ago."

"You're kidding, right? There's no way you're thirty-five. You could easily be twenty," said Cindy.

"Thanks, that's very kind, but most people get my age wrong because of my size—or rather, the lack of it."

"So, you've never heard of Jack Kerouac? Really?" asked Randall. "Beat poet, writer, iconoclast."

"Alcoholic, mama's boy, anti-communist," added Will. "Randall has a tendency to lionize. Myself, I find that a two-dimensional perspective of anyone will cause grief."

"I may have heard the name, but it has no context for me. I guess I need a trip to the library."

"No need," said Will and pulled a book from the leather satchel at his feet. "Have a go at this," he said and handed her a well-worn copy of *On the Road*.

"I can't take this unless I can return it," said Brenda.

"That's the plan," said Will and warmed her with another smile.

"You have a British accent," said Cindy. "When did you come over? After the war?"

They chatted for over an hour, interrupting her meal often as she described her wartime experiences in London and then her jobs in Ottawa and now here in Vancouver.

"Didn't it bother you that you were working on a war machine that was designed to kill people? I mean, you went through the Blitz, then there you were back east, making an aircraft that supports the American military industrial complex. A bit hypocritical, don't you think?" asked Will, a challenging cant to his tight grin.

"That's one perspective," she replied. "But what saved us in the Battle of Britain were fighter pilots taking down German planes. The CF-105 was designed to take down Russian airplanes carrying nuclear weapons to bomb us. I didn't see it as a moral dilemma. I saw it as protecting myself yet again against foreign aggressors— mostly men, I might add—responding to their egotistical obsession to crush and dominate the people where I live."

"And now there are no CF-105 planes in the air?"

"Correct. Now the threat appears not to be bombers, but nuclear weapons stuck on the end of rockets that can be sent from continent to continent. The preferred responses now are missiles to take down missiles. It seems we're spiraling into an endless game of one-upmanship. It doesn't bode well for the future."

"So now you're building bridges. There's a metaphor in there somewhere," said Randal.

"Not for much longer. It's just a contract job really, and then I'll be looking for work. In fact, I'm looking for work now even though I'll still be employed for a couple of weeks yet."

She stabbed at the last piece of toast awash in maple syrup.

"Let's go down to the water when you're done," said Cindy. "It's too nice a day to spend it inside talking."

The three friends stood, and Will met Brenda's gaze, "Ándale, epa," he said. They were quite possibly the only words that would have impelled her to join them.

The four walked down the hill on Arbutus Street in two-by-two fashion, Cindy and Randall, Brenda and Will.

"You spoke Spanish back there."

"Speedy Gonzales," he said. She looked confused.

"Bugs Bunny! You know, the cartoons. Speedy always says, 'Ándale, ándale, arriba, epa!'"

Will laughed at her befuddled look and said, "Man, you gotta get out more."

At Kitsilano Beach, they sat with a large, bleached fir log at their backs. They removed their shoes and dug their toes in the sand while a light breeze of warm sea air tousled their hair.

"Party next Saturday Brenda. Are you in?" said Randall.

"I'm not really a party person," she said.

"When was the last time you went to a party?"

"I guess it would be the evening of the first Avro flight, though it was more of a company social than a party, like back at university," she said, choosing to omit her wedding celebration.

"So, what you're saying is that you haven't been to a real party for donkey's years," Randall said. "That can't be healthy."

"You have to come," said Cindy. "It'll be fun, I promise."

"You shall come," said Will. "I insist."

§

The event was held at a large Tudor style house, built in the nineteen-thirties on West Tenth Avenue, across from a red-brick elementary school. The home had been converted into apartments, and though the party was on the main floor, the warm evening had induced attendees to spill out into the front and back yards. The hosts were an assemblage of Maritimers: two lads fleeing Newfoundland outports and one from Cape Breton. They were well into their cups when Brenda and her group arrived, their accents so thick that she was hard-pressed to parse what they were saying. It appeared to matter little, as they gleefully received the newcomers with slaps on the back, blurry welcomes, and laughter.

Cindy took Brenda under her wing and introduced her to so many partygoers it all became a haze, at which point she just let go and fell into the revelry. Brenda had brought a bottle of wine with her, carrying it around by the neck until to her surprise she found it was almost empty.

"What's that?" she asked Adam, one of the hosts, as they stood in the crowded kitchen. There was an odd-looking pastry dish beside her. Her head was feeling heavy and thick, so she leaned against the Formica countertop.

"Dat, my dear girl, is flipper pie."

"Really; what's in it?"

"Flipper."

"No, really," she said. "What's in it?"

"Da flipper of a seal. Back home, we make it from harp seals, but here on the West Coast, the fishermen will come across a harbour seal. The seals eat the salmon, so the fishermen are none too fond of them. A buddy of mine gets them for me. Have a bite," Adam said and reached into a drawer for a fork.

With her normal inhibitions diluted by the chablis, Brenda seized the utensil, dug into the dish, and shoved a forkful into her mouth. The taste was feral, tidal, and musky. The image of fatty kidneys and liver wrapped in fermented seaweed flooded her thoughts. She wanted to spit it out, but Adam was gazing at her with an intent and hopeful look on his face, as if his maritime culture was on culinary trial. Brenda managed to force herself to swallow.

"An acquired taste, I think," she said and quickly washed it down with the dregs from her bottle. The thick nimbus of cigarette smoke swirling around the room reacted badly with the wine and flipper pie sitting dangerously in her stomach. Brenda felt an overwhelming need for fresh air. She made it as far as the back porch, before vomiting over the railing. A cheer went up from those partygoers standing in groups in the back yard.

Suddenly, Will was behind her and laid his hand across the small of her back, and began to rub in small, concentric circles. "I'd say it's probably about time to call it a night," he said quietly.

Together, they walked the seven blocks to her apartment building, and by the time they arrived, the rhythm of her moving legs had brought back a faint semblance of sobriety.

"Thank you for walking me home."

"My pleasure. Shall I come up?" he said as a crooked smile sprang to his lips and his right hand slipped across her shoulders.

Through the leaden mist, Brenda slowly raised her gaze, and then shook her head. "Next time, I'll drink tea."

The smile slid from Will's mouth. Brenda slowly turned and unlocked the door to her building. "Goodnight Will," she said, and then stepped inside and closed the door.

21

1960

The following Saturday morning found the foursome seated at the same café. "We're going to visit my uncle's cabin on Denman Island for the Dominion Day long weekend. Want to come?" asked Cindy.

Brenda's contract would end on the last day of June, though the bridge would not officially open until the twenty-fifth of August. Brenda was at loose ends, having no job offers from any of the engineering firms in town, and had spent her free time reading the Kerouac book and another Will had loaned her, *Walden*, Thoreau's classic discourse on utopian living. Both had spurred a discomfort about her current circumstances—mental, physical, and geographical. It was a new decade, and she had toyed with the idea of returning to Windermere, despite her disdain for retracing steps she had already trod. Yet, whenever the thought of returning to England entered her mind, a contrary belief immediately crushed the idea. There was something coming. And it could only be found here.

Brenda only had to be open to opportunities and to be bold. Both Fiona and Michael had taught her to be unflinching in pursuit of happiness. She would follow their lead.

"Yes, I do. Count me in."

Jammed into Randall's pickup truck, they crossed the Lion's Gate Bridge and wound their way along Marine Drive to Horseshoe Bay, where they caught the early ferry to Nanaimo. They drove up the Island Highway, and at Parksville both the sun and the tide were out. Randall pulled into the parking lot and, laughing and hollering, they all ran out onto the sand and chased seagulls from the tidal pools. To the delight of her companions, Cindy suddenly shrieked wildly as she stood in the knee-deep water. Little flatfish had wriggled beneath the soles of her feet and tickled her toes.

At the Dairy Queen, they grabbed burgers and sundaes, piled back into the truck, and headed up the highway, passing both the Big Qualicum River and the hamlet of Bowser, whose name drew a cascade of dog jokes. At Buckley Bay they waited for the *Catherine Graham* to arrive and carry them across the last marine leg of their journey, a one-mile hop to Denman Island. They stood in the sun and watched herring gulls harass a bald eagle that sat on the seaweed-covered rocks. Ignoring the gulls, the eagle intently ripped apart the carcass of a ling cod that a fisherman had filleted and left for the crabs.

The group's attention was suddenly snapped away by the sound of an old, rusted-out pickup with no muffler pulling up behind them. Oily blue smoke spewed from underneath the vehicle until a loud explosion stilled the engine. The roar was replaced with the dissonant hiss of steam venting from under the hood and through the grill, as though a geyser was the last act in a daytime pyrotechnical display.

The driver leapt from the cab and began to ineffectually wave his arms about in the vapours, all the while issuing execrable words of admonishment to the now defunct vehicle. After a minute, he paused, and then seeing the four travelers standing outside their truck, he gave the hissing hulk a flat-handed smack on the hood, raised his arms, and shrugged his shoulders. An embarrassed grin rose to his mouth.

"You've got what looks to be about seven minutes," Randall said to the man and nodded to the approaching ferry.

"To do what?" asked the driver.

"To move everything from the back of your truck into the box of mine."

"We'll help," Brenda said, and with that, introductions were made as the group transferred ten bags of Portland cement, several hundred linear feet of dimension lumber, several lengths of copper pipe, and ten boxes of ceramic tiles before the ferry slipped gently into the dock. The three men pushed the rusted wreck off to the side, and then the man, who had introduced himself as Wolf, spoke some urgent words to the ticket agent, who apparently knew him well. Prompted to board, the travelers jumped into Randall's cab as their passenger climbed onto the pile of construction materials in the back, and they moved across the ramp onto the ferry.

"You guys are life savers. Can't thank you enough," Wolf said as he climbed down from the box and onto the ferry deck. He stood beside Brenda, and as he took time to formally introduce himself and shake everyone's hands, she was able to see that he was older than Brenda had originally thought. He had a lean torso, wiry upper arms, and dark hair longer than was fashionable, and when she had first seen him in jeans and a sweat-stained tee shirt, he looked to be in his twenties. But now in close proximity, she guessed he was closer to her age.

"Is that a European accent?" Brenda asked.

"The Netherlands."

"A post-war émigré?"

"Yup. Many Canadians died to liberate my country, so when I chose to leave Holland after the war, Canada seemed to be the best choice."

"So, are you building a house here?" asked Cindy.

He nodded. "I'm a contractor. I'm building a cabin on the east shore for someone."

"Where exactly?" Cindy asked.

"Just south of Fillongley Park on Dalziel Road. What about you people? Are you here for a holiday?"

"For the weekend," said Randall.

"We're staying at my uncle's place on E Road, so we'll almost go past your site on our way. How nifty is that?" said Cindy.

A short few minutes after the ferry docked, they dropped Wolf and his materials at the low-bank, beach-front property. The project was well underway, and the owner would have a spectacular view of Hornby Island a mile away across Lambert Channel. He hosted a tour of the building under construction, which still lacked windows and a complete roof.

"So where do you live while you're building?" asked Will.

"Oh, I'm over on Hornby. I commute by boat," he said.

Will looked down the beach at a rowboat pulled up on the shore.

"You're kidding me. You row that thing back and forth all the way over there every day?"

Wolf laughed. "No, no. That's my boat out there on that buoy," he said, pointing to a lap-strake skiff with an outboard motor. I just row the punt out there and swap it out when I'm coming and going."

"So, do you have family over there?" asked Cindy.

"No, I'm staying on a farm with a nice elderly couple, and I do farm work in lieu of room and board." He looked out over the water and Brenda could see the wanting in his gaze. "I'm saving up for a place of my own."

"It's so beautiful here. I can see the attraction," Brenda said. "It reminds me of a place in England where I grew up during the war. Peaceful, quiet, safe."

For the first time, their eyes met, and she felt an electric pulse run up her spine as he held her gaze.

Will saw the look and, intentionally shattering the moment, said, "I think I'd go crazy living here. What do you do for entertainment? I mean, there are only so many times you can go beachcombing or stargazing. Am I right?"

"Yeah, there's not much here to keep the teenagers amused, but some of us have already had more than a lifetime of excitement," said Wolf.

"We can never have enough of nature," said Brenda.

Will turned to Randall and Cindy and said with an edge to his voice, "Oh, so now she's quoting Thoreau. I better not lend her my copy of *Mein Kampf*, or there could be trouble." He laughed and searched the faces of his friends for encouragement.

Wolf's brow arched. He paused before speaking, taking the measure of the group, and then said, "I doubt if chopping down her tree will make yours grow any taller."

"Hey buddy, I was just joking," said Will and defiantly puffed his chest. "No need to get huffy."

Ignoring Will, Wolf turned to Brenda. "My apologies to you, Brenda, it was improper for me to comment. I am sure you are quite capable of dealing with such…matters."

"Yes, I am. But I appreciate the intent," she said. Her scar flaring red as she turned to glare at Will.

Cindy cut the tension, "Well we should probably hit the road. Lots to organize before dinner."

"Randall," Wolf said, moving forward with his hand outstretched, "I want to shake your hand again for springing to my rescue and transporting all this here. It was very kind and an immense favour. All of you, thank you."

With his elbow hanging out the passenger window, Will disregarded the parting wave from Wolf as Randall guided the truck up the drive. Cindy directed the vehicle to E Road, and several minutes later, as they neared Heron Point, she had Randall pull into a short, gravel driveway.

"This is it," she said and spread her arms wide.

A small cabin sat nestled under a grove of fir trees, and as they clambered out of the cab, they were struck by the smell of dry grass, conifers, and the sea. To Brenda, it was perfume of the highest order.

Cindy led them inside the cabin. It was a bare-bones structure with a kitchen composed of a simple wooden countertop and unplumbed sink. Water came from a hand-pump well outside. There were two small bedrooms and a sitting room with a fireplace and a foldout sofa bed. The toilet was in fact an outhouse, sited under the branches of a spruce tree near the water. It was all quite simple and functional without the slightest pretense of elegance or modernity. In her youth, Cindy had spent many summer days at the cabin, and to her it was familiar, comfortable, and free of flaws or shortcomings. To her guests it was quaint, charming, and primitive—so unlike their usual lodgings that it added to their sense of distance and secession from the familiar urbanity of the big city.

From the truck they unloaded the cooler, bags of food, and the sleeping bags Cindy had sourced from her family. Taking control of the sleeping arrangements, she said, "Randall and I will take the bedroom on the right, Brenda, you get the one on the left. Will, you get the sofa bed."

Will responded with a smile and then said, "Sounds good… for now." As might Groucho Marx, he bobbed his eyebrows.

Brenda shook her head and quietly released her breath.

They changed into their bathing suits and made their way to the sunny, tumbled-stone beach. The sea was flat, and Brenda could see bits of seaweed—wrack, kelp, and sea lettuce—dotting the surface. Little puffs of warm air caused the slightest of ripples. A seagull standing on a log that floated fifty yards away watched the group warily as Cindy led the way out into the water via a foot-friendly path through the stony foreshore.

When the water reached her mid-thigh, Cindy dove forward and quickly bobbed to the surface, wearing a broad grin. Randall followed and was quickly joined by Brenda. Will hung back and dragged out his entrance till finally he simply floated onto his back while taking care not to submerge his head.

A seaweed fight broke out between Randall and Cindy, who lobbed handfuls of the dripping green and brown algae at each other.

Having never swum in the sea, Brenda quickly became aware of how much more buoyant she was than when swimming in a lake or freshwater pool. She lay on her back and idly floated, sculling with her palms to keep her body moving along the surface. The sky presented to her was blue and scattered with a few puffy white clouds. An occasional muffled yelp from Randall or Cindy came to her ears, but the water muted almost everything except the thumping of her heart. It took Brenda some moments to identify the feeling that had washed over her, and then it came to her; she felt that she had returned home to a place she had never known.

She drifted her way shoreward until she could touch bottom. Brenda stared down through the water at her toes. There was so much more to see on the ocean bed compared to the pristine lake bottom of Windermere. Here were seaweed, barnacles, orange and purple starfish, and scatterings of clam and oyster shells. Little bullheads and perch darted about as her feet moved slowly, step by tentative step. Everywhere she looked vibrated with life; gulls called, and an osprey perched in the bent top of a craggy hemlock tree to the left of the cabin.

"Seal!" shouted Randall, pointing to a head that popped up close to the seagull on the log.

"It's a harbour seal," said Cindy. "Cute and harmless."

"Shark!" yelled Will.

Brenda's head snapped around at his call.

"There aren't any sharks here," said Cindy. "Don't be an idiot."

"You never know," he said and then laughed.

"I do know and there aren't. At least not the kind that you mean."

§

"It may sound great, the equality of the masses, but the truth is there are people who will always transcend the system, whatever it may be. We've had this argument too many times, Will. There are always people willing to put in the extra effort or able to see how things really work and then make a way for themselves to rise above everyone else. Sometimes it just has to do with opportunity and timing. Being in the right place at the right time with the right idea," said Randall.

It was the second evening of the weekend, and their bodies and faces were varied combinations of weathered reds and tans. They had finished the last of their food but for some sad-looking tomatoes, brown-edged lettuce, and enough eggs and bread for an early breakfast before heading back to the city.

"What do you think, Brenda?" asked Will. "Is stripping the capitalist yolk from the necks of the proletariat the way to create a new world order? One that puts the people in charge? Or as Orwell has said and apparently Randall believes, are some animals more equal than others?"

Brenda looked over her shoulder from the sink, where she was washing the last of the cutlery.

"As I see it, the great thoughts and ideals of men are swept away by the realities of hunger, dirty diapers, and lack of sleep. The words of Nietzsche or Marx can look noble and paradigm-breaking on the page but when it comes right down to the nitty gritty of life, *real* life, it's the women who always get stuck with the scut work while the philosophers wax poetically about the way the world should function. And then of course they run around and start wars when they don't get their way." Brenda wrung out the dish cloth and hung it to dry. She turned to take in the men slouched on the sofa. "For instance, all weekend, Cindy and I have prepared the meals, cooked the food, and done the dishes while you two have drunk the beer."

"Hey now," said Will rising in his seat, "no need to get angry. We could have done the dishes. Take it easy."

"I'm not angry. I am simply stating things as they are worldwide and in this cabin. If you want to philosophize on the plight of man, the first place to start would be the plight of women."

"You know, you could have asked," said Will.

"Why should I have to ask? Then it's simply you two doing Cindy and me a favour, deigning to stoop to our level. If you truly believe in the equality of the masses, dismantling this class or caste system you're always on about, it's the everyday that counts, not some big pie-in-the-sky intangible political system."

"Careful or you might be mistaken for a harpy," said Will and smirked. He winked at Randall.

Brenda sighed heavily and then said, "So when you condemn Diefenbaker or Eisenhower, it's under the guise of thoughtful criticism, but when someone assesses your behaviour, your university-trained critical reasoning skills kick in to provide you with what, name-calling as the optimal response?"

"And here I thought you were a bridge builder," said Will, whose smirk had now morphed into a sneer. The muscles in his jaw rippled.

"And here I thought you were an egalitarian," came her sharp reply. She glared at him.

"I think Brenda and I should go for a walk," said Cindy as she put away the last plate. "C'mon, Brenda."

"That really wasn't about politics was it?" asked Cindy as they walked along the beach just below the tide line. The sun had set, and the evening light was soft and waning.

"No. It was Will and me being upset with each other."

"Because?"

"Because after dinner last night, I turned down his offer of sex. I like him only as a casual friend, not as a potential lover. We were nowhere near climbing into bed together, at least not from my point of view. Since the day we met, his number one priority has been to get into my pants. Not develop a friendship, not to let a relationship evolve. I find him arrogant and controlling and he throws tantrums when he doesn't get his way. I've met that before and I've learned my lesson."

"He has told me that he really likes you," said Cindy.

"Well I guess in his mind then, that because he really likes me, I have an obligation to him. I do not. Last night he told me that I had given him expectations that I suddenly and unfairly refused to fulfill. He didn't take the rejection well."

"And now what do you think?"

"Well, I think he made it pretty clear just now that he doesn't respect me or my opinions. Will is years younger than me and has a lot of growing up to do."

"He was just sounding off. You hurt his pride."

"So be it. I'm glad, really; it saved me a lot of time and distress to sort him out so quickly." She bent down and picked up a sun-bleached periwinkle shell, rolling it around in her palm. "I'm at the point in my life where I don't need to suffer fools gladly."

"So, no hope for him, then?"

"None. I'm looking forward."

"To what exactly?"

She held the shell between two fingers and then let it drop. "A leap of faith."

22

1960

The next morning, the sky was cloudy and appeared to match Will's mood. They loaded the truck, and as they moved to get into the vehicle Brenda said, "I'd like to sit by the window."

Will's mouth opened as if to speak, thought better of the idea, and then quietly slid in next to Cindy. In the cramped cab, he did his awkward best not to let his thigh or shoulder come into contact with Brenda.

"Bye bye, cabin," said Cindy as Randall pulled out onto E Road. At the sharp left bend, E turned into Denman Road, and a couple of hundred yards later, at the Fillongley Park turnoff sign, Brenda said, "Randall, can you pull over here please?"

"Really?" he said. "You have to pee already?"

"Really," she replied.

He sighed and pulled the truck over. Brenda got out and reached into the back of the vehicle for her satchel. She squared her shoulders, looked across Will at Cindy, and said, "Thank you so much, Cindy. I can't tell you how much this stay has meant to me. I'm so glad to have met you. Have a safe trip home."

"What are you talking about?" said Randall. "You can't just leave. Where are you going? How will you get back to Vancouver?"

"Randy, just drive," said his girlfriend. "She'll be fine."

"Forget her," said Will. "She's crazy."

Randall shook his head and despite his own protests pulled the truck back on the road and guided it towards the ferry.

Brenda watched the vehicle disappear, then turned onto the gravel side road. She felt a flutter in her chest as she looked up at the street sign. It read, Swan Road.

It was just over a mile to the building site, and with every step, the feeling of anticipation grew. She didn't second-guess her actions. If it worked, it worked, and if it didn't, then a world of other possibilities would open up instead.

The clouds had thickened in a dark, menacing sky, and as she made her way onto Dalziel, the rain began, first as little explosions on the dusty road and then suddenly as torrential sheets of water. Brenda looked down several driveways as she made her way along the shoulder of the road, hoping that each one led to her destination. She was drenched. Finally, there it was, looking somehow less magical as the water wept off the bare plywood sheathing that covered most of the roof.

He had his back to her. She smiled as she saw him, outfitted as he was in a droopy rain hat and heavy green slicker, but wearing shorts and leather work boots. An oversized Christopher Robin, he held an umbrella in his left hand.

She breathed in the moment, savouring the few precious seconds of boundless hope and knowing that when he turned, her life would change.

"Need any help?" she asked.

Wolf spun and stared at her in unruffled silence. His eyes locked onto hers as they had on the Friday afternoon, and while full seconds ticked by, she watched as a gentle smile came to his lips.

"More than you know. It looks like maybe we both do. Come in, you're soaked."

She followed him into the cabin. The east side entrance area and kitchen were out of the weather, but the west side was still open to the elements. Brenda looked up to see beams and trusses supporting nothing but air.

"That was supposed to get covered over today, but I don't like going up on the roof when it's wet and slippery."

"Nor should you; too many have tried and died doing that sort of thing." She looked at a sheet of plywood laid flat over two sawhorses. On top lay the blueprints, curled in a roll. Brenda spread out the plans and scanned them intently. "Did you have these drawn up?"

"No, I just follow them. Unlike many buildings on this island, this one is actually going to be built to code."

"I can see that. These were actually drawn up by an architecture firm in Vancouver," she said. "I applied for a job there last week," and saying that, flipped to another elevation. "This is not going to be just a primitive little cabin. It will be quite elegant. Small but very nice."

"You're an architect?"

"No. One better. I'm an engineer."

He nodded, then seeing that she was shivering, asked, "Would you like some coffee? I have some here in my thermos."

"I would love a cup, thank you," she said.

"And what about a change of clothes? If you're stuck, I've got a spare shirt here somewhere. It might be a bit punky, but it's dry at least."

"I do have some alternate clothes at hand," she said and pointed to her satchel.

"Great. While I pour, you can change in the master bedroom on the second floor. The view is spectacular," he said and pointed up to the area where the rain tumbled in through the open roof.

Brenda grinned and instead found a water-free corner by the front door and changed into jeans, a sweatshirt, and a jacket. In sandals, her feet were white from the cold and wrinkled from the rain, but without an alternate pair of footwear, she simply had to make do.

"You can't be building this all by yourself? Surely those beams weren't manhandled by one person?"

"No, I have a crew of two. They have the long weekend off, of course. The other day I was just bringing in supplies to keep ahead of them."

Savouring the rhythm of their conversation, Brenda thought for a moment, then said, "That truck has seen better days."

"Haven't we all. But thankfully that was not my truck. Brendon, one of my crew, drove all the way to Chilliwack to see his parents, but he figured that his truck wouldn't make it that far, so we swapped. Turns out he was right."

Brenda sipped at the coffee; it was hot and sweet.

"So, you're looking for a job, you say? Can you swing a hammer?"

"I am," she said. "And I can."

They worked well together and framed in a space for the hot water system and a pony wall near the main entrance. At midday, his sandwich and cookies were shared, and they finished off the last of the coffee. It was still overcast by the time they had completed the carpentry, but the rain had stopped, and the winds had died down. It would be a bumpy ride to Hornby Island, but not dangerous.

"So, are you still game for this?" asked Wolf as they walked together down the beach to the rowboat. "We could probably find someone at the park to take you to the ferry."

"In for a penny, in for a pound," said Brenda as she tossed her satchel into the rowboat.

"And that means what exactly?"

"It means that I'd like to keep working with you."

Together they slid the rowboat into the water with the intent of paddling out to the bigger motorboat tied off at a bright orange buoy just off the shore. Brenda sat in the stern of the little rowboat, and as he stroked the oars with his back to his destination, a smile broke across his face.

"What?" asked Brenda.

"Nothing, really. I was just thinking that considering how the morning started, it's turned out to be a beautiful day."

Wolf shipped the oars as they nudged up against the larger craft. He tied off the rowboat, then clambered into the skiff, followed by Brenda.

The outboard motor roared to life after several pulls on the starter cord.

"Probably a good idea to put this on, just in case," he said and held out a lifejacket to her. She slipped it on over her head and did up the ties. Wolf sat on his for padding.

The ride across the channel was fast and bumpy as the hull skipped across the tops of the whitecaps. On a couple of occasions, when Wolf anticipated an encounter with a particularly large wave, he cut the speed, waited for the swell to pass under them, then gunned the motor once more. In short order they were around to the lee of the north point of Hornby, where the water flattened out. A minute later, Wolf eased the throttle and pulled the craft up to a second rowboat, where they reversed the action of exchanging boats. Knees to knees, they rowed ashore and Wolf secured the punt above the high-tide mark. He led the way, following a trail up through tall grass and a steeper portion through some fir trees to a large farmhouse sitting proudly on a small prominence.

For the second time that day, Brenda felt a stab of anticipation as, satchel in hand, she followed Wolf up the front stairs to the porch. They doffed their footwear and stepped through the front door, making their way to the kitchen; thick, rich aromas filled their noses.

"Look what I found," said Wolf to an elderly lady stirring a full pot on the stove. The woman looked up as Brenda stepped out from behind him, wearing a tentative smile.

"Oh, my goodness, aren't you the cutest little thing," she said and wiped her hands on her apron. She advanced and said, "Hello, I'm Doris."

"Brenda," she said and held out her hand.

"Oh tish," the elderly woman said and threw her arms around the new arrival. "Welcome. Fred! We have company."

In response, there was an irregular thumping on creaking stairs that followed the slap of slippers on the hardwood floor. A white-haired gentleman sporting suspenders that held up very wide-wasted pants limped through the doorway. There was something of Christmas about him.

"Who have we got here?" he said and quickly took the measure of the newcomer.

"Brenda Leamington, sir. I'm very pleased to meet you both."

"Oh, my goodness, polite as well as pretty. Too good for you, my lad," he said and gave Wolf a bit of an elbow.

"She's an engineer and I've taken her on with the Denman house. I was hoping you might be willing to put her up here for the duration."

"Well, I don't know," said Fred slowly. "We are a little cramped for space. I suppose we could toss some straw in the chicken coop." He looked at Brenda and winked. "Mind the rooster though."

"Don't be a silly bugger, Fred. She can have her pick of the spare rooms." Doris looked at Brenda and said, "There are two empty rooms upstairs. The smaller one looks out over the water, and the one in back gives a grand view of the orchard. After dinner, you can make your choice."

Standing in the center of the group, it struck Brenda that perhaps she had overstepped her mark. That the reality was, she had no idea what she was doing.

"My appearance has just come out of the blue for you," said Brenda. "I feel now that this is a huge imposition. I'm so sorry, I've just been foisted on you."

"Sweetheart, here on this island, Fred and I live for the sound of other voices. I have heard everything he has ever had to say, too many times to count. Surely you can give an old lady a break from the repetition. At least for a short while."

23

Netherlands, 1921

Anton de Pont, city councilman and an elder with the Great Church, was proud of his rank and position. On this day as he walked home from evening prayer, he pondered the authority and power that the church had invested in him. It was right and just that God and the community had seen fit to anoint him in this position; frankly, he thought, his prominence in the town was most rightly recognized, for after all, even the clerics didn't have the stomach to truly address the sinners. Words of damnation just were not enough.

After the Great War had concluded, Anton had found the road to elevated civil status to be most easily travelled by swatting at challengers not with his fist or his finances—although he was not averse to using either—but with the razor-sharp instrument of theological might. He had found through experience that biblical chastisement, moral suasion, guilt, and a lofty sense of piety more than amply sufficed for beating his challengers and fellow townspeople into submission. Of course, this principled position required him to sin in the relative concealment of his home, but surely God allowed the truly righteous to let off a little pent up zeal.

Anton coveted the mayor's chain of office. "But only to better serve you, oh Lord," he said to the darkening night. The mayor was a popular man, however, and was not in the least interested in stepping down anytime soon, nor even in choosing not to run in the upcoming election. Anton felt his heart pounding more heavily as the sense of frustration began to build. He would have that job by whatever means. "It's mine. Why else am I here, Lord?"

By the time he crossed the threshold of his home, his stomach was churning and the taste of frustration was nasty and bitter. His wife, Grietje, immediately read the signs and as he settled in his favourite chair brought him a tumbler of jenever, the Dutch version of gin.

In short order, he finished the drink and called for another.

"That was the last of it, my darling," said Grietje. "I'll get another bottle tomorrow."

The speed with which Anton flew from his chair was matched only by the velocity with which his hand smashed into her face. Collapsing to the floor, his wife found herself within easy striking distance of his boots.

Hearing her mother's screams, her father's shouts, and the scraping of furniture across the floor, their daughter, Angelien, burst into the room and yelled at him to stop his assault. Anton turned from his now insensate wife and in one motion grabbed his teenage daughter by her long blonde braids and dragged her down the hall.

Later, Anton ran the short distance to the police office and exploded through the front entrance.

"Some bastard Romani has beaten my wife and raped my daughter!" he yelled at the man at the desk. "Call a doctor. Get a search party together. It'll be one of those gypsy scum camping down by the canal!"

Resources were quickly assembled, and a group of angry men soon set out to arrest the villain.

"Angelien told me that the culprit had dark hair, medium build, bad teeth, and a beard," Anton told the chief of police as they marched a platoon of officers towards the water.

"Don't worry, Meneer de Pont, we'll get him," replied the chief of police; deferentially, he had chosen to use the Dutch version of 'milord' to address the elder de Pont. "I guarantee it."

An hour later, a frantic-looking, dark-haired young Romani man sat in a jail cell. Danior Sanchari's face was bruised and swollen; several teeth had been knocked out, and blood matted his black beard.

"My wife is too traumatized to testify, and I will not have my daughter brought up on the stand to relive her ordeal," Anton told the judge the following week. "I will tell the court what both my wife and daughter have told me." He took a deep breath and with well-rehearsed grace swept his right hand over the top of the glistening pomade that held his thinning black hair in place; he looked like a man nobly reluctant to be the provider of such unseemly information. But Anton's moment of drama was suddenly interrupted.

"I regret to inform the witness that hearsay evidence is not acceptable to this court," said the grey-haired judge from his bench. He also was an elder with the church, and a bit too self-righteous for his own good, Anton had always felt. Now the pompous prick was interfering.

Anton's dark brows quickly knotted at the rebuke, and he snorted from the witness box and looked out over the sea of familiar faces jammed into the courtroom. Seldom had anything this salacious involving a prominent member of the community been brought before the courts. This was high drama and would fuel kitchen table discussions for a generation; Anton knew he simply could not show the slightest trace of shame.

"Your testimony alone is what you are here for today, Meneer de Pont," said the judge. "Please proceed."

"As I said previously," began the prosecutor once again, "can you please describe to the court the sequence of events as you experienced them on the night in question?"

"I was returning from a meeting with my fellow elders of the church, and as I entered the foyer of my home, a man came running down the hall. He smashed into me, knocked me down, and fled down the street. I heard my wife's cries from the kitchen, and I went to her. She was in rough shape. The bastard had beaten her pretty badly," he paused for dramatic effect. He could read the audience, the intense anticipation evident in their faces for what would come next. "She told me to go to Angelien. I went down the hall and found her." He let his voice catch in his throat as he said, "I found the poor thing on her bed, her clothes had been ripped from her body... Sorry, I don't want to go on."

The gallery was swept with pity for the poor father having to announce to the world that the purity of his virginal daughter had been violated.

"Please, Meneer de Pont. The court must hear all of your testimony, as difficult as it may be."

"She was weeping, and my sweet little Angelien lay on her back, legs wide apart. She had been despoiled by that monster," he said and pointed at the man in the dock.

"You recognize that man?" asked the prosecutor.

"Absolutely. I got a clear look at his face before he threw me to the floor. The lights were on in the foyer, and I will never forget those dark, cruel eyes. Never."

The prosecutor finished with a few more questions. Then the defense attorney rose and asked, "Meneer de Pont, when your daughter was shown a photograph of the accused, she simply shook her head and said, 'That's not him.' Can you explain that?"

Anton could feel the weight of the gallery's attention shift to his shoulders. He forced himself to breathe in slowly and then relax.

"Well, as the judge has said, I cannot testify in my daughter's stead, but I know she has been terribly traumatized, so I'm not too concerned about what she can or cannot remember. But speculation is not needed here because I, on the other hand, have an excellent memory, acute eyesight, and fear no repercussions from my testimony."

The gallery murmured its approval. Anton repressed a smile he felt building in his lips.

"You did not actually witness the defendant attacking your daughter?"

"No, I came home moments too late to protect her."

"So, then it is entirely possible that the defendant could have been passing by your house and had simply heard a commotion and tried to intervene. That perhaps the real offender had fled earlier."

"That's a lot of possible and perhaps," said de Pont. "Why would he run from me?"

The attorney nodded and looked down at his papers, then said, "Do you find it strange that the accused denies ever being at your home? And do you find it strange that there are none of his fingerprints anywhere in the home, only those of your wife and daughter? Oh, and yours, of course," he said, looking pointedly at Anton. He continued without waiting for a response.

"And do you find it strange that the rest of the Romani clan at the canal have testified that the accused was with them all evening on the night you claim he assaulted your family?"

Anton turned his gaze from the lawyer to the gallery. "Actually, I find none of it strange. These Romani mongrels all lie, cheat, and steal. They stick together like the pack of wild dogs they are and will do anything, I repeat anything, to take advantage of the good will of our community."

He saw heads vigorously nod in agreement. Encouraged by the murmurs of approval building in the gallery, he would take them all to the last step. They were on his side now, and they could taste the sweetness of righteous indignation in their own mouths.

"We have all been put at risk by these heathens. Despite many calls from our community and church leaders, our mayor has done nothing to address their continued presence and the endless wave of crimes they commit. They might come after your wife or daughter next time. We need to send a message to the mayor that this type of behaviour will not be tolerated!"

The gallery broke into applause as Anton gripped the edges of the witness stand, his knuckles taut and white.

It was not long after Sanchari was sentenced to life in prison for rape and attempted murder, that Angelien showed the first signs of her pregnancy. The word spread through the community, and townspeople were quick to express their condolences to Anton.

"It's God's will reminding us that all our women are at risk of these rampant dogs," he replied with his clear and powerful voice. "Let us heed his warning."

As it turned out, Anton had played the anti-Romani card into the hand of his nemesis. A few short weeks before the election, the mayor had the chief of police organize repeated violent raids on the encampment, the result being the dispersal of the caravans to other communities. The mayor was re-elected, and Anton was forced to contemplate a new path to power.

During the pregnancy, Angelien was not seen on the streets; her seclusion and confinement were absolute. But when Wolfgang was born, Anton fell in love for the first time in his life, and he let everyone see his pride. God had blessed him with a son to perpetuate the de Pont name.

"God works in mysterious ways, his wonders to perform," he said to his wife. "You refused to bear me a son, but the Lord has provided. Just look at his clear eyes and strong jaw."

To the amazement and awe of the community, Anton appeared to dote on his heir. His acceptance of this spawn from the Romani rapist was seen to be the pinnacle of Christian charity, and Anton never missed an opportunity to been seen as a humble and pious servant of the church who had turned the ultimate cheek. At home, of course, Wolfgang was subject to his father's rages, and as he grew, the boy soon learned the combined power of a leather strap and the word of God, most often dealt out at the same time.

His mother could not help but love Wolfgang, and his grandmother knew well enough not to be caught disciplining him in any way. As long as he was able not to displease his purported grandfather, life for Wolfgang was tolerable, at least until he reached school age. There he encountered another level of hell. The other boys were well informed of his alleged vile Romani beginnings and bullied him mercilessly, both subtly and overtly. Every day, without exception or quarter, they came after him with taunts about his purported gypsy bloodline. His Christian upbringing had taught him to be kind and caring, but no amount of tolerance or cheek-turning acquiescence seemed to stem the tide. To his father's frustration, Wolfgang became a shy and introverted boy, and he developed a stutter.

Not long after receiving a bicycle for his birthday, Wolfgang found himself out riding in the country lanes between the farms and the canal on a beautiful day, free from his family, the school, and the politics of hate that were surging through his town. The sun sparkled off the shiny new paint, and he rang the little bell just because he could. He stopped at an intersection and chose to go left towards a grove of weeping willows that offered shade and a dry spot to sit and eat his lunch. Wolfgang leaned his bicycle against a tree, sat down by the canal, and let go a long-held sigh. It was not long before a pair of ducks swam by, and Wolfgang tossed them a little piece of crust before he finished his sandwich. In the treetop, a songbird began a series of long and complicated trills, and he lay back to listen, to see whether he could identify the bird. Instead, he fell asleep.

The dream found him atop the spire of the Great Church, looking down at people being swallowed by the wide oaken doors. They were marching two by two, the women wearing hats with gauze fringes, the men doffing their fedoras as they crossed the threshold. In the cemetery he could see a hole in the ground, a grave, and he wondered whether if he were to give himself a good running start from the roof, he could land in it. The distance was great, but he felt it would be worth a try. Yet no matter how hard Wolfgang kicked or pulled at his legs, his feet seemed to be stuck to the hard, unforgiving slate. Finally, he gave up the idea of a leap and looked up as a crow flew by his head, then landed in a tree down to his left. It began to mock him. The bird was joined by another, and together the pair began to laugh and deride him in fluent Dutch, calling him Romani scum and bastard rapist spawn. The words became louder and louder. Wolfgang felt a poke in his ribs.

"Wakey-wakey, mongrel trash."

Wolfgang snapped awake and stared up at Deiter de Groot and Reiner Bergman, the mayor's son and his sidekick, the son of a local banker. The wealth of their parents fueled the boys' sense of superiority, and together the pair executed their self-appointed mandate over school lunch times and after-school hours by tormenting Wolfgang as might a cat with a nearly spent wren. They were older and bigger than Wolfgang; Deiter was already showing some facial hair and his voice was deepening. Wolfgang brought himself up to a stand and readied to face the inevitable. To the pair, harassing this pathetic failure had become so droll that the act had lost its wild pleasure-making flair and spirit, becoming mechanical and almost dull, despite the frisson of excitement at the outset of each episode. Wolfgang hoped that at some point the bother would outweigh the effort, but they always seemed able to follow through regardless of the emotional trauma it caused him.

"So, what have we here, Wolfie? A new bike?"

Wolfgang stood silently. The inevitable beating would be less severe if he didn't respond or fight back. He had tried that tack on several occasions and was met with an almost cheerily vitalized response, as if his objection was license to crush him with even greater fervor.

Deiter grabbed the bicycle by the handlebars and swung it with all his might into the willow tree. The steel frame warped on impact, and as it fell to the ground, Reiner stomped on the wheel rim, bending the front spokes into inoperable scrap. Deiter grabbed the carcass and tossed it into the canal.

"Maybe a bit of a scrub will wash off the gypsy scum from his nice new bike," said Reiner and slapped his pal on the shoulder.

"Oh!" Deiter said, interrupting his own forced laugh. "I forgot this." He swung the back of his hand into Wolfgang's face with a resultant smack. The smaller boy felt his nose erupt with blood that spurted over his mouth and down his chin.

"I guess we'll be on our way, Wolfie."

"Have a nice walk home," said Reiner as the two mounted their own bikes and rode off towards the town.

After the bleeding stopped, Wolfgang stepped out into the shallows of the canal and retrieved the bent steel hulk of his birthday present. He worked on it for some time until finally he was able to push the wobbling skeleton home.

On the long walk to town, Wolfgang played out the consequence of every scenario he could possibly present to his parents. Knowing the explosive temper of his father and the way of the schoolyard, every choice but one came back to more physical torment, from either the boys or his father. Anton met him on the doorstep and quickly scanned the damage to both the bike and his son.

"I c-c-came around a c-c-corner and there was a herd of c-c-cattle all across the road. I was going too fast and c-c-crashed into one. I'm s-s-sorry, father."

A look of anger flared across the man's face, quickly morphing into disgust. "Just like you to run into a damn cow. What a waste of money you are." He turned and re-entered the house.

What had started with Anton as love and devotion had turned to vitriol and hate as his son grew and failed to meet his father's biblical expectations. This latest event evidently was the last straw, and he sent the progeny of his rage to a private boarding school, out of his sight and out of his life for years.

The lessons Wolfgang continued to learn in the schoolhouse cloakrooms, out of the earshot of his teachers, were retained and then utilized later, for the war changed everything. Never one to miss an opportunity to pursue political power, Wolfgang's father joined the infamous Nationaal-Socialistische Beweging, the only political party the Nazis permitted after their invasion of the Netherlands in the spring of 1940. It was not long after the arrival of the German army that Anton recalled his son to his side and inculcated Wolfgang in the verities of Hitler's National Socialism. Finally, he could be someone his father would be proud of, and the teenager set about to wholeheartedly embrace the Aryan way and free himself from the self-loathing and anger of a lifetime of being held unworthy.

24

1960

The intimate group of four were sitting at the dining room table after enjoying their first meal together. Doris had made a hearty stew, with bread just out of the oven. A bottle of Fred's homemade blackberry wine stood empty on the table.

"This wine is amazing," said Brenda and emptied the last contents of her glass. "I normally find red wine too acidic, but this is quite sweet."

"Thank you," said Fred. "Wait till you try my apple cider or my raspberry or blueberry wine."

"Careful or the compliments will make his head swell," said Doris, laying her hand on her husband's forearm. "If something can't run away fast enough, Fred will ferment it."

"Never sleep in or you could find yourself in a vat in the basement," said Wolf. "Almost happened to me once."

Brenda rolled her eyes and, smiling, turned to Doris. "So, have all your children left the island?"

"All five. The two girls are in the Victoria area, with children of their own. The eldest boy is a shift manager in the pulp mill in Port Alberni. The youngest fishes out of Campbell River, and the middle boy is in the Royal Canadian Mounted Police. Currently he is stationed in Prince Rupert," said Doris.

Fred chimed in, "The last one left the nest about eight years ago, and we were quite at our wits' ends until Wolfgang came along, what, two years ago?"

Wolf said, "Almost three now."

Fred nodded and added, "Keeping this place going takes a lot of work and it was getting quite out of hand, what with my hip."

"Brenda," began Doris, "I don't know what your intentions are or how long Wolfgang's project is expected to last, but Fred and I will be happy to give you the same setup as we have with him: room and board in exchange for work around the farm. It is hard work, mind, and you're a wee thing, so it might not be what you English call 'your cup of tea.'"

"It is a very kind offer," said Brenda. "I know I can handle the challenge of the work, but I still have my place in Vancouver paid for until month's end. Will it work for you if I commit to staying for three weeks and then at that time assess how we're doing?"

"Daring and cautious all in one stroke," said Fred.

Doris clapped her hands together and said, "Oh it will be so nice to have another woman in the house."

Brenda turned to look at Wolf; he wore a soft, hopeful smile.

After dinner, Doris took her by the hand and led her up a double flight of oak-railed stairs. "This house was built many years ago, so the only plumbing up here is off the main bedroom. You'll have to use the facilities downstairs. Here is the larger room."

The walls were papered with a floral theme, and there were two single beds along the walls and a pair of matching chests of drawers. A framed black-and-white photo of a calf sporting a 4H ribbon hung above one bed, and a well-rendered watercolour painting of the house from the perspective of the beach hung on the other wall.

"This was the girls' room."

Looking out the window, Brenda could see an orchard that led up to a wide pasture boasting sheep and several Hereford cattle. She noted a large vegetable garden surrounded by ten-foot-high wire fencing, a chicken coop, and a duck pond. A tractor and hay wagon were parked outside a large weathered but otherwise healthy-looking barn.

"It does look like quite the handful," said Brenda.

"When the kids were younger, they pretty much ran the place while Fred was off logging. That's what made this all work financially, him working for MacMillan Bloedel to bring in the extra cash."

Doris let her fingers slowly run the length of the nearest bedspread and then paused for a beat before closing the door and guiding Brenda across the hall.

"Fred and I are down there on the left; Wolf's room is at the other end of the hall. I think you'll like this one best; it would be my choice."

The room was narrow but boasted a wide picture window that ran the length of the wall facing the ocean. Standing by the glass, Brenda was presented with a view of the water through a scattering of large conifers. The surface of the water was steely grey and dappled with rain that had begun again.

"It reminds me so much of Lake Windermere; that's where I grew up," she said to Doris. "You're right. This is the room for me."

For Brenda, the three weeks flew by. While Wolf worked with his small carpentry crew, she assumed the role of project manager, sourcing and ordering materials, coordinating building inspector visits, and taking the ferry to drive up to Courtenay or down island for specialty supplies. Then in the evenings she worked on the farm, feeding the animals, weeding in the vegetable garden, and painting the outside of the house, while Wolf repaired the fences, reroofed the chicken coop, and stowed hay in the barn. It made for intense and physically draining days, and each night she fell into bed with her mind whirling around a cascade of things to do the next day.

Early in the morning of the third Sunday, at low tide, Wolf took Brenda out in the rowboat to a sunny little bay, where they dug littleneck clams and stripped mussels off an old piling. On the return trip, he shipped the oars as they passed over a reef, and after tying a heavy metal lure to the end of the line, he handed her a fishing rod. Wolf showed her how to let the line out till the jig hit bottom.

They sat quietly enjoying the moment till Brenda broke the silence. "Glisky. The sea is glisky today."

"I might agree with you if I knew what glisky meant."

"It's Cumbrian for that," Brenda said and squinted as she pointed at the bright glare that sparkled off the rippled sea surface. She continued to bob the line, feeling the thud of the lure as it contacted the ocean floor.

"I learn something new every day when I'm with you," he said.

"And that's a good thing?"

"It's a very good thing. In fact..."

He was interrupted suddenly when Brenda felt the rod suddenly bend as line swiftly peeled off the reel in an exciting shriek.

"What do I do? What do I do?" she said wildly.

"First thing is to relax. Second thing is to turn the handle on the reel and wind it in," he said and broke into a broad grin.

As the line slowly returned to the reel, the furious bobbing of the rod stilled until she felt only a nodding dead weight resisting her efforts. Then up from the deep came a large, orangey-coloured rockfish, the jig hanging from its wide and voracious-looking mouth. As the fish spotted the boat, it once again fought to free itself and peeled off a short run of line. Brenda wrestled it back to the surface till finally Wolf slipped a dip net beneath it and swung it into the cramped little boat.

"Careful of those spines along his back; speaking from experience, I can tell you that they'll really hurt if he sticks you."

Lifting up a foot-long wooden club, he dispatched the seven-pound fish with one swipe, disengaged the hook, and laid the cod in a metal box that he pushed back under his seat.

"Well done!" he said. "I believe we now have the makings for a fine bouillabaisse."

When they returned to the beach, Wolf showed Brenda how to safely carry the fish with her fingers under its gills, then he filled a bucket with sea water for the clams to self-rinse. While Brenda carried the fish up to the house, Wolf toted the bucket of clams and the small sack of mussels. Doris was delighted. "A night off from the kitchen! Wolfgang is going to make us his special dish tonight, I see."

"Brenda caught the fish. Brought it in like a pro."

Fred heard the commotion in the kitchen and joined them. "Ah, nice fish. I'll take care of it, shall I?"

"If you would Fred, I'll go to the garden," said Wolf.

Brenda watched as Fred skillfully removed two boneless fillets from the fish. He wrapped the skeleton and skin in newspaper and handed the package to Brenda. "At least a foot deep in the rows where we've already harvested lettuce, if you would be so kind."

She found Wolf in the garden, pulling up some new potatoes, leeks, garlic, and onions. He already had tomatoes, basil, and some fennel in his woven wooden basket.

"This morning was so much fun; thank you," she said, patting the last shovelful of dirt over the buried fish carcass. "I can see why you love it here." She looked up through the orchard and across the pasture, then turned and looked back at the house. Doris was watching from the kitchen window and gave a little wave.

He grinned, his tanned face open and buoyant. "That was my hope."

"Oh my god, that was amazing," Brenda said as she dropped her spoon in the bowl that she had emptied for the second time. "I couldn't eat another mouthful." A large serving dish brimming with empty clam and mussel shells sat in the centre of the table. Both Doris and Fred joined Brenda in voicing their hearty approval.

"It's the Sambuca that does it," Wolf replied. "It gives it that extra little kick of anise."

"Well, personally I would have said it was the specially caught rockfish that made it memorable, but if you think it was just the liquor that should take credit, I'll indulge you," she said and then covered a burp with a smile.

"It was my last desperate push to convince you to stay," he said and met her gaze.

"Let's go for a walk," Brenda said and stood to clear the table.

Doris waved her away "I'll do that."

"No, Wolf and I do the dishes, that's the deal."

"Out!" Doris replied and flicked the back of her hand in their direction.

"And don't come back till you get the right answer," added Fred.

Side by side, Wolf and Brenda walked up the drive. A doe and fawn stood nibbling on browse where the pasture met the forest, and Wolf reflexively scanned the deer fence around the vegetable garden he had reinforced the previous spring. There were no chinks in the armor, so they carried on past where the access road began. The sun had set behind the mountains on Vancouver Island, and the air freshened as the temperature dropped. A little red squirrel high in a conifer scolded them as they passed, interrupted during his meal of fir cones.

"He does a fair Doris impersonation," said Wolf.

Brenda laughed and then abruptly went quiet as Wolf reached out and took her by the hand. They continued walking in silence, feeling the warmth of their palms mated together, until he said, "I like you very much, Brenda. We've spent a lot of time together, every day all day for three weeks, and I get the sense that you enjoy my company as much as I enjoy yours."

"I do very much. But there's something you need to know about me. I learned from my last relationship that I can't hold back anything. I've got to come clean and be completely open with you at the outset. And I have to say, it's really hard to do this. Trusting you with what I have to say is fraught with risk. Risk to a potential relationship with you and a personal risk to me." She paused and looked up at his face. "I'm scared."

Wolf pondered for a few moments, then replied, "Brenda, you've been through the war and I've been through the war. You may have experienced some bad things in the years before we met, and as far as I'm concerned, the past is the past."

Wolf looked in her eyes and said, "I just don't care about past lovers and blunders. If you feel obliged to tell me something in order to find some kind of release or comfort, I'm fine with that; I'll be there for you. Or if you want to keep it close to your chest, then that is your prerogative; I don't have a need to know. But as I see it, our lives together are commencing today; we are starting anew, and everything previous in our lives is wiped from the slate."

The evening sunlight backlighting her hair compelled him to reach out and touch it.

"We can't forget our pasts, but surely we can leave them behind us."

"You'd be happy with that? Me not confessing my sins?"

"There is nothing that you could say about your past that could possibly influence how I feel about you. Everything I need to know about the kind of person you are, I've seen in the last three weeks. To me, that is the real Brenda. If it has been a heavy burden, let go of the past; we have such a wonderful future before us."

Brenda thought for a moment and asked, "And what about you? Are you needing to get anything off your chest?"

Wolf felt his gut go tight. "No. The invasion of my country by the Nazis was horrendous, and I have no need to revisit that past. We need only think of the prospect of a wonderful life together," and then he leaned down and kissed her upturned face.

They married on a sunny day in September. Doris and Fred, his carpenter crew Brendon and Glen, their girlfriends, and many island residents attended the ceremony on the beach. A minister from Denman Island officiated, and the vows were overseen by an eagle sitting on the crag of the big spruce tree. The wedding register was signed "Brenda Margaret Leamington" and "Wolfgang Rost de Pont," and with a wisp of reluctance, Brenda surrendered her bedroom view of the sea for a much grander and more spacious room with Wolf at the end of the hall.

By the end of October, the construction project had been completed and two more begun on Hornby, one a clone of the Denman building and the second a much grander house on Tribune Bay. Brenda also took on drafting work for barns, garages, and even a barge that some landowners wished to construct.

In early November, at the dinner table, surrounded by her new-found family, Brenda announced that a baby would be due in June. Fred opened a bottle of his best elderberry wine.

A week before the due date, Doris had insisted that Brenda and Wolf stay in Comox, citing the vagaries of the ferry service and lack of proper medical services on both Denman and Hornby. Having experienced Noel's easy arrival two decades earlier, Brenda was not concerned about having a home birth, but in the end, Cecily Fiona de Pont was born on the twentieth of June at the regional hospital.

25

1967

The farm was breathing in. Lambs were gamboling in the pasture and the garden was sprouting. To Brenda, the day felt full of possibilities. She sat at the sunlit kitchen table with Fred, enjoying a morning cup of coffee. Wolf had gone to a building site and had taken Cecily with him in the truck, dropping her off at school. Doris was upstairs preparing to start her day, although normally she was the one to start the percolator in the morning.

"What's on your agenda today, Teensie?" asked Fred. He had assumed the right to tag her with a nickname to celebrate her diminutive stature, and despite her original reluctance, Brenda had accepted it for what it was: a way to voice his affection.

"I have an appointment to meet a chap at Phipps Point about a landing-craft-cum-barge-cum-ferry project he's entertaining. And then I must contact the shearer about the sheep. After that, the garden is asking to be hoed. And you?"

"The barn. I am going to hobble out there and work on that stall for Cecily's pony. Doris has almost finished sewing up that saddle blanket for her. Where is she anyway? Her coffee's getting cold."

"I'll go look," said Brenda. She climbed the stairs and called out. There was no response. She knocked on the bedroom door and hearing nothing, slowly opened it, expecting to find Doris asleep under her duvet. The room was empty, the bed made. Brenda called out again and then gave a gentle rap on the bathroom door, also getting no response. Carefully, she opened the door and found Doris fully dressed and slumped on the floor.

§

Just three weeks after the funeral for Doris, Fred suffered a massive stroke, and after a long stay in the hospital in Comox, he was transferred to a long-term care facility in Victoria, where his daughters would be close.

The following Saturday, Cecily was sitting at the kitchen table working with her arithmetic textbook. Heavy footsteps on the porch preceded her father's appearance. His form filled the doorway.

"Why so glum chum?" he said, as he moved to the sink to pour a glass of water.

"Bad news, I think. Mummy got a phone call ten minutes ago. She hung up and just started crying."

Wolf made a grimace. "Where is she?"

"Down by the water, I think. I'm just guessing though."

Wolf nodded and headed down the path to the shore, where, as suggested, he found his wife sitting in a weatherworn Adirondack chair above the tide line.

"What's up honey?"

"It's Fred. He died in the night," she said and burst into tears.

Wolf sat on the gravel beside his wife and reached out to rest a consoling hand on her knee, all the while fighting to keep his composure.

"It's so sad," she said, and brought her hands to her face, covering her eyes. With that gesture, Wolf felt the bottom fall away. Apart from his wife, the only adults who had ever truly loved him, were gone. Until that moment, he had been unaware of the magnitude of the void that their absence would leave, and he wept.

It was several minutes before he could speak again.

"They had a good long life, Bren. Their last years here have been some of the best—Doris told me so. I don't think they would have traded their life here with us for something different; if anything, having us here extended their stay."

"I know," she said and then allowed herself another round of weeping. Wolf held her hand and waited for her to settle. Her moist, reddened eyes met his gaze and she said, "Doris told me while we were bathing Cecily on the day we brought her home that Fred had decided to put up the 'for sale' sign years ago. Their youngest had left and they thought that they would go to Victoria to be closer to the girls. But then you came along and gave them hope. You gave them a reason to stay as well as the means."

"Well, I think we both can take credit for that," he said and sighed.

"When Lawrey and my parents died, I was completely cut adrift. My aunt Fiona rescued me, mothered me, and gave me a home, yet I didn't fit, not really. I always felt like an add-on. But you, Doris, and Fred took me in and made me part of a family that was more like what a real family should be, with trust and caring and unwavering support. Funny thing is, with my own parents I came to realize that their love was conditional and always contingent on what I could do for them, not what we could do for each other."

"The times were different back then; parents were different."

"Maybe, but I don't think it was like that for Doris's children. I'm going to miss the two of them so much."

After Fred's funeral in Victoria, there followed long and protracted discussions with all five of Doris and Fred's children about the fate of the farm. The youngest son, Gavin, was keen to take over the property, but the other four were eager to sell to Brenda and Wolf. Gavin's only asset was his fishing boat and as a consequence of his passion for rye whiskey, he was hard pressed to keep it fueled and afloat. At family meetings and in long-distance telephone calls, many of which were collect, he railed against the intransigence of his brothers and sisters and their wish to simply hand over the family home. But with no capital in hand or equity that a bank would consider sound, he finally succumbed to his siblings' demands and agreed to the sale.

With Wolf's savings and the remains of Brenda's trust as a down payment, they were able to acquire a mortgage and become owners of the farm. For the first time in her adult life, Brenda finally felt grounded; she had a husband, a daughter, and her own home. Life was rigorous and challenging. And it was a life that bound the three together.

 followed by

ϛ

Brenda looked up from hoeing the vegetable garden and glanced at Cecily sitting on an old, weatherworn, three-legged stool that Fred had slapped together years earlier. In her lap was a small metal saucepan into which she was dumping the first hulled peas of the season. For Cecily escaping grade one, it was the first time she was experiencing the release and joy brought by the end of school, and summer was now expanding outward in an apparently endless spiral.

"You should probably try and put as many of those in the pot as you do in your mouth," Brenda said to her daughter.

"Ha ha, very funny," Cecily replied, then said, "Who's that?"

Brenda turned to see a man, in his thirties she guessed, walking down the drive. He wore a Bee Gees tee shirt, cut-off jean shorts, and dusty sandals. His longish hair refused discipline.

"Hello!" he called and then waved as they met his gaze. He made his way to the garden and smiled through the deer fence.

"Our camper van has broken down, and I was hoping I might use your phone to call for help. We're about a quarter mile from the top of your drive."

"Oh dear," said Brenda. "We don't have the kind of garage that you're hoping to call on Hornby; most people here are do-it-yourselfers. Help would have to come from off island. My guess is that they wouldn't get here till tomorrow, what with the ferries."

The man frowned, then said, "That's the price of getting away from it all, I guess. You get away from it all."

"Cecily, go get your father, please. He's in the house."

Her daughter placed the pot on the ground, dashed out of the garden, and with pigtails bouncing sprinted to the house.

"Daaad!" she called as she shot up the stairs and disappeared inside.

"My name is Peter. Peter Grant," the stranger said and held out his hand. "I'm here with my wife and daughter for a week."

Brenda introduced herself, and when Wolf and Cecily emerged together, she introduced them to the stranded tourist. After a few quick questions about the engine failure, Wolf said, "Probably the best thing is for me to get the tractor and tow you down here. Then we can have a look at it within arm's length of my tools."

As the men and the tractor headed up the drive, Brenda turned to her daughter and said, "Better get to those peas; we'll be six for dinner."

It had not taken long for Wolf to diagnose a jammed float in the carburetor. Peter and his family had been driving dusty gravel roads in the mountains up by Campbell River, and some grit had found its way into the fuel system. An hour later, with the problem solved, they were all sitting at the table, enjoying a barbequed salmon, new potatoes, peas, and salad.

Peter's wife, Christine, and daughter, Ronnie, had been welcomed, and Cecily was delighted to be gifted a girl of her own age to entertain.

"Can we go for a swim after dinner, Mum?"

"Fine by me. Christine?"

The woman's daughter first flashed her gaze at her father, then turned a high-beam stare of expectation at her mother.

"Just watch out for killer whales," she said.

Both girls simultaneously rolled their eyes and pushed back from the table.

"Clear first," said Wolf and nodded at the dirty dishes on the table.

"Really?"

"Really."

"I'll help," said Ronnie, and together the girls had the table cleared and were out the door in less than a minute.

Later, the adults sat in chairs on the deck and watched their daughters below in the water, splashing about and swimming in the shallows. This night would cement a friendship between the families that would last for many years. The Grants would visit Hornby every summer until the girls were in their teens, and numerous reciprocal trips were made every year to Victoria.

26

1973

"Ah, here you are," said Brenda as she poked her head through the door to the workshop. Wolf's first real contribution to the farm, soon after his arrival, had been to assist Fred in building this appendage to the back of the barn. Over the years, the workshop had become fully equipped for woodworking as well as mechanical repairs to the tractor and harvesting equipment. It was essential to the smooth running of the place, and Wolf could often be found there taking something apart or putting something together. It was also his haven for listening to very loud music. Brenda stepped into the shop and winced at the aural overload. Wolf turned down the volume on Led Zeppelin.

"What's that you're working on?"

"Well, you're always going on about sailing your little punt around Lake Windermere, so I thought I'd build Cecily a little sabot for her birthday," said Wolf. "Y'know, something that she can sail out to the Point and back."

"Do you think she's old enough?"

"Yeah, I think so. Twelve is a good age, and she's a bright girl that loves a challenge. Besides, she has sailing in her blood and a mother to teach her how."

Late on the eve of Cecily's birthday, Brenda and Wolf surreptitiously carried the completed craft down to the beach. He had painted the hull white and had carefully added a stylized black swan on the transom, with the head, neck, and body making up the capital "S" of Swan. Stepping back to enjoy her husband's handiwork, she said, "Wow, that takes me back. So many memories."

There was no sound associated with the recollection and the images slid lightly into focus, thin and grey. There was no….what was it? Resonance. Yes, that's it, she thought. Reed's death no longer resonated. It had no more heft than the memory of tying her shoe for the first time. Brenda reached out and brought the back of Wolf's hand to her lips. Meeting the warm glow of his eyes, she said, "Cecily is lucky to have such a wonderful father."

The next morning, they led their daughter down the trail to the shore and introduced her to her own boat.

"Oh my goodness! Oh my goodness! Oh wow!" was all Cecily could manage.

"Before you take it out on the water, you have to learn all the wind theory and the name of every part of your little ship," said Brenda. "It's important to understand what makes a sailboat sail, otherwise you'll never go where you want to go; or worse, you could capsize. And of course, you'll always be wearing your life jacket."

"I know, Mum, I know," said Cecily, waving a hand to silence her mother. "But look at the oars, Mum. They're beautiful."

Cecily picked one up and was delighted to show her mother a mahogany swan inlaid into the curve of the spruce blade.

"It's amazing, Daddy. The whole thing is amazing," she said and then threw her arms around her father.

"Mum will teach you how to sail it," he said, returning her hug. "She's the sailor."

It took Cecily little time to learn the sailing vernacular, and her parents challenged her at the dinner table each evening for a week. Satisfied with her daughter's grasp of the theoretical basics, on a bright Saturday mid-afternoon, Brenda found herself in the family rowboat in the middle of the bay while Cecily hoisted the sail of her own little boat, made it fast, and maneuvered away from the shore.

A light breeze moved the vessel along nicely. As Brenda had learned from Fiona, Cecily learned to guide the Swan through all points of the wind following cues called out by her mother. It took several tries to get the hang of jibing—tacking downwind—but overall, the first lesson went well.

"That is so much fun!" she said to her mother as she shipped the oars and stepped out at the shore.

"And you didn't sink, not once," Brenda said gaily, then laughed joyously upon seeing Cecily's smirking lips.

As the summer came into full blossom, Cecily made time for herself every day to get out on the Swan. She loved the technical aspect of sailing—reading the wind and setting the sail to optimize the forces that pushed her forward. Gradually, as Cecily's proficiency increased, Brenda's need to oversee every moment of her child's time on the water waned. She had relentlessly hammered home the boundaries of her daughter's sailing domain, and Cecily felt comfortable keeping within the marker buoys that Wolf had set out. But with the heavier winds of autumn and the cold of the salt spray came the decision to end the sailing season. As the three of them carried the Swan back to the barn for the winter, Cecily's mind charged ahead to the following spring and the rampant urge to expand her navigable territory.

"Next year, I want to sail to Galleon Beach and back."

"Well, honey, one step at a time. That may be a bit far," said Brenda.

Cecily was silent as they opened the barn door, hefted the boat inside, then propped it and the mast up against the wall.

When they had finished hanging the sail from a rafter, Cecily said, "How long is Lake Windermere, Mother?"

Brenda eyed her daughter. Cecily called her Mother, not Mum, when her dander was up. "Ten miles or so, I think. But I wasn't allowed to sail the length of it at your age, if that's what you're thinking."

"Well I bet Galleon Beach is not even a mile from our place. And next year I'll be a teenager."

"And that means what exactly?" asked Wolf, as he propped the oars against the wall.

"It means that I'm growing up and that you'll have to give me some rein."

Wolf snorted and said, "Spoken like a true Leamington."

"But I'm a de Pont."

"True enough, but you're your mother's daughter through and through.

27

1974

"There! I did it, Mum. Galleon Beach and back."

"Well done, sweetie!" said Brenda, looking up from the sink as the kitchen door swung open. A wave of relief had washed through her at the sound of feet leaping up the back stairs.

She could see that Cecily was glowing, partly from pride and partly from the wind and sun. Her thirteenth birthday had been the previous day, and in Cecily's estimation, her best gift was permission to sail out of her parents' line of sight for the first time. Wolf was on a job site and Brenda had busied herself in the kitchen the whole time while her daughter was out on the water. She had forced herself to stay away from the beach and hopping from foot to foot in the sand as she anxiously awaited Cecily's return. The making of bread dough took her mind off the thought of her daughter bobbing alone on an arm of the Pacific Ocean, but with the loaves in the oven, her mind had run to visions of capsizing amidst rogue waves.

How had Fiona felt when Brenda took herself down the lake? Brenda had never really considered her aunt's perspective before. How had Fiona found the wherewithal to so calmly defend her against the police investigation into Kevin Reed's death? How was she able to let her go to Canada? Someday, Cecily would launch herself from here. How could Brenda survive that? It had been too long since she had written her aunt, and she reminded herself to put pen to paper.

Cecily pulled the elastic band from her ponytail and shook out her hair. "It was easy. Sailed on a beam reach on the way there, tacked up into the wind for a bit, and then I ran on a reach all the way home. Piece of cake."

"Speaking of which, there is some of your birthday cake left. Would you like a piece?"

A minute later, with cheeks bulging and crumbs tumbling from her lips, Cecily asked sloppily, "Where'sh Dad?"

"He's still at the mall project in Courtenay. You can tell him all about your expedition later," said Brenda, handing her daughter a napkin and a glass of milk. "He'll definitely want to hear a detailed account of the Swan's big adventure."

The following Sunday, the sky was blue and lightly streaked with clouds, and Cecily pushed the Swan off the beach below her house, waved to her mother and set sail for Galleon beach once again. The wind was stronger than on her previous outing, and the little vessel made, what was to her, remarkable time. It seemed a waste of a good sail to turn around so soon after setting out, despite her mother's edict that she was only to go to Galleon and back. Cecily kept her hand on the tiller, the land on her right, and continued her outing. Short minutes later, she slid by Grassy Point, where she let out the main sheet, turned south and with the wind behind her, ran along the shoreline. She was careful to dodge kelp beds and stay well away from rocks and reefs. Cecily had run along this shore with her father in the runabout many times while fishing, so although the coastline was familiar it was also foreign and exciting, as it was she alone who set the course.

A large ketch sailed by, heading north, its sails taut and snow-white hull looking splendid as it beat into the increasing wind. A heavily bearded gentleman at the helm of the yacht doffed his hat as Cecily waved a greeting. Both crafts held to their courses.

Though the wind continued to freshen, it wasn't till she saw a fishing boat, a trawler heading north and pounding into the building seas, that Cecily realized getting back home was going to be a much bigger challenge than running with the wind. She would have to beat her way, tacking into the wind time and time again, to make it back to Grassy Point, followed by what would then probably turn out to be a wild reach home. Yet every time she tried to turn her boat around and head up into the wind, the little craft tipped wildly in the rolling seas and threatened to capsize. The wave tops were white and breaking with foam, and the biggest threatened to curl right over the stern and fill her boat.

It was then that she saw them coming, a pod of orcas. Their glistening black dorsal fins sliced through the water, and Cecily estimated that there were eight of the whales, half a football field away and closing. In the bright sunlight, she could see the spray periodically rising from their spouts, but the wind and rampant crashing of the waves around her swept away the sounds of their approach. The largest of the group, a mature female, led the pack in an unswerving procession directly into the waves and toward the little boat. As an adult orca had twice the mass of a pickup truck, there was little doubt in Cecily's mind what would happen in a collision between her little boat and the matriarch whale.

"And then I'll be in the water with them," she said to the wind.

Covered in a fine layer of sawdust from the workshop, Wolf stepped into the kitchen and met Brenda's concerned look. "She should be back by now, don't you think?" she asked, glancing up at the wall clock.

"Yes, and there's a lot more wind out there today than the last time she went out. I've been keeping my eye on the wind for an hour. It's blowing at least fifteen knots now."

He glanced out the window and peered through the trees at the water. "I'll take the runabout and buzz down to the Point while you get on the radio and see if anyone on the water has seen her," he said. Their eyes locked for a brief moment. "Don't worry, Bren, she'll be fine. You taught her well."

"Just go," Brenda said as she turned and fled to the den and the VHF marine radio.

The outboard motor started on the second pull and Wolf headed out into the chop, the aluminum hull slamming and banging as he angled the craft through the waves. He told himself that surely nothing bad could happen on such a beautiful sunny day. The Swan was sound, Cecily sailed skillfully, and well, this just couldn't turn out badly. But as one might bring along an umbrella to ward off rain, for the first time in memory, Wolf slipped into a life jacket before heading eastward along the top of the island.

Brenda had heard from the "Colali." The captain of the white ketch reported on the marine radio that his vessel had passed the Swan some ten minutes earlier and that all was well with the little craft. He was able to confirm that she was heading south, a course that continued to lead her away from home.

With the keys in her hand, Brenda ran from the house and jumped into the truck. As the vehicle disappeared up the dirt drive and the dust wafted away in the breeze, the telephone rang in the empty house.

Cecily yelped as the leading animal rose for a breath a mere body length from the Swan; its massive black back was the size of a car roof. The orca dove and slid effortlessly beneath the boat as its companions passed on either side. The last of the group rolled as it approached, the side of its head momentarily free of the water. It eyed the little craft in passing. Cecily was stunned. She had caught the eye of the beast and could see that the whale hadn't just noticed the boat; in those two seconds, it had actually looked at the boat with an intelligent appraisal. From under the water, the boat could be mistaken for a short, stubby log but above the waterline there was so much more to see, and the orca had taken it all in. Cecily felt as though touched by a mystical hand.

A couple of thudding heartbeats later, the young mariner and the whale pod were separated by a rapidly expanding distance that freed Cecily to focus on the task at hand. The pitch of the waves was now hurling the little craft down the slope of one wave and into the trough of the next. She was in danger of broaching and flipping. If Cecily kept on the current heading and was able to avoid capsizing, she would end up running the length of the island and might swing around the lee shore. But that would take at least another hour she guessed and was only a viable option if the waves did not continue to grow ever larger.

So, she thought, it's now or never. Time to come about. Cecily slid off the seat and settled into the bottom of the hull. With her mass lowered, the vessel would be more stable as she pushed the tiller hard to the starboard side. She initiated the move, and as the boat swung to come around, it rocked viciously as a cresting wave crashed into the hull. Gallons of water dumped over the gunnel and the sailboat began to roll. Cecily shrieked wildly and then slammed the tiller back across to bring the bow back to the original down-wind course. Her heart was pounding, and her breathing came in fear-driven gasps. She grabbed the little plastic bucket at her feet and began madly bailing with her free hand.

Her only remaining safe choice now was to gently steer the sabot downwind at an angle towards the shore and find a little cove or other secure haven. Ahead on her right she caught sight of buildings along the shore, and she heaved a great sigh when she spied people on the rocky foreshore. With the current sea conditions, the Sea Breeze Lodge would prove too challenging a landing, but she knew that if she held her course, a refuge was at hand. A few perilous minutes later, leaving the wind and waves behind her, she snuck into the shelter of Tralee Point and eased her boat to shore. It felt so good to stand up and stretch. A broad-waisted woman wearing a wide grin approached with a black lab at her side. The dog had a stick in his mouth, sand on his coat, and a tail wagging with hope of more fetching to come.

"Bit lumpy out there!" the woman said. "Can I help you pull her above the tide?"

Cecily smiled broadly and said, "Yes, it was getting a little much."

She shrugged out of her life jacket and put on her sandals. "That would be very kind. Thank you."

Together they managed to wrangle the boat up the beach to safety.

"Thanks so much for your help."

"I'm impressed with you being out in that wind. Your parents must be very sure of your abilities," she said and tugged the stick from the dog's mouth.

Cecily simply nodded and said, "Speaking of which, I should go and call them to come and get me. Thanks again," she said and with a little wave made her way up to the trees and over to the lodge.

Brenda reasoned that if Cecily was already south of Grassy Point as reported by the captain of the ketch, the next logical haul-out point was Hidden Beach. She drove hurriedly, flying by a stunned islander who had been inching along in a rusty old patchwork Ford. Arriving at her destination, she leapt from the truck and ran to the water's edge. The beach was empty, not a soul in sight, and the waves were rolling straight onto the shore. It was obvious to Brenda that there was little chance of any small craft successfully beaching here. She raised her hand to her brow and scanned the horizon. The little sailboat was nowhere to be seen. To the south, the only vessel nearby was their runabout with Wolf at the helm, diligently making his way along with the sea swell.

The familiar and overwhelming panic she had felt in searching through the firestorm for Lawrey swept through her body. Her legs suddenly felt weak and began to tremble. Brenda screamed into the wind. She screamed out her daughter's name. She screamed at the seeping black terror. She screamed at herself for letting her daughter out on the water.

It would be so easy to let herself collapse onto the sand and simply give in to the cresting wave of hopelessness. Instead, she spun around and ran for the truck, where her hands were shaking so wildly that she struggled just to put the key in the ignition.

Wolf continued to scan the shoreline and the horizon in front of him. He saw a pod of orcas coming his way and swung out to give them a wide birth. Propellers and whales don't mix, and on any other day he would simply have cut the engine and enjoyed their passing.

There had been no sign of his daughter or her boat, and to Wolf that was a good sign. The sabot was wooden, had no ballast and could not sink—capsize maybe, but not sink. In the heat of last summer, they had practiced testing what it would take to tip the boat over and fill it with the sea, so his daughter did know its limits. Cecily was a grand swimmer, the sea was not viciously cold, and she was wearing a life jacket. She knew to stay with the boat if she foundered; he had told her so, as had Brenda. It all boded well for a positive outcome, yet there was a frisson of anxiety tightening in his gut as he continued his search.

Up ahead was the resort; if he didn't find her there or around the next jut of land, he'd pull in and call the Coast Guard. Wolf made his way around Tralee Point and into calm water, where he was greeted by the sight of the Swan safely high and dry above the tide line. His daughter sat beside the little vessel. Seeing him, she sprang to her feet and wildly waved her arms above her head in greeting.

From through the trees, he saw Brenda emerge, pause, and then rush to Cecily. Instead of the expected hug of reunion, Brenda grabbed her daughter by the shoulders and shook her, all the while yelling something. He could not hear the words from where he stood, but the message was obvious.

"Mother stop it!" Cecily shouted. "You're hurting me!"

"You don't know what hurt is, you silly girl. How could you be so stupid?"

"I was just sailing. You said I could go sailing!"

"Don't play innocent with me, young lady. You're miles from where we said you could go. You've no idea what we've been through!"

Brenda released her grip but held her hands out in front of her as might a boxer.

"Well, the wind came up, and rather than risk flipping over, I did what you always said to do. 'If you get in trouble, find a safe place to shelter and we'll come and get you,' quote, unquote, and so that's what I did."

She set her jaw, puffed out her chest, and glared at her mother.

"And did I tell you to sail over to the windward side of the island and get mixed up with wind and seas that were beyond your skill level? Did I tell you to put your father's life at risk searching for you? Did I not specifically tell you that your route was to Galleon and back?"

"Why are you so freaked out, Mother? I went for sail and pulled in here to get out of the wind. I even called home from the resort as soon as I got here. Twice. I called twice. If you had stayed home, you'd have known that I was safe half an hour ago!"

"Don't blame me for your bad decision to not turn back when you knew you should have! You made a silly choice and you cannot hide that fact. You silly, silly girl!"

"Better silly than crazy!"

"Do not get lippy with me or you'll regret it," Brenda said. Her face was pale with rage. "You are grounded until further notice. The Swan is out of bounds until your father and I decide what to do with you. I am so disappointed in you."

After beaching the runabout, Wolf approached his family with long strides and his face set in steely focus. From the shoreline he had seen them arguing, and he was sure that Brenda had already taken several strips off his daughter; did he need to pile on as well? Stepping into the midst of the whirling fury of mother and daughter, Wolf suddenly felt a concern that things might be said, things that might be regretted later, words that would be hard to take back. Reflexively, he placed his hand on his wife's forearm as Cecily's shoulders began to shake while tears peeled down her cheeks.

Brenda whirled and spat, "Don't you dare take her side on this. Those crocodile tears are just water. She may be Daddy's little girl but she is in big trouble, trouble of her own making. There will be consequences. You know there must be consequences!"

Wolf felt the sting of her misdirected fury but nodded. "I agree. Clearly a lot has been said already that I've missed. Let's deal with the boats and get ourselves home. We can deal with consequences there."

Choosing to avoid a lumpy and tedious boat ride home, Wolf used the Swan to tie off the runabout on a mooring buoy. He would navigate the powerboat home the next day when the wind had settled. The family of three sat in the too-close confines of the truck cab. Little was spoken the whole way home; the only sounds were the rattle of the Swan and its contents in the back of the truck.

Wolf and Brenda agreed that the Swan would be in dry dock for a month. Cecily took the news dry-eyed and without comment; her only reaction was to purse her lips and glare at her parents. Later that day, Brenda was dumbfounded to hear her daughter laughing and gabbing on the phone to one of her friends. Brenda resented as well as marveled at the girl's resilience. It struck her that to Cecily, the whole episode had been a bit of a lark, an adventure for the telling. For Brenda, however, her core felt ravaged, brittle, and hollowed out; it would take days for her to recover. The incident had been a reflection from the black mirror of her youth, so it was not a surprise that night when she woke in the moonless darkness from a dream.

"Are you awake?" she whispered.

"I am. You woke me with your thrashing and jerking. Dream?"

"Yeah, a bad one. I was drowning." Brenda paused and then said, "I'm sorry I barked at you. Today was just too familiar and traumatic."

"I could see from your reaction that it was not just today's events you were battling."

"No, it was partially about Lawrey and the bombs. But if something had happened to Cecily, I honestly don't know what I would do."

"Well, nothing bad did happen and nothing will."

"Maybe I love her too much. Maybe it's more than love. Maybe I'm just too protective."

Wolf rolled onto his side and wrapped her hand in his own work-roughened hands. "Can a parent love too much?"

"How much is too much?" asked Brenda. "And if I do love her too much, how do you unlove someone?"

"I don't know, Bren, but there is no limit to what I would sacrifice for you two."

28

1977

"Mum, I think we should have it on the Saturday, not on the actual day," said a teenaged Cecily, bouncing into the kitchen.

"Have what dear?" asked Brenda as she put away some dishes.

"Don't be a drag, Mum," she said and wrapped her mother in her arms. "My birthday party, silly. Sixteen is big and I want to have all my friends here, so we should have it on the weekend instead of on the real day."

"What kind of party were you thinking then?"

"Something fun. I don't know. Maybe we could have a salmon barbeque, but that's not really all that special; we always do that."

"I'm sure we could manage something a little out of the usual. Whatever it will be, we'll need a lot of food to fill all those stomachs. How about a lamb roast? Dad could do an open fire and roast it on a spit. We could have The Islanders come and play; I hear they do good covers of Elvis Presley songs."

"Mum, are you serious? Elvis Presley? Do you not even listen to the radio nowadays?"

When the big day arrived, balloons were hung from every vertical surface and hundreds of lights were strung from tree branches. When it was all set up, Brenda and Wolf asked Cecily to join her outside the barn.

"We've got a little present hiding in there for you, sweetie."

Cecily immediately thought of a horse—a full-sized quarter horse or maybe a palomino, for she had long ago outgrown the pony. Instead, when her father swung wide the heavy double doors, a light blue Volkswagen Beetle sat quietly awaiting its new owner. The aging car was a little worse for wear, what with several rust spots and a scratched windscreen where the previous owner had neglected a faulty windshield wiper, but Wolf had ensured its mechanical soundness.

"Oh my God!" shrieked Cecily. "You are the best parents ever! I can't believe it, my own car. Dad, will you take me to town to take my test next week?"

Her father nodded and said, "No use having a car if you can't drive it."

There followed celebratory hugs and kisses and several trial runs up and down the drive. Having driven the tractor for years, Cecily had no problem with the standard stick shift. Brenda's proud smile almost matched that of her daughter.

Soon after, as Cecily and her father were staking out some Tiki torches, a familiar car edged down the drive. "Ronnie!" screamed Cecily, a huge smile filling her face. "Ronnie, come and see my new car!"

The Grants had arrived, and after a whirlwind of hugs all round, followed by a grand tour of the vehicle, the teenagers left their parents outside and ran to Cecily's bedroom to catch up and dress for the party.

Guests arrived from Denman and from all over Hornby. The gathering had become more than a mere birthday party; it was a social event for islanders to launch the summer holiday season. A disc jockey who had been hired—a high school boy named Cliff from Courtenay who did weddings, birthday parties, and school dances, managed to generate enough sound and mayhem to entertain all the teenaged guests. Wolf did indeed roast a lamb on a spit and with mountains of potato salad, fresh bread, garden vegetables, and platters heaped with potluck contributions, even the boys were left sated.

The party was scheduled to end at eleven, and at a quarter to the hour, Brenda and Wolf were sitting with Peter and Christine and other friends on the balcony, looking out over the water. The thump thump of the music rattled the windows, and the occasional shriek of a girl was heard, followed by a burst of laughter.

"Sixteen, Wolf. How can she be sixteen? It was just yesterday we were changing diapers or teaching her to ride Patches or to swim."

"Yeah, I know, and it won't be too long before she launches herself out of here. I can see her off at a university taking a degree in something and then, just every so often because she's living her own life, she'll come back to us for a whirlwind visit."

"Hopefully she'll... what's that?" Brenda said, interrupting herself and pointing to a flash of light out on the water a mile distant.

Wolf leapt to his feet. "Call the Coast Guard. Vessel on fire off Grassy Point," he said, then sprinted for the beach. He flung the rowboat into the water, slotted the oars into their locks, and rowed with all his strength for his power boat. He rowed as his arms screamed. He rowed for redemption.

29

1943

As an executive member in the NSB, Anton had executed his influence to have his son accepted as the youngest member of the Nederlandse Landwacht. In the Stormban IV Section under Commander N.J. Alblas, Wolfgang was tasked with checking personal identity cards, the *persoonsbewijs* issued to every citizen over the age of fifteen. Special attention was given to members of the Jewish community, whose cards bore a large J. At the beginning of the war, all Dutch Jews were identified. Later, their assets were seized, and then finally as the war progressed, they had been rounded up and shipped off to the transit camp at Westerbork before heading to their final destination in the camps at Mauthausen or Auschwitz.

Wolfgang had become a watcher, a shadow. On this cold moonlit night, he stood out of sight near the mayor's house, as he had every Saturday night for the past two years and every night for the past two weeks. He wore black; his uniform-issue motorcycle boots were black, as were his pants, shirt, overcoat, and leather belt and chest strap. His breath crystallized in the cold winter air.

From the brick chimney came the signs of a crackling fire in the living room or library. The mayor and his family were enjoying their evening. Wolfgang pictured the father, a brash, portly man, perhaps reading files of city business, being joined by his socialite wife in a hot drink. He also imagined the man's supercilious son, Deiter, sitting beside them as they gloated in their deception, thinking they were so far above suspicion as to be unreachable. In contrast, years of absorbing cruelty and subjugation had led Wolfgang to form sophisticated skills of vanishing into his environment, evasive and ever vigilant to potential sources of menace and jeopardy. He had learned to shrink from the light and to abhor becoming the nucleus of attention. This proficiency led him to understand the mindset of the hiders: Jews finding refuge in the bosom of anti-Nazi citizens.

Finally, as he began to shiver, Wolfgang was rewarded by a wisp seeping from the smallest of vents at the distant end of the roof. At first it came as just a little puff; then it became a continuous plume of steam and smoke the size of a foxtail. They were being ever so cautious, just another little fire for warmth, as they had done on only the coldest of nights. The heater would be made of an empty lard can or something similar joined to an old piece of pipe, and the thought of them burning sheet music of Mendelssohn or Mahler as fuel brought a true and sardonic smile to Wolfgang's lips. The family would be huddled against the heater with hands outstretched as they attempted to absorb every little bit of warmth dissipating into their attic hovel. At this image, Wolfgang's smile faded, and he turned away and headed for home.

The next morning found him joining Anton at a breakfast of ersatz coffee and dry toast. Wolfgang sat across the table. His left leg bounced with anxiety and his chest felt tight. He would have to speak soon, or his stutter would prevent him from speaking at all.

"You would like to take down Mayor de Groot." It was a statement, not a question.

Anton looked up from the newspaper at his pimply faced son. "He is incapable of leading this community, so yes, if there was a way that I could take his place, I would. But there is no election pending." He went back to his reading.

Wolfgang fought to find the strength to continue. "I can, or rather, we can. Do it together, I mean."

Anton shuffled the paper into a semblance of its original folds and flipped it onto the table.

"Wolfgang, I find it highly unlikely that at this time, without divine intervention, I can unseat de Groot. Further, a history of stuttering, acne, and identity checking on street corners does not significantly position you to support my career plan or the NSB mandate."

Wolf nodded as if in agreement but continued, "I have been conducting a long-term surveillance effort on de Groot's home." Rather than just blurt out the information, he wanted Anton to acknowledge that he could in fact be of use to the family prospects. He wanted him to ask.

"Good for you. And what have you found? That his son is stealing potatoes or that his wife has a lover?"

"No. It's more significant than that."

"Out with it then boy, for God's sake!"

Wolfgang took a deep breath and said, "They are hiding a family of Jews in their attic."

In a heartbeat, Anton's face went from snide indignation to intense eagerness. "What are you talking about?"

"All the signs are there. Yesterday, I was checking papers, and although I know Deiter de Groot because we went to the same school, I asked to see his papers. I expected him to try and flip me off. Instead, he acted all friendly, but he had a hint of fear in his eyes."

"So what if he was scared? People get intimidated by a uniform, even with you in it. How is that significant? How does that equate to Jews in the attic?"

"Deiter has never been nice to anyone in his entire life. He's the mayor's son and figures he's God's gift to the world. Normally he would rather die than treat me with deference, never mind respect. After I checked his papers, he actually thanked me and wished me a good day. So that is one thing."

"And?"

"The amount of food going into the house is greater than what one would expect for a family of three."

"He's a big man is our de Groot, eats like a pig."

"No. This is significantly more."

Anton shifted his weighty gaze to meet his son's eyes. "And that's it?"

"No, sir. On very cold nights, smoke comes out of the tiniest of vents in the roof. I think they have a little coal heater that they fire up. But only on the coldest of nights."

"You're sure?"

"Yes, sir. I have been watching." And here Wolfgang paused, unsure how explicit he should become in providing details of his obsessive surveillance. "I have been watching for some time. There is a pattern that all leads to one conclusion. The de Groots have people in the attic."

Anton shifted in his chair and with his left hand distractedly played a little arpeggio on the tabletop. "You realize of course that if you are wrong about this, there will be consequences?" He paused and held the boy's gaze. "Severe consequences."

Wolfgang nodded, then in a firm, even voice said, "I am not wrong." As the words slipped from his lips, Wolfgang suddenly came to the realization that although he could feel his heart thudding in his chest, he had not once stuttered throughout the conversation.

"Alright then," Anton said, his voice rising in eagerness. "I'll call the Sicherheitspolizei."

The following morning, Wolfgang and Anton stood side by side in the snow, across the street from the mayor's house. Together they watched as first the mayor himself was led out of the home by police, immediately followed by his wife and Deiter. Two minutes later, the four members of the Bergman family emerged at gun point and were escorted to join the de Groots in the waiting van. As he stepped up to the van, Reiner Bergman caught sight of Wolfgang and his father. With his hands shackled behind his back, his only acknowledgement was a brief nod before he was thrust into the vehicle.

As a terrier-faced officer approached them, Anton rested his hand on his young son's shoulder. Wolfgang imagined he could feel the affirmation seeping through Anton's leather glove and the fabric of his own coat. It filled him with pride, an emotion both new and exciting.

"Four Jews, Meneer de Pont. You'll be getting the thirty guilders reward for the lot of them. Sadly, no price on the head of the de Groots, but be assured they'll be heading to Westerbork with the Jews."

The man turned, barked a few orders, and re-entered the house to seek out other possible treasure.

"So, you know those two boys, do you?" asked Anton.

"Not really. We were at the same school, but they were two years ahead of me. Our paths crossed once or twice."

The older man nodded and said, "Well, Wolfgang, you have done a great thing. You have opened a door I thought would never crack, and far be it from me to hold back God's praise when it is well deserved. We'll make a great team if you can keep this up."

For the first time in his life, Wolfgang felt the warming bloom of approval and acceptance. As the sensation settled, it filled him with hope and the thoughts of a possible future in which he would command his own destiny. As the van pulled away, it took very little effort to squelch the pulse of remorse festering beneath the joy.

30

1977

Within minutes, Wolf had swapped out the boats, and he guided his powerboat at full speed towards the foundering vessel in mid channel. There was a moderate chop on the water, and the light aluminum craft bounced through the night and slammed its way across the wave tops. As he approached the fire-lit scene, Wolf cut the throttle and assessed the blaze. If he approached from downwind, he would be assailed with blinding smoke; if from upwind, he would drift onto the burning vessel. The engulfed yacht was broadside to the wind, and as he slowed, he guided his own vessel to its bow.

"Ahoy!" he called. There was no response. He called again and again while scanning the water with his flashlight, guiding the beam up the hull where he saw two small figures huddled near the anchor winch. Wolf eased his boat under the high curve of the bow above his head and yelled at the pair.

"I need you to jump into the water. I'll pull you out!"

The figures stood unresponsive to his entreaty. They were children.

"Jump into the water. Right here," he shouted and pointed.

"I can't swim!" screamed the smaller of the two; her voice was desperate and panicky. She appeared to Wolf to be about four.

"Pick her up and drop her!" he yelled to the boy. "I'll get her. You need to do it now. Hurry!"

Wolf took a nervous glance down towards the stern, to where the gas tanks sat rapidly rising in temperature. He had no idea how much longer it would take before the stored fuel became superheated.

"Now!"

The young boy, perhaps seven or eight, grabbed his little sister by her hands, eased her over the bow rail and let her fall, screaming all the way. As she hit the water, Wolf grabbed her jacket by the scruff and in one motion hauled her aboard. He looked up.

"Now you!"

The boy nodded and hurled himself into the water, and Wolf dragged him over the gunwale and into his boat. The little girl was wailing in the bow, and the boy lay on the bare metal hull, panting for breath.

"Who else is there?"

"My mum and my dad," said the boy between gasps.

"Are they still on board?"

The boy said, "I don't know about my dad. My mum got burned and she jumped into the water."

Wolf did a quick estimation. He glanced at his watch; it had been eleven minutes since he had put the rowboat in the water. Assuming that the woman had jumped in at that time and that the vessel was not then under power, the wind and tide drift would mean that she could be anywhere between the burning vessel and several hundred yards to the north.

He called out again above the roar of the flames and listened for an answer. Hearing nothing, he turned to the boy and said, "I need you to listen, only listen. I'll do the yelling, but I need you to listen for your mum or your dad. Can you do that?"

The boy nodded.

"What's your name, son?"

"Mark."

"Okay, Mark. You are doing really well. Both of you are, but I need your sister to be quieter so that we can listen for your parents, okay? Can you see if you can get her to calm down, to stop crying? That would be a big help."

The boy pulled himself up and then climbed over the middle bench and reached out for his little sister. She immediately threw herself into his arms and muffled her cries in his embrace.

Wolf kicked the motor in gear and slowly moved upwind and away from the burning fibreglass hull. The flames and smoke arched in a high windblown curve into the sky as only a distant slice of moon bore witness to the little rescue vessel slapping and bobbing into the waves.

From the stern, Wolf continued to call out and listen for a human sound above the murmur of the outboard motor. He scanned the water with his flashlight. Minutes slid by as he slowly weaved a searching course upwind and away from the burning yacht. A flash of hope immediately soured as for a moment he thought he had seen the woman, but it turned out to be a tangled mass of bull kelp floating at the surface.

"I think I heard her!" shouted Mark from the bow. "Over there," he said and pointed ahead and starboard.

"Mummy!" he shouted.

Then Wolf heard it too, a gasping call from the moonlit sea ahead. He guided his vessel forward, giving the motor a little twist of throttle.

"Mummy!"

Suddenly she was beside the boat, and as Wolf reached out to grab her, a sheaf of loose skin slid off her bare forearm and into his hand. Wolf recoiled and flung the sticky mass into the water. He looked down at the figure gasping below him; her arms were splashing spastically. He cut the motor. Without power the boat rocked wildly, but Wolf managed to grab the woman by her shirt collar and swung her aft. He fought to pull her over the narrow gap of gunwale beside the motor. As though heaving a bale of hay, he yarded her torso up and over, then grabbed her pants at the beltline and yanked her lower body and legs into the boat. She lay in a twisted mass, unmoving and silent on the floor of the runabout. He stood gasping for breath. Aware that time was slipping away for the woman, he pulled the cord to restart the outboard motor. As he did so, a tremendous blast filled the air as two hundred yards to the south, the engulfed gasoline tanks exploded in a massive ball of white and orange flame.

Wolf stood transfixed by the conflagration until moments later, a large vessel rushed toward them, sweeping a great searchlight beam onto him and his boatload of traumatized passengers.

31

1977

Local Hornby Island building contractor Wolfgang Rost de Pont (pictured above) is being celebrated as a hero for his actions at approximately 11 P.M. on Saturday night. From his home near Grassy Point, where his daughter Cecily's birthday party was under way, de Pont witnessed the vessel "Cee Maid" in distress and made his way in an aluminum runabout to the vessel a mile offshore. Once on the scene, de Pont found the yacht fully engulfed in flames, but he was able to rescue the two small children of Miles and Susan Cummins from certain death. De Pont was also able to pull Susan Cummins from the water, who had suffered second and third degree burns to significant portions of her body. A Canada Coast Guard vessel responded after receiving a mayday call from the burning boat as well as several calls from locals who had first seen the boat on fire. A Labrador helicopter stationed at Comox was dispatched and transported the mother to St. Joseph's Hospital, where she is currently in critical condition. The "Cee Maid" burned to the waterline and sank in deep water. Despite hours of searching by the Canada Coast Guard and numerous local boaters, the body of Miles Cummins has not been recovered.

When asked for a comment, de Pont, an immigrant from Holland, declined to respond, though witnesses credit him with saving the lives of the three boaters. "Without Mister de Pont's quick response and heroic conduct, there is no question more lives would have been lost," said Captain Eli Marsden of the Coast Guard. He also expressed the need for all boaters to have the appropriately rated fire extinguishers on board at all times, though it is yet to be seen whether a single extinguisher would have been of help in this case.

An investigation into the cause of the blaze is ongoing. It could not be determined by press time whether the vessel had been insured.

Cecily read and reread the article splashed across the front page of the *Comox Valley Times*. "It even has my name in it, Mum," she said proudly. "We should buy several copies. I want to cut one out and send it to Ronnie."

Brenda smiled and then sipped her morning coffee. "Let's plan a special dinner for Dad tonight. He deserves it."

"We'll make him a hero cake," said Cecily.

Wolf received all manner of accolades from island residents as he met with clients, suppliers, and neighbours. Even the ferry crews sounded the vessels' horns and announced his presence on board as he crossed over on his way to Courtenay to pick up construction materials. There were demands for radio interviews and newspaper articles, all of which Wolf declined. It took a week before the notoriety ebbed to a more tolerable level, despite Wolf's strategic efforts to downplay his role in the event.

On the tenth day after the rescue, he was sitting in the kitchen after dinner. Cecily had finished the dishes, and Wolf and Brenda were working on the newspaper crossword puzzle. The phone rang and Cecily dashed to the hall to answer. "It's for Superman," she said, returning, and as her father rose, she sat in his chair to take his place.

He was on the phone for a short time, and when he returned his face was drawn and his jawline was tight. With their eyes on the puzzle, Brenda and Cecily did not see the look of defeat, the slump of the shoulders, and the disquiet in his eyes.

"I have to replace the sparkplugs on the tractor," he said dully and stepped outside.

Lying in bed that night and sensing his unease, Brenda rolled onto her side and placed her hand on his chest. "Everything okay?"

Wolf released a big sigh and said, "Just feeling a bit bushed after all this big to-do."

"We are all so proud of you. You saved three lives."

Wolf sighed heavily and then reached for the feel of her hair. "I wish this had never happened or that someone else had been the hero. I'm not comfortable with being at the eye of the storm."

"Notoriety is not what it's cracked up to be, but don't worry, it will all just fade away soon," she said and kissed him goodnight.

As the moon tracked across the night sky, Wolf stared up at the dark ceiling, all the while positing plans to evade the imminent tsunami that would wash away his life. The feeling in his stomach, so familiar in his boyhood, had returned and was joined by a disturbing hissing sound in his ears. Finally, the blush of the sun seeped into the eastern sky; he slipped from the room and made his way to the desk in the office down the hall.

"Where's Dad? Gone to the job site already?" Cecily asked her mother later as she poured milk on her cereal.

"He got up early and caught the first ferry. He has to see a lawyer; something to do with a supplier defaulting on his contract."

"There you see, Mister de Pont, this is pretty much a boilerplate will. If you predecease your wife, then your assets will go to her, and should you both die, everything would be held in trust for your daughter until she is an adult," said Cameron Marshall, LLB.

The lawyer had spun the document around and passed it across his desk for his client to review. "You've indicated that neither of you have close relatives, and that in the extremely unlikely circumstance in which all three of you were to pass, then you've indicated that the assets are to be evenly distributed to the War Amps and the Centre for Israel and Jewish Affairs. When we had this will drawn up for you and your wife twelve years ago, those were the stipulated conditions. Is there anything you'd like to change?"

Wolf looked up from the page he was reading. "No, I just wanted to familiarize myself with the conditions. Time has skipped by, and I wanted to have a quick peek as I'd pretty much forgotten the details," he said and placed his hands flat on top of the document. "It all seems perfect," and he slid the document back to its author. "On another matter, there is a supplier of longstanding with us who has failed to deliver goods, despite receiving a cash advance more than two months ago. I need you to write a letter to rattle his cage..."

Brenda thought of Wolf as a balanced, taciturn man, but over the next few days she saw his normally quiet, introspective nature collapse into a nervous, withdrawn shell. Two weeks to the day after the boat fire, the reason became clear and she met him on the porch as he came home from work. In her hand was the day's copy of the *Comox Valley Times*, and spread across the front page above the fold was the headline "Local Hero Identified as Nazi Collaborator." Without speaking, she hugged him and then handed him the paper.

Wolfgang Rost de Pont, recently lauded for his heroic rescue of three boaters from their flaming yacht in the Strait of Georgia, has been identified as a Nazi collaborator by a survivor of the Holocaust in World War II, in which more than six million Jews were systematically murdered in the world's greatest mass genocide. Avi Brickner, a researcher with the Institute for Netherland Wartime Atrocities, has reviewed records collected in Amsterdam after the war and has identified de Pont as a member of the dreaded Nederlandse Landwacht, which was found responsible for identifying thousands of Dutch citizens sent to the gas chambers in Auschwitz. Meticulous lists kept by the Nazis at the concentration camps in Europe detail the names of the 125,000 Dutch Jews and non-Jews sent to their deaths, including members of Brickner's own family.

When reached for comment by the Comox Valley Times, *de Pont's only comment was, "I was just a teenager at the time, and teenagers do stupid things."*

Brickner's response to the comment was brusque and to the point: "Yes, teenagers are known for making bad decisions, but this wasn't cheating on a test or smoking behind the barn; this individual's actions sent people to the gas chamber." Brickner went on to say...

Wolf let the paper slip from his hands and reached out again to hug his wife. To Brenda, Wolf smelled the same, he felt the same, and everything about him was the same, but for the feeling that everything around him had changed.

"Where's Cecily?"

"Alicia and Jill took her to the Community Hall. *Carrie* is showing."

"D-d-d-does she know?"

Brenda nodded. "She's devastated."

"A-a-a." Wolf closed his eyes, took a deep breath, and released it slowly. "A-and you?"

"I'm still processing it."

His head bobbed weakly. "I think I'll g-g-g-go into the g-g-g-garden and hoe for a bit," he said and turned for the steps.

"Wolf, I have never heard you stutter before. Is that new or from bygone days?"

Humiliation bowed his head. Unable to meet her gaze, he simply shook his head and said, "I don't feel like t-t-t-talking right now—if that's okay?"

"Of course, luv. We can talk later." She entered the empty house alone and looking for a distraction, made a cup of tea. Then, standing at the kitchen window, Brenda watched the stooped and broken shell of her husband hack fitfully at the dirt. Her tea went cold.

The ringing of the phone yanked her from her musings. It was a short call. When Wolf finally came back into the house, she told him, "They've dropped you from the ferry-dock improvement project. 'Given the circumstances' they said." Wolf just nodded and climbed the stairs. After a few minutes, Brenda heard the bathtub begin to fill.

32

1977

As midnight approached, Cecily had her friend Alicia drop her at the top of the drive. She had dried her eyes yet again and watched as the little car's taillights disappeared into the night, all the while hoping that the reality that had slammed into her earlier would vanish as quickly. But she knew she had not even climbed to the top of the worst of it yet. Her father's side of the story was yet to be heard, and didn't newspapers always sensationalize everything? She would talk to him, to clarify. But what could he say? He as much as admitted to the worst of it in the article.

Cecily looked down at her home, silhouetted against the moonlit sea, and was struck with the realization that her childhood had ended. There would be no going back to the shelter of parents as gods, defenders against all comers. From this moment forward, she alone would be making the decisions that defined her future.

She slipped out of her shoes and silently opened and closed the door behind her. The house was dark and quiet, and a wave of relief swept over her; her parents had always said that things would look better in the morning, so she would talk to him tomorrow.

Cecily climbed the stairs, a panther in the silence. Her eyes were adjusted to the darkness and she could see that their bedroom door was ajar. Her parents were waiting to hear her come in, to confirm that she was home and safe.

Cecily leaned to the crack to whisper her arrival but instead heard her mother say, "...so I killed him. He sank to the bottom of the lake and I just sailed away. The police came asking questions because someone had seen me in my boat. They didn't suspect that it was me that had killed him; how could they? I was just a tiny little waif, a female one at that. So you see, we both have done things in our past that in the light of day don't reflect well on us."

"Brenda, the Nederlandse Landwacht was our v-v-version of the home guard in England, but it wasn't designed to serve the same purpose. Our mandate was to terrorize transgressors and track down Jews, not rescue citizens from the horrors of war. When I joined, I was a teenager, but I knew what I was doing, and I was good at it. These people I tyrannized were n-n-normal people, good people, no different at all from our friends here on Hornby. They weren't like the man you killed; they were just regular people."

He paused while, just a few feet away, Cecily calmed her breath and waited for her father to continue.

"After we met, years ago, you asked why I had never married. That is the reason. I thought I didn't have the right to happiness; those people I condemned to death will never return to life. What I did will never be undone. It took a long time for me to come to terms with myself, and I hold no illusions that p-p-people will easily make the same journey. Especially Cecily."

"Your daughter loves you, Wolf, and she will come to understand."

"Brenda, we've taught her to be caring, incisive, and insightful, and she has become just that. She knows the difference between right and wrong. I don't want her to have to compromise all that just because she loves me."

"You want her to hate you?" asked Brenda. Cecily could tell by the shuffle of sheets that her mother had shifted her position. She envisioned her mother peering into her father's eyes. Her heart was pounding wildly in her chest.

"Love shouldn't be some kind of trump card that erases m-m-moral failure," she heard her father say.

"Well then, at what point are we able to forgive?"

"I don't know, Brenda. Maybe there are some things that you just cannot erase from the blotter of your life. Maybe the cost of forgiveness for some things is too high."

He paused in thought, made a decision, and then continued. "I followed the path I did because I was seeking approval from my father, a tyrant who raped his daughter and in doing so, fathered me. The day before I left for Canada, my mother, who it turns out, is my sister, informed me of the sordid tale of my lineage. J-j-just imagine finding out that about yourself." Tears streamed down his face. "There is no way that I will set my daughter on a confused and tortured path to cover for, or to make up for, my sins. My sins, Brenda. I'm just not worth it."

"Of course, you are worthy of being her father. There must be some route through this. Surely. What can we do?"

"I don't know, sweetheart. I don't know."

But as he lay beside the warm body that ached to give him solace, he did know what he would do.

Cecily silently slipped back down the stairs, loudly opened the door, then slammed it shut. "I'm home," she yelled as she climbed up the stairs for a second time and stomped down the hall to her room. Her limbs trembled as she slipped into her bed.

At school the next day, a hulking, indolent sophomore, clicked his heels together as she passed. Cecily heard him murmur, "Guten tag!"

Her first class that day was English and before Mister Manning waltzed into the room at the sound of the bell, as was his wont, Mickey Peters stood up and, doing a quite passable imitation of the teacher, grabbed the pointer, smacked it on the wide oak desk, and said loudly, "Today we talk about the Nazzies!" The boys in the class erupted with guffaws. Most of the girls in class joined in with tittering and whispers. Cecily was stupefied.

Math class passed without event, as did chemistry, but when she walked to her locker to grab her bagged lunch, she was met by a felt-penned swastika scrawled across the grey metal surface. The artist had crafted the tines pointing in the wrong directions; nevertheless, the message was exquisitely clear.

Her female classmates, girls she had thought of as friends, actively shunned her or at best kept their communications with her to terse and unengaged utterances. Even the amity of her best friends, so supportive the night before, had cooled. In the cafeteria, they had wielded the scimitar of shunning and cut themselves free of her company. Cecily was stunned by the betrayal. Left alone, she spent the rest of the school day in overwhelming solitude.

As she headed for the bus at day's end, Kevin Zohlner, a short and awkward teen wearing black-framed eyeglasses with thick lenses, held the door open for her. She had seen him for years suffering the brunt of the other boys' mockery, but only now could she relate to his torment. He had the countenance of a trampled garden. "It-th not going to thtop. They enjoy it too much," he said quietly, his lisp thick and moist. "For what it-th worth, in my experienth," and he paused till she met his eyes cowed from years of unrelenting bullying, "It just doesthn't get better."

It was late in the night, possibly three or three thirty Cecily guessed when she heard her father slip out the door. He had left two letters on the kitchen table, one each for Brenda and Cecily, and earlier in the day he had sent a letter to the editor of the *Comox Valley Times*, though he had no illusions that it would be published.

He started his truck for the last time and made his way to St. John's Point Road, eventually easing to a stop in the gravel parking lot at Helliwell Provincial Park. Wolf sat for several minutes in the dark cab of the truck, pondering how it had come down to this; which other branch of destiny's river could he have chosen that would have still ended up in his life with Brenda or at the very least a life that allowed him to ease into old age without having to carry this perishing weight of guilt, sadness, and remorse. Was it even possible to choose, or did the tributaries of his past sweep him well beyond choices? Was the betrayal of Deiter and Reiner really the starting point of the fall from his moral center, or had it been before that, when the bullying began? Had he been more forceful in his resistance, more physical or vocal in his condemnation of his oppressors, would that have changed the flow of his life in a more positive direction? Or should he have even more quietly suffered the slurs and beatings, absorbing them as might one of the biblical martyrs his father so vociferously championed? Indeed, what should one expect from a six or a sixteen-year-old child?

The engine ticked as it cooled, till finally Wolf opened the door, dropped the keys on the driver's seat, and with a flashlight pointing the way, stepped out into the darkness. The trail to St. John's Point was familiar, and he easily picked his way along the path through the shadows in the fir and oak forest. Nearing the open face of the cliff, he lengthened his stride and picked up his pace, breaking into a trot and then running at full tilt. He could feel the rush of fresh ocean air in his face and the roar of blood in his ears until finally, he could no longer feel the ground beneath his feet.

Cecily's features were unwaveringly bitter as she stepped into the kitchen, a suitcase in her hand. "Where's Dad?"

Brenda looked up from the open letter she held; she was sitting at the kitchen table. Her face appeared tortured in the morning light, and it was clear to Cecily that her mother had been weeping for some time. She ignored the obvious distress. "I asked, where's Dad?"

Brenda was able to manage, "He's gone." Then she leaned forward and collapsed on the table. She continued to weep.

"What, the Nazi bastard has run off? Not man enough to stay and face the music?"

Brenda's shoulders heaved.

Cecily's face had ripened to a well-reddened fury; raging with self-righteous indignation, she spat, "And what about you? My own mother a killer! Oh yes, Mum, I heard you tell Dad, like you were fighting for the right for who was the worst human being between the two of you. You disgust me, both of you!"

The tsunami overwhelmed her now, and there was no stopping Cecily. "I can't believe the hypocrisy. I can't believe the lies. I can't believe that you are my parents! I don't want you to be my parents. I don't want you to even think you are my parents."

She slammed her shaking hands onto the table. "It sounds like I'm lucky to get out of this family with my heart still beating. Who knows, perhaps had I crossed some imaginary parental line, you'd have taken me out in the rowboat and drowned me too!"

Brenda pushed her torso up and managed to meet the white-hot glare in Cecily's eyes. "It wasn't like that. I was about to be—"

"Oh great, here come the excuses. Wasn't it you that told me there are no excuses for bad behaviour? Wasn't it?"

"Cecily, I have to tell—"

"I am not going to stand here and listen to this garbage. You have no idea what I went through yesterday at school. They all hate me, so I'm leaving! I am taking my car and driving down to Victoria to live with Ronnie. I'll finish school, go to university, and as far as I'm concerned, I am no longer part of this family. I just wish my last name wasn't de Pont. There'll be no escaping it, thanks to you two."

Unable to choke out a response, Brenda simply held out an envelope with Cecily's name neatly printed across the face. Her daughter snatched it from her hand and continued yelling, "I don't want to see you, I don't want to hear from you, and I certainly don't want a stupid letter from my Nazi father."

Cecily ripped the envelope and its contents into pieces and flung them at her mother, then picked up her suitcase and walked out of her mother's life.

33

Brenda stroked Lacey's ears as though removing a dusting of flour from her right thumb and forefingers. The dog remained in deep REM sleep, her forelegs twitching in active pursuit of what was most probably a squirrel.

"I am so tired, Colin, so I think I will have to call it there. Besides, there's not a lot more to tell. After Wolf's funeral, which only a few close friends attended, I rented out the farm to a bunch of hippy types, and then I came back to the mainland and found design work at UBC on the Tri-University Meson Facility and other projects. I spent the rest of my career bouncing from research grant to research grant—whoever would have me, basically."

I thought for a moment, hesitating to broach the subject of her daughter. I was concerned, not just merely curious, whether the rupture with Cecily she had just described had in fact been their last point of contact.

"And Cecily?"

"Oh, I sent letters and birthday cards to her, of course, care of Ronnie's parents, but for years she never replied. It was all very one-sided. I visited her in Victoria, but we never really talked. All our meetings were stilted, uncomfortable, and superficial. She made it very clear that our relationship would be distant and marred by my past, at least as she knew it. Christine Grant let me know when Ronnie and Cecily were graduating from university, and I went down to watch. My daughter saw me standing outside the building after the ceremony finished but turned away to be with her friends."

"And after that, did she make any efforts to at least touch bases with you?"

"Minimally. She and Ronnie went travelling after university. I didn't get any letters, just the occasional postcard. I think she appreciated the brevity the cards offered. While trekking near Cebu, she met a young Australian man."

Lacey stirred from her sleep, yawned broadly, and stretched. Brenda fingered a paw, met my gaze, and continued, "I was shocked to receive a wedding invitation from Airlie Beach several months later. I wasn't surprised that she was getting married, but I was stunned that she wished to include me. Queensland was a long trip, but I attended and was introduced to the family, who were obviously innocent of both my past and that of my husband. I could tell by how graciously they embraced me and treated me throughout my stay that Cecily had not briefed them. She is, after all, her mother's daughter."

She saw the look on my face—concern and maybe more than a little sadness.

"Don't even try to feel sorry for me. I have had a good and eventful life. I can't imagine living a life where nothing happens. Of course, had I a magic wand, I would have waved it a little differently, but you cannot change your past. Everybody is faced with what newspeak calls 'life lessons.' Even if you make it through with a charmed, uneventful life, free of *Sturm und Drang*, the boredom and emptiness of never overcoming a single significant ordeal would be a horror to endure. Life is supposed to be a challenge."

Brenda's breathing had become laboured, and I could see that this visit had taken a severe toll on her physically and emotionally. Her tiny frame seemed to have collapsed even more deeply into the bed, so I picked up Lacey and placed her on the floor, where she stood stunned till she came completely to a functional level of alertness. At this same time most evenings, Lacey is down for the count, but she managed to shake herself awake and we said our goodbyes.

The door next to Brenda's room was open and the light was on. I paused in deliberation; the training session and Brenda's visit had left me drained, but there are no do-overs in hospice care. If you miss an opportunity, the door slams in your face. I decided to knock and then stuck my head in to check on Alice, the resident.

"Oh good, you're awake. When I came by on Thursday afternoon, you were sleeping. Do you feel up for a short visit?"

"I do, but my skin is really sensitive today. It's like it screams when something rubs against it. Would you mind if the dog stayed on the floor?"

She was dressed only in a thin hospital gown and lay on top of the sheets with her head propped up on pillows. She strained with each word from a tortured throat. Her condition had rapidly deteriorated since our last visit.

"Not at all. She'll just flop down here," I said and downed Lacey with a motion of my hand. The recliner chair was forgiving and comfortable.

"I've been thinking a lot these last few days, and I wonder if I might share something with you?" she said.

"Be my guest. I'll help if I can."

"It seems pretty clear to me that there is no God."

"You have indeed been doing some thinking. What brings you to that belief?"

"Sadly, it is not a question of belief; it is a statement of fact. Evidentiary. Conclusive. Though I must say, it is not a conclusion I'm terribly keen to arrive at, but the math is there." Alice paused for breath, her voice thickening with exertion.

"Math?"

"Statistics. Let us say that if there is a God—Christian, Muslim, Jewish, whatever—and that one of those is the one true God, one would expect this mighty power would respond to desperate prayers from deserving, faithful individuals."

She paused to catch a breath before continuing, "The assumption is that an omnipotent being hears our pleas and actively responds to those deemed worthy. Otherwise, why pray? Organized religions make prayer a fundamental pillar of the belief system. Am I right?"

I sat forward in my chair and said, "Prayer plays a major role in many religions, of course, and I think many patients find peace and strength through prayer."

"So, if one of these Gods is the one true God, logic would say that prayers would be answered by that deity, but not prayers said to so-called, false gods. My question to you then is, when statisticians look at cancer death rates, do you think they see Christ coming in ahead of Allah, Buddha, or Vishnu?"

I considered the question while well aware that I was being pushed into a tight theist corner.

"As far as I know, you're correct; cancer death rates don't appear to vary significantly based on religious belief. However, I think some theologians might dispute the nature of the prayer itself. It being self-focused."

"Well of course it's self-focused! What's the point of praying if it doesn't provide some benefit to the person doing the praying?"

"Perhaps the prayer might better be answered if it were petitioning for understanding rather than a cure."

"The only understanding I want is an understanding that the cancer is gone. I have no desire to understand that an omnipotent, caring God that has the power to cure my cancer chooses not to do so," she said, her hands balling into fists. Alice stared at me, intense and challenging.

I probably should have let the matter drop at that point, but she seemed to want me to continue, so I said, "It might be argued that responding to a particular prayer simply doesn't fit into God's plan."

She snorted and then coughed before taking a few moments to catch her breath. "God's great plan? He can't have it both ways. If the plan is immutable, then why are we taught to pray, that prayer can make a difference? If it's not immutable, then prayer should have an impact—except as you've pointed out, it doesn't."

"As far as I know, prayer does have an impact for the faithful, regardless of the faith. Many find great solace in prayer."

"Well, good for them. So as long as you believe in something, anything, you're better off?"

"That appears to be the case."

"Placebo effect," she said, and then was wracked by a coughing spasm. Alice covered her mouth with her hand and as the attack ended, she wiped her bloodied palm on a towel she kept by her bedside. "Might as well believe in fairy dust."

When she had resettled, I said, "You're suggesting that the act of belief is what creates the benefit and not what one believes?"

"Precisely," rasped Alice.

Just then, one of the nurses popped in to check her vital signs. We took a brief hiatus until she had finished jotting down the findings in the case notes.

After she left, I said, "One certainly sees the effects of belief on the playing field. Winners believe they will win, and they do. Losers lose."

"So where does that leave me?"

Here there be dragons, I thought. Christopher Hitchens I am not, so it was time to dodge and weave. I said, "Right where you believe yourself to be, I suppose."

A look slowly settled on the sick woman's face, a look that I could not read: fear or perhaps resignation or even simple exhaustion. Then, just as it quickly as it had come, the look was replaced with a brightening energy. "So, what God do you pray to, Colin? What do you believe?"

I considered the question, weighing my response carefully. We volunteers are always told to respond honestly and frankly with patients. But anything medical was out of bounds, and theological issues were supposed to be for the chaplain to untangle. I was beginning to regret getting lured into this conversation, so I gave her my standard answer: "I'm not a religious person. I just come to chat, really."

"It must be tough though, meeting us patients. We talk about whatever comes to mind, and I suspect that you come to actually like some of us, but we all die on you. Despite your best efforts, we all die."

"You've met Gordon, the chaplain, haven't you? He's a multi-faith clergyman and is much better suited than I am to discuss spiritual matters with you. Shall I mention to him that you'd like to talk?"

Alice thought for a moment, then said, "Sure. Why not get it direct from the horse's mouth? Of course, I might just give him a piece of my mind, you know."

"I know he will be happy to take you on."

She nodded, then said quietly, "There are some people that I'd wanted to say some things to for years but never had the courage to say till recently. It's funny—now that I know I'm dying, I feel almost fearless in that respect. When one is stripped of status, dignity, looks, and all things worldly, about all you have left is honesty."

Alice paused for breath, and I held her juice container for her as she tilted her head forward to take a sip. Her eyes closed, and for a moment I thought she had drifted off to sleep, but she continued quietly, "I'm suddenly in the enviable position of being able to be absolutely frank with anyone and everyone. The people that intimidated me before hold no sway in my life anymore; it took getting cancer to make me realize that I do have control of my life."

Slowly her eyes opened, and her voice quavered as she said, "The downside of course is that it won't last too much longer. Perhaps some of my…newly found spirit will rub off on someone and they'll take it to heart and take more control in their own life. Even that's not my concern, though, y'know?"

I nodded.

"It's not my job to enlighten my family. That's their job," she whispered. "I simply look forward to each day now as an event completely free of shackles. I used to fret about money, about my career. I drove myself to the point of exhaustion in a passion for a big house, fancy car, and the trimmings. It turns out the only things that really count are a warm, dry place to sleep and a good IV line."

I smiled and helped her to take another sip. She then lay unmoving but for her chest rising and falling. "Of course, the perspective is different," she continued quietly. "You could make the argument that those things aren't important now simply because I'm dying, but I like to think that the reason they're not important is because they just are not important. Plain and simple. That is a lesson I've learned in all this."

I met her eyes in understanding.

"Are you married, Colin?"

"Widowed."

"How long?"

"About two and a half years."

"So you know death?"

"I do."

"Met him, don't like him?"

"Indeed."

"Grieving isn't easy, is it? Memories fade; that's what so painful about them.

"For me they don't; that's what's so painful about them."

A grimace came to her chapped lips, but when I met her gaze, I realized it was intended to be a smile.

"You know, I'm lucky I get to die this way. I could have had a heart attack or died in a car accident or something, and then I would never have had the opportunity to experience this clarity, to feel this connection to my family and friends."

"There must be great comfort in that," I said.

We settled into an amiable silence once again until she reached out her hand and squeezed my fingers. She raised her pale, watery eyes to mine and said, "Whatever comes next, I'm not afraid. I'm ready for it."

34

Lacey shuffled into the house, made her way to her water dish, then flopped down in front of the unlit fireplace. I flicked on the television to catch the news, but I didn't listen to what the newscaster was saying, my mind kept dipping into the pool of Brenda's life.

They train us volunteers just to focus on providing companionship and social interaction. Giving hands-on succor or any kind of help outside the hospice, such as taking trips to a bank to deposit a cheque or watering their lawns, is strictly forbidden. It is far too easy to be swept into the vortex of a dying person's life and to develop emotional attachments that eventually cripple your ability to be a good volunteer. I knew this. I knew it as a philosophical construct, I knew this as an emotional pitfall, and I knew this from direct experience. Yet I couldn't help myself.

That night, I dreamt of my wife; it was the first time since she had died that her dream self was healthy and without the deadly weight of cancer. I wasn't really there, not as a participant—this was just a scene I had been blessed to watch. She was sitting with an imagined middle-aged Brenda, and they were talking about the challenges of raising girls. Neither had confronted the trial of managing growing boys, but they came to the same conclusion that girls were the greatest test of one's will. Then suddenly they burst into laughter and fell together, holding each other through spasms of giggles and head-thrown-back guffaws.

I startled awake with a broad smile on my face. It was the middle of the night and Lacey was snoring loudly, so I gave her a bit of a nudge and we both settled in till morning.

The sun was shining when we woke, and I felt a weight had been lifted. With a cup of tea beside me, I turned on my laptop. In my naiveté, I thought that with a few keystrokes, my search would be done. It turned out not to be so. I tried a general Google search, then Facebook, Instagram, Twitter, and even LinkedIn but couldn't find her. I clicked away at every other site I could think of, but Cecily Fiona de Pont did not exist. The thought struck me that perhaps she had died, so I tried Obituaries.com with no result. If she had changed her name when she married, then I was hooped. There were too many women named Cecily in the world to fire off a missive to each one, so I turned off my computer and took the dog for a walk.

When we returned, there was a phone message on my machine. Still old school, I have a landline even though I have a cell phone, which I seldom keep charged. I had been more than content to shed the electronic shackles when I retired and settle back into communications over which I alone have dominion.

"Hi, Dad," said my daughter when I called her back. "I just called to ask if you'd like to come for dinner tomorrow?"

"I'd love to."

"Really?"

"Yes, sweetheart, I would love to come."

"You are sure? You'll come this time? You won't bail at the last minute?"

"I promise, luv. Is there anything I can bring? Wine or dessert or something?"

"No, we'll be good for all of that. Bring Ginger, though, okay? I haven't seen her in so long."

When, as a rescue puppy, Lacey was first brought into the house, the whole family struggled with changing her name from Ginger. When we finally reached consensus that a new start should beget a new name, it wasn't long before our youngest, for whatever reason comes to the mind of a teenager, decided that she alone would default back to the dog's original name.

"You sound good, Dad. Lighter somehow, whatever that means."

"I feel good, sweetheart."

We chatted for a few minutes, then said our goodbyes. As I hung up the phone, an unbidden thought crystallized, and I went back to my computer. In seconds I had found her: Cecily de Pont did not exist, but the Internet informed me that though she had assumed her husband's name when she had married, she became Cecily Fiona Leamington when she divorced. She had chosen a link to her past, changing her surname to match that of her mother. That meant something, surely.

I nuked a mug of tea from the pot and sat in my chair. It took some time to settle on how best to approach the subject in an email.

Broaching a lifetime barrier of disdain on one side and unrequited love on the other was something far above my pay grade, so I finally settled on less is more.

I wrote:

Dear Ms. Leamington,

> *I am a volunteer at the local hospice here in Steveston, British Columbia, where I recently met your mother. I understand that you have not been in contact with her for some time so I thought you might not be aware that she is in her very last days. Should you decide to meet with her, you may wish to speak to the Director of Care.*

I reread it numerous times and sweated for several minutes on how to close. Imagining how she might feel receiving such a note from out of the blue, I decided on something simple.

With caring,

Colin Driscoll

Then I included the contact information for the facility, took a deep breath and clicked send.

My tea was now tepid, so I went up to my bedroom to suit up for a bicycle ride along the dike. As I rode along the gravel embankment and looked out over the tidal flats, at some distance I spied a lone coyote trotting through the marsh grasses. I stopped pedaling and rolled to a stop to watch as he pounced on a frog or vole. With his dinner dangling from his mouth, he continued to a grove of willows and disappeared from view, leaving me to consider the potential consequences I had set in motion. There would be repercussions, I knew; you don't go sticking your ladle into a stew like this without some kind of ramification. I had been volunteering now for some time and had derived considerable benefit from the process. If I'd overstepped my bounds, then I would be okay with having to call it quits and find some other line of volunteer endeavour. This seemed to me a watershed moment, however it salted out, and I found that I was at peace with what might be in store for me.

Early on Wednesday evening, I packed up the dog and drove in to Kitsilano, where my daughter Olivia and her boyfriend rent an apartment on the third floor of a three-story walk-up. It may even be close to where Brenda used to live those many years ago. Fortune favours the brave, they say, but I was pleasantly shocked to see an empty parking spot directly in front of her building; finding parking in Kits is notoriously difficult. I took Lacey for a short walk to drain her bladder, then we went up for dinner—well, I went up for dinner, she went up for crumbs. Before we left home, I had fed her the special diet food she is on, but Lacey is always on the mooch for more.

Olivia met us at the door and Lacey gave her an excited greeting, even throwing in a bit of a whimper as she wriggled about before click-click-clicking her way across the hardwood floors into the living room, where she gave a hearty greeting to Greg, Olivia's boyfriend. He is a nice young man and has been a rock for my daughter throughout the last couple of years. Greg stuck out his hand for a shake, but I went in for a hug instead.

The kitchen was redolent with the aroma of garlic and marinara sauce. "It smells fantastic in here," I said. "Lasagne? Mum's recipe?"

Olivia nodded. "Plus a little something. I sautéed the ground beef with a little Thai chilli sauce," she said and then got down on the floor to commune with Lacey.

"Wine?" asked Greg.

"I think I'll wait till dinner, but I'd love a glass of sparkling water if you've got it."

The kids brought me up to speed on their lives, and Olivia gave me the goods on what her sister, Leona was up to. Or at least her version of it, as I'd heard the true tale from the source herself that morning.

"Toronto, Dad. I know she'll hate it there. She's worse than you for wanting peace and quiet. Leona will go crazy if she's not within spitting distance of something to climb."

"Well, it's her choice, sweetie, and post-doctoral fellowships are only for a couple of years. Not to worry, we'll wind her back in."

"I hope so, but what if she meets some guy and ends up living in Guelph or somewhere?"

"Well, then we'll just have to visit her there then."

"You seem awfully flexible about this all of a sudden, Dad. A month ago, you got upset if the mailman didn't push the envelopes through the slot all the way."

"I've been learning a little bit about perspective lately, I guess. Letting things go has been my problem since your mother died, and I've finally got to the point where I feel that letting go isn't forgetting or not respecting what has come before. Mum always said that I should live a good life after she was gone. I think that's the best thing I can do to honour her memory."

"Do I hear a build up to something?" asked Greg.

"That's what I like about you, Greg—smart and good-looking in one package."

He laughed but Olivia looked at me with concern.

"Lacey and I have been rattling around in the big house alone for too long now, and as you say, I've a love for the outdoors. So, I'm thinking of selling the house and moving to Vancouver Island. No idea where at this point, but I'm thinking Saanich or Maple Bay, maybe the Qualicum area. With what the current property is worth, I should be able to buy a little place on the waterfront and even have a little money left over."

As I looked at my daughter, I could see her eyes begin to brim with tears. "Mum is gone, and now you and Leona are going. Our whole family is falling apart. It's not fair," she said and buried her face in Greg's chest.

Brenda's father's diatribe on fairness sprang to my mind, but instead I said, "I know it may seem that way now, sweetie, but I'll come to visit all the time, and you can pop over by ferry or plane. They do harbour-to-harbour seaplane flights to wherever I wash up over there. I know this comes as a shock, but I just can't live in that house anymore. It feels empty. And if I'm going to move somewhere new, I want it to be…I don't know…an adventure."

I guess I should have waited till after dinner to announce my plan, but the conversation just seemed to lead me that way and I couldn't hold back. It took a while, but we managed to salvage the evening based on what turned out to be a fantastic main dish and Caesar salad.

First thing the next morning, I called a realtor and we set a time to meet the following day. Then I gave Lacey a bath in preparation for her visit to the hospice. For an old girl, she gets pretty wound up after she gets out of the laundry sink. I managed to get the towel around her wriggling body to capture most of the water dripping from her fur. It was like pinning down an electric sausage, and she squirted out of my grip, shook madly, and tore off into the family room, where she rubbed her face along the carpet and galloped back into the laundry room, holding a squeaky toy in her mouth. We played indoor fetch for a while till she tired of the game, and then I had at her with the hair dryer, which she actually quite enjoys. When she was dried, there was just enough time to slip into my yoga togs and make my way to the community centre.

It took a lot of non-effort to still my mind. The class had started, but there were so many thoughts and ideas spinning in my head—mountains of things to do to sell a home. I had difficulty focusing on what the instructor was saying, and by the time I finished the class it felt like I had missed the best part. Normally at the end I feel that I could just drift off into a nice, luxurious nap, but on this day, I felt a new, unbridled vibrancy pulsing through my core.

Lacey was parked at the door when I returned, but she was asleep and of course didn't hear me come in, so I grabbed a quick shower and made my lunch. The smell of garlic in the slices of turkey summer sausage slapped onto my sandwich must have drifted over to the front entrance because as though an alarm clock had gone off, she pulled herself up to a stand and hobbled to the kitchen. All the racing around earlier in the morning had taken its toll on her joints, and I could tell she felt a bit achy. The thing about dogs is that they live in the moment. Had I given her another bath right then and there, she would have repeated her high-energy antics, oblivious to the discomfort it would cause later. There are a lot of positive things to be said about the workings of the canine mind, and living in the now is, I think, one of the most important. They never dwell on past failures, long ago embarrassments, or puppyhood censures from a parent. Nor do they fear the future.

Despite veterinary guidance to the contrary, I tossed her a piece of the meat. She sat there in polite attendance by my feet and stared gamely up at me, awaiting further manna from my hand.

We said our hellos at the hospice. The Director of Care was absent from her office, and I felt a little ambivalent about this— mildly relieved to have dodged what I thought would probably have been a tense meeting. I had expected potentially heated admonitions that ultimately resulted in my termination from the program, and yet I was contrarily upset that I had not had a chance to defend my position. I stepped in to see the Volunteer Coordinator. She was her usual self and gave me the rundown on the current residents, who had died and who had arrived; Brenda was not mentioned till last.

"The lady in one one six, Brenda Leamington, you visit her often, don't you?" asked Marnie.

"Yes, we have nice long visits."

"Her daughter popped in yesterday afternoon for a visit. Unfortunately, Brenda is almost gone. She's not responsive and will most likely pass anytime now."

I felt a thud of disappointment. My vision of a difficult but ultimately satisfying ending for the two women was dashed.

"Okay, well I guess we'll go and do some visits." I stood to leave her office.

"Colin?"

"Yes?"

"Elizabeth is really good at her job as Director of Care and she's here for a reason. She's a buffer that is there to serve the patients and to protect you from distraught families who sometimes get overwrought and threaten legal consequences. Next time, please just forward your concerns or information on to her. It's in everyone's best interest."

I nodded and felt my ears burning. Suddenly, the urge to defend my interference evaporated. "There won't be a next time, I promise," I said.

Lacey and I continued down to the nursing station and, nose to the floor, she scanned the surface for errant morsels while I chatted with the staff and then read the recent updates to the volunteers' notebook. Brenda had slipped from consciousness two days ago. Had I been smarter, or had I attempted to track down Cecily earlier, perhaps the outcome would have been better. Or perhaps not. I closed the book.

"Marnie said that Brenda's daughter came by yesterday for the first time. How did that go?"

Her nurse, Pamela, rocked her head from side to side. "So so. I think she was disappointed that she didn't get a chance to talk to her mother."

"Is she coming back today do you think?"

Pam looked at the other nurse in the chair beside her, who simply shrugged.

"Don't know."

"Okay. I think we'll go and see the new chap in one eleven." I gave Lacey's leash a tug.

A few visits later, we knocked on Brenda's door; hearing no response, we entered. Between the two unmet curtains, only the narrowest shaft of sunlight slipped through the gap and illuminated the shape under the sheets. Her face had become a dark brown colour with deep, sickly yellow undertones, and she was breathing slowly and not at all smoothly. I lifted Lacey up onto the bed and she gave Brenda's right hand a swift couple of licks before settling in beside her.

"Good afternoon, Brenda," I said. "Just wanted to pop by and see how you're doing."

She gave no sign of hearing my words, but I continued undeterred. "I heard that Cecily came by yesterday. I hope that was nice for you."

I sat down in the big recliner chair by the bed and adjusted the tilt until I was comfortably prone. Her chest moved only every few seconds and as I looked at her throat where fire had etched its mark, I could see Brenda's pulse beating reedy and thin.

There are no emergency intubations in hospice care, no crash carts, no Code Blue. The medical staff are not there to save your life; their role is to give you a good death, and the best deaths involve chemicals. Not to say that the patient is given an unwanted push. No, the drugs are there to alleviate suffering, and without drugs at the end of life, it's not always pretty. There are drugs that help you from drowning in your fluid-filled lungs, drugs for terror and anxiety as you sense the train coming down the tracks, and of course drugs for pain. Their side effects can include respiratory suppression—which can be your first-class ticket out. With the drugs you slowly fade away till at some point, you're no longer with the living.

"Brenda, this will probably be our last visit together for one reason or another. I have to tell you that I have really benefited from your story. Literally more than you can or will ever know. In fact, I think this will be one of my last visits to the hospice, because I've pretty much decided to head west across the strait in search of greener and wilder pastures."

Neither Brenda nor the dog responded to my voice, and as I listened to Lacey's gravelly snore combined with the ragged, irregular breaths from Brenda, I felt a wave of fatigue sweep over me. Last night had not been a good night for sleep. Not for the usual reasons, though. No, I had been too excited about the possibility of starting anew, while all manner of ideas danced in my thoughts.

Now, though, the effects of the short night and the physical impact of the yoga class pulled me into a deep sleep.

35

"Well, I think that's the last box," I said as I loaded it onto the back of the moving van. My wife looked on and said, "Great, I'll call the cleaners; they can come tomorrow and give the house a good and final cleaning."

"My back's a bit stiff with all this lifting," I said.

"That's because you're getting old."

"True enough."

I met her gaze and asked, "Are you coming?"

She shook her head. "No, I don't think I can. Not this trip."

"I can't leave without you."

That look came to her eyes, the one where I knew that if I pushed even just a little bit harder, a terse rebuke would fall from her lips. I had learned that look when we were dating those many years ago; it came with "no means no."

CRAIG MICHAEL SMITH   334

"What about the dog? You should take her," I said. "After all, she really has been yours all along. Lacey has always preferred you to me. Of late, I've just been a bad substitute."

"No, you keep her for a while longer. She can come and live with me soon, but not just yet."

"Right then, I guess I'll be off." I turned to get in the moving van.

"Colin?"

I turned my head.

"Colin? Colin? Sorry to wake you." Pam, the afternoon shift nurse, had her hand on my shoulder and gave it another squeeze to rouse me.

"Brenda's daughter Cecily is here," she said and then took a step back to reveal a woman in her late fifties or early sixties. She had fine features that fit her greying blonde-highlighted hair, which was pulled off her face with a tortoise-shell clasp. It took a couple of moments to pull myself back from deep in my dream, but then I stood and held out my hand to introduce myself.

"You sent me the email," she said. Her voice was warm and deep, without edge; it didn't feel like an admonishment. I could tell she was from away by her accent.

"Yes. That was me. Brenda didn't ask me to do it; I just took it upon myself. I'm sorry if it was inappropriate of me. I just thought that perhaps you might want to hear her tell some of the background of her life. Things that maybe she hadn't told you when you were younger, things that might clarify how she ended up here." I looked at Brenda and then added, "I guess it's a little late now for her to do that."

She nodded, and I wasn't sure whether that meant she was letting me off the hook or whether she was just acknowledging my admission of meddling. A call bell rang from another room and Pam excused herself to attend to the appeal, leaving us standing and facing each other. I wasn't sure whether I should simply exit with another round of apologies or go through my typical visit routine. As usual, Lacey came to my rescue.

"Is that your dog?" she asked, looking at the small form splayed out on the bed.

I watched Cecily's face carefully and detected a slight spark come to her eyes when I said, "She is. Her name is Lacey and she is a fifteen-year-old professional sleeper."

Cecily approached the bed and slid her hand along the dog's back. I have always found a hint of the exotic in left-handed people, and I watched with interest as her jewelry-free fingers fondled Lacey's paws. Then she crossed the room and grabbed the edge of the curtains. "Do you mind? I'd like to let a little light in."

"I think that's a great idea," I said.

Cecily moved her arms as might a magician at the completion of a stunning trick, and sunlight filled the room. Then she turned and looked around for a place to sit and found a fold-up chair in the corner, which she opened and then sat upon.

"Please take the recliner," I offered, still feeling my way.

"No. I've found it inadvisable in the past to separate a man from his chair. Makes them twitchy," she said and met my gaze. Her eyes had the same green sparkle as her mother's.

I smiled and sat down in the same chair where I had been dreaming; Cecily's lips reflected my own grin.

"You've been married before, I take it?"

"Divorced some years ago. You?"

"Widowed. About two and a half years now."

"Children?" she asked.

"Two grown girls. You?"

"A boy. He finished university and fled to New York. Arbitrage is his calling. God knows why."

There came a stilted silence. I wasn't sure whether she felt obliged to be here so that she could tell her friends that she had transcended her lifelong aversion to her mother and fulfilled her daughterly duty, or whether Cecily truly needed to find closure somehow and understand both hers as well as her mother's past.

"I've been visiting your mother on Thursday afternoons for about a month now. We've had some nice chats."

Again, came the nod. To this point she had not acknowledged the presence of her mother, but now she shifted her gaze, and I could see Cecily's face soften as she looked at the collapsed little body wheezing and sputtering in the bed beside her chair.

We sat in the quiet for some minutes, just listening to and watching the last moments of Brenda's life.

Then I said, "For what it's worth, she felt tremendous regret for not pursuing you more rigorously to let you know that you weren't in possession of the full story. She knew that she had failed you as a mother, but for some reason known only to her, she let you slip away. I suspect she felt it was just easier to let it go and not have to fight you or fight for you. As the years went by, the inertia became unassailable. Brenda felt shame in that."

"She told you about what happened on the day I left?" Cecily said, eyeing me carefully. The pitch of her voice had gone higher and her eyes had reddened.

"She did. That and more. It's the more part that I think you might be interested in hearing."

I would tell Cecily later how what she did next was one of the most courageous things I have ever seen someone do; she reached over to pick up her mother's yellow, wasted hand and said as her eyes brimmed over, "Can you tell me now?"

Just then, Pam leaned into the room to ask how things were going and heard me say, "It was a yoga day when I first met Brenda, and based on my experience, I expected her to die by month's end..."

Epilogue

As I sit here on the veranda, looking out over the ocean, I can feel her presence. Brenda passed away three years ago, and the path to this place seemed almost inevitable. It started with me being a conduit to Cecily's familial past and evolved from there, with the two of us eventually finding a new start together.

Brenda had never sold the farm. She'd continued to rent it out and had had a little one-bedroom cabin built on the property in the early nineteen eighties. She'd come here whenever time allowed and always took several weeks in the summer to unwind and, I think, to be close to her memories.

Last spring, Cecily and I travelled to England—first to London, where we met with Noel's children, and then up to Windermere by train. Of course, Fiona and Michael had long since passed, and Noel had died ten years previously from lung cancer, but his children were happy to meet with us and we got on very well. We've invited them to pop across the Atlantic and come for a visit here on Hornby. You never know, they just might come; the cabin makes a great guest house—a little rustic, maybe, but it has a special feel.

Here for a visit, Olivia and Greg are married now and are down on the beach, playing with their two-year-old son Marshall. There's a lot of hooting and laughing echoing up from the water, and Cecily and I can't help but smile as we sit here, looking down at the beach. When I think of how strong my love is for them, I imagine how a grizzly bear mother feels for her cubs and wonder what I'd do if someone I knew sent my children off to a death camp. Every person reacts differently, but I'm pretty sure the perpetrator would feel my wrath: an eye for an eye. That leads me to think that Wolf had examined his new and unwanted notoriety from every angle. What greater way for someone seeking revenge than to harm his family and leave him to suffer their loss. He didn't know, of course, if anyone was coming for him, but by taking himself out of the picture, he had effectively removed his family from being a potential target.

Or perhaps he just couldn't live with himself and the shame of it. Second guessing a dead man's motives is a fool's errand, so I've let all that go. It's hard for Cecily, though; he was her father, after all. She has spent all her adult life coming to terms with the two sides of the man. Having never met the young man who embraced the Nazi ideology, it's so hard for her to reconcile a genocide collaborator with the loving, caring father who taught her to swim, bought her a pony, taught her to drive, and saved the lives of children on a burning boat. For a few heartbeats on her sixteenth birthday, he wasn't just her dad—he was a god, a hero for all to admire. And then suddenly, he wasn't.

Cecily's little sailboat is long gone, but I'm building a little sabot for my grandson. I'm using spruce wood as well as red and yellow cedars to slowly put it together. By the time it's completed, Marshall will be big enough to learn to sail. Far more easily, I could just buy a fibreglass version, but there's something inherently satisfying about using my hands to craft a little boat for him. I'll paint it white, and in fancy black script I'll write "Swan" on the transom.

Not long after Cecily and I moved here, Lacey's heart began to fail. She spent a lot of time resting outside on the lawn, just keeping her eyes on a little red squirrel that lived in a big Douglas fir by the house. He'd sit on a nearby branch and boldly scold her. In response, she'd sprawl on her back and lick her lips, which for some reason really set him off. Over time, her lungs became congested despite the vet's best efforts. Deep into a cool spring night, she climbed down from our bed while we slept and made her way downstairs. We found her in the morning, lying inert in the middle of the hallway. I don't know whether it was because her sweet little heart suddenly gave out or she simply lay down, thinking that this was as good a place as any to just stop.

THE END

Acknowledgements

All the characters in this story are fictional except for the test pilot of the Avro Aero, Janusz Zurakowski. The town of Sterness on Lake Windermere exists only in my imagination.

My thanks to the staff at the Woodward Biomedical Library at UBC for digging up the old medical texts that informed the treatment of Brenda's wounds. Thanks also to Jonny Rook, head plantsman at the Cumbria Wildflowers plant nursery in Carlisle, for suggesting a suitable plant to bloom at the right time on the fictional Beddall Holme.

I am indebted to my first readers, Shannon and Bev, who dared to tread where many would not. Marcus, your editorial insights provided refinements far beyond my imagining. I owe many thanks to my mother, who gifted me with my first library card at an early age – it started then. My greatest thanks go to my wife, Linda, and my daughters, whose support for all my endeavours is always unbounded and suffused with limitless love. I am a lucky man.

If you have enjoyed this novel, rather than letting it gather dust on a shelf, please pass it on for a loved one to read or, be bold and surprise a stranger. Thank you for being one of my readers.

craig-michael-smith.com

Manufactured by Amazon.ca
Bolton, ON